THE ART OF LOVE AT BLACKWATER POND

The Art of Love at Blackwater Pond

Terri Gilbert

For my family, who are all great story-tellers.

Author's Note

The Art of Love at Blackwater Pond is a stand alone novel, but does contain references to characters and events from *The House at Blackwater Pond* (2024). I did not set out to write a series, but as I finished the first book, Sarah's character insisted she had a story to tell. In learning her story, that idea became thematic. Everyone has a story, but sometimes what we believe to be true about ourselves is more fiction than fact.

Sarah is on a quest to find a home for herself, a goal that seems almost impossible for many people today. Although the housing crisis is, perhaps, not as severe in Tennessee as it is in many parts of our nation, I see your struggles and hear your frustration.

This book is a work of fiction.

Chapter One

Sarah Peters rummaged through the floorboard of Liam's car, holding one deep-rose-colored, lace infused, dyed-to-match bridesmaid's shoe, desperately looking for the other. *Why am I so disorganized? How can a shoe just disappear in a sixty-minute drive?*

"Sarah! Found it!" her sister Elizabeth's voice called from the front door of the wedding venue. Sarah jerked her head up, bumping it and dislodging a few dark brown curls from her bun. She slammed the car door and rushed to the left side of the double-curved staircase leading to the doorway of the stately Federal house where her brother would soon be married. Vaguely aware of another car door slamming and muttered curses coming from the right, Sarah raced up the stairs, reaching the door at the same time as the source of the cursing.

And wheezing. There was definitely wheezing. Sarah eyed the man with concern, despite feeling a little superior because she certainly wasn't out of breath. "Are you all right?"

"Er, uh, yeah," he said, ending with a whistle. "Here for the"—gasp—"wedding."

"Right," Sarah said slowly, opening the door. "After you." Just my luck, she thought, eyeing the man hunched over with a fist to his chest, messy dark hair half-covering a bumpy red complexion. This guy had to be the missing groomsman, the man she'd be partnered with. Everyone else had been at rehearsal last night, but he had not. *Just my luck,* she thought again. After six months without a date, naturally she'd get stuck with a wimpy, wheezing, spotty slob with coffee all over his shirt. Sarah shook her head. It didn't matter. She was on a hiatus from men anyway.

After a string of failed relationships, Sarah had decided to take a break from dating and figure out what she really wanted in a relationship. That had seemed like a good idea until everyone around her started getting engaged or married. Now she just felt lonely.

AN HOUR LATER, Sarah stood in the bride's dressing room of Blackwater Manor frowning at her reflection in the mirror after applying another coat of lip gloss. Behind her, Sarah could see her sister and three other women clustered around Meg, the bride-to-be, soon to be her sister-in-law, who was sitting on a reproduction rose-upholstered fainting couch. *Everybody is just so happy,* Sarah thought with disgust, watching the women gush as Meg read aloud the note James had written for their wedding day.

James isn't usually so eloquent. Wonder who wrote that letter for him. Her older brother had never dated anyone seriously before Meg, a cute and perky schoolteacher. After hearing about Meg's all-too-frequent computer problems, Sarah and Elizabeth had clued James in, and the rest was history. Sarah grimaced. *If James can find true love, why can't I?*

Sometimes Sarah felt like the only person in the world without love. She had sworn off men six months earlier when Brandon, the bartender, blew off their planned weekend in Nashville. Feeling unimportant and unappreciated, Sarah had ended the relationship, vowing to discover why none of the men she dated ever turned out to be Mr. Right. James, Elizabeth, and even their mother Jillian had gotten engaged last year.

Sarah's mother and Andy Harrison had each inherited a half-interest in the house at Blackwater Pond where Sarah currently stood. As local workers refurbished the house, Jillian and Andy had uncovered the mystery of Andy's birth, the history of the house, and their love for one another. Re-purposing the Federal-style manor house and grounds as a wedding venue created an income stream to fund their plans to create a museum honoring the home's unique position in local history. As word spread about the planned wedding venue, a new inn and two florists had opened, helping to revitalize the small town of Belford, Tennessee. The museum would open late in the summer, with plans for the grounds to eventually house artists and writers.

Andy and Jillian's wedding in December had been the first to be held at the manor. It had been lovely, and Sarah had been happy then. Liam and Elizabeth's engagement had shaken her though. Elizabeth, at twenty-seven, had been dating Liam since she was seventeen, so everyone *knew* they'd get married—just as Sarah knew she shouldn't have been surprised, but she was. Somehow, she'd imagined that she'd get married before her younger sister. *Why can't I find a good guy? Elizabeth did. Meg did. What's wrong with me?*

One of Meg's coworkers giggled, poking Sarah in the back. "Darlin', you need to turn that frown upside down."

Who talks like that? Sarah turned. *Oh, the kindergarten teacher. Of course.*

"You're going to give yourself wrinkles if you don't stop frowning."

Thinking wrinkles were the least of her problems right now, Sarah dug through her bag for her phone, so she could pretend to check her messages and get away from the plump young woman standing before her. Sarah sighed. "I'm sure you're right, Josie." She had to find a way to be more cheerful during the ceremony, but thinking about her 'partner' didn't help. His absence last night had made Sarah feel more alone than ever, and today, the guy had stuttered and stammered every time she looked at him.

Sarah closed her eyes in an attempt to dislodge her negativity. *He's Meg's friend, someone she loves, and looks shouldn't matter anyway. I shouldn't be so judgmental.*

"Wasn't that just the sweetest letter? 'You'll be my valentine forever,'" Josie yammered in the background as she looked in the mirror and smoothed her strawberry blonde hair.

"Lining up in two minutes, ladies." Sue Ellen Ramsey poked her head in the dressing area. A tall slender woman with iron gray hair, Sue Ellen was one of two wedding directors on staff at Blackwater Manor. Weddings were big business, and Blackwater Manor was proving to be a popular venue, especially with brides from nearby

Chattanooga. Since it had opened to the public just six weeks earlier, the manor had hosted two small weddings. Even more incredible, they'd already booked twelve weddings for spring and summer.

Sarah fell in line behind the annoying Josie, her own sister Elizabeth, and a petite young woman named Rachel, whose beautiful long, shiny black hair was pulled back in a low ponytail encircled by a thin braid. Meg's sister Trish, as maid of honor, would walk in unescorted right before Meg and their father. Since there were ten people plus the bride and groom in the wedding party, the bridesmaids would walk in with the groomsmen, then sit in the front row. Only Trish and Eric, James's coworker and best man, would stand up front with the bride and groom. Relieved she only had to plaster on a smile for the walk down the aisle, Sarah had been delighted to hear these arrangements until she'd learned who would be sitting with her. Meg had decided to put "couples" on either side of the aisle.

As the music started, Sarah took another look at her escort, Arthur whatever-his-last-name-was. She could not imagine a geekier, less interesting guy. Even if she had not sworn off men, nothing about Arthur attracted her. *So much for my fantasies of meeting a handsome, eligible groomsman.* The shortest of the groomsmen, Arthur kept nervously tugging his dark brown hair over one side of his face, which was covered in a bumpy red rash. He even wore stereotypical thick black-rimmed glasses with honest-to-goodness tape on the nose piece. As Sarah looked at him, he blushed, wheezed, and pulled at his shirt collar before pushing the glasses back on his nose. *It's one afternoon, not a relationship. He's a perfectly nice guy or he wouldn't be in the wedding party.*

Despite her feelings toward her escort, Sarah smiled politely and took Arthur's proffered arm for the walk down the aisle. She was determined to appear happy, no matter how miserable she felt inside, no matter how often he tripped over his too-long pants. *Honestly, his whole suit is swallowing him, despite the shirt being too tight. Did he miss a fitting? Does he not care how he looks? Stop the negativity. This is James and Meg's day. Smile!*

Waiting their turn to walk down the aisle, Sarah looked around the large room where the wedding was to take place. Vases of pink roses and baby's breath filled niches in the wall. Last night the room had been filled with round tables and hundreds of twinkling lights. Today, sunlight filtering through the bare limbs of trees outside cast dancing shadows on the dark wood floors, and rows of white folding chairs faced a wedding arch at the front of the room, where her brother James stood, smiling broadly, flanked by the pastor and best man. Sarah smiled at James. Her big brother was getting married!

"Jeez, it's like the death curtain from the Ministry of Magic." Arthur snorted.

Sarah grinned and glanced at him with new appreciation. *Another Harry Potter fan!* He wasn't wrong. Although not black and tattered, the sheer curtains covering the arch were billowing softly.

Wearing a more genuine smile as they advanced down the aisle, Sarah spotted her parents and grandparents. Sarah's mother and Andy had been married just over two months. They were seated next to Sarah's dad, who had turned into such a recluse that Sarah was surprised he and his girlfriend Stacy were in attendance. Also in the family row were both sets of grandparents, who rarely traveled and had not spoken to each other since her parents' divorce almost five years ago. *Mom and Andy look so happy and vibrant and polished, like burnished jewels, while Dad and Stacy just look old.*

Sarah loved her dad and she really liked Stacy, but she didn't see them very often. They led quiet lives centered around work and whatever was on television. *At least they have each other.* As everyone stood to watch the bride and her father walk down the aisle, Sarah had to force a smile because she felt so lonely.

Taking her seat between Arthur and Liam, Sarah sighed heavily. Liam didn't notice, but Arthur whispered, "Hey, are you okay?"

Sarah shot him an annoyed look and hissed, "Yes," as the preacher welcomed everyone to the ceremony. Noticing Arthur rubbing his thighs and clenching and unclenching his fists, she grew increasingly annoyed. As Meg's father walked to his seat, Arthur suddenly started scratching his chest and upper arms furiously. Sarah turned away with disgust.

"Sorry. Poison ivy," Arthur whispered.

"Shh!"

After a prayer, the preacher called on Trish, who read a poem about marriage, and then the best man, who sang a song about love never failing. Sarah watched James, whose face portrayed the depth of his love for his bride.

Meg was lovely. She wore a simple white A-line dress with a v-neck lace bodice. The multi-layered chiffon skirt had an irregular hem falling just above her ankles, showing off a pair of Kate Spade sling-backs that Sarah knew for a fact cost more than Meg's wedding dress. Meg's curly blonde hair was pulled back in a loose braided bun adorned with baby's breath.

The preacher smiled as he eyed the congregation over the top of his half-rim glasses. "Meg and James wish to say a few words to each other before reciting their vows."

Meg turned to James and took his hand in hers. "The foundation of learning is the ABCs, so I decided there should be an Alphabet of Love too." The congregation murmured their approval as Meg began: "A is for after where happily ever we'll B, because I love you, you C.

"OMG," Sarah whispered.

"No effing way," Arthur muttered at the same moment.

They looked at each other and grinned.

"D is for darling, which you'll call me-E."

Arthur leaned close to Sarah and whispered, "Ugh, cringe."

"Obvs," she responded without looking at him.

Sarah's grandmother, sitting behind her, poked Sarah's shoulder. Sarah glanced back and mimed zipping her lips.

Beside her, Arthur pulled out a pen and wrote "Ooh, trouble" on the wedding program.

Sarah grabbed his pen and quickly scribbled "ikr."

Meg's rhymes continued. "F is for forever, because Gee, H is for heart you, I forever . . ."

Arthur retrieved his pen and wrote, "lmao."

"Smh."

Somehow, they managed to not make a scene, but it was touch and go for a bit as the rhyming continued. After Meg recited, "S is for secrets shared in the sun, and T is for tummies, we each have one," James laughed out loud, so Sarah was sure no one heard her groan. Meg finished her speech with "Z is for zebras of which we'll have none." The audience chuckled and applauded.

James brought Meg's hands to his lips and kissed them before speaking. "Meg, you make me laugh, turning the darkest day into sunshine. Your love warms my heart and makes me want to be a better man. You know just how to respond when I get cranky and frustrated with work or ignorant people. I'll always be there to solve your computer problems and pave the way for whatever roads we decide to follow." James released Meg's hands, pointed to his eye, then made a heart on his chest, as he continued, "I heart you." Everyone laughed again.

At the ceremony's conclusion, Arthur offered his arm to Sarah, saying, "Well, that was fun." They snickered quietly, then followed the bride and groom up the aisle to the foyer.

Sarah appreciated Arthur's quick wit and their side conversation had amused her. Before wandering off to find Meg and James, she smiled and said, "ttyl," wondering if everyone had found the ABCs as moronic as she and Arthur or if others had found it cute.

The wedding party gathered in the entry foyer for candid photographs. As Sarah hugged her new sister-in-law, Meg whispered, "I just knew you'd hit it off with Artie. Isn't he great?"

Sarah was startled but smiled and agreed with Meg's assessment before hugging James. Surely Meg wasn't serious. Okay, they'd had a few laughs, but she was not interested, thank you very much. She slipped into the crowd before anyone else decided she and Arthur were a couple.

Spying one of the bridesmaids at a punch bowl, Sarah hurried in that direction. "Rachel, right? How do you know Meg?"

"We work together. I'm sorry, which sister are you again?"

Sarah wasn't surprised by Rachel's question. She'd heard variations of it most of her life. Even their mother said she and Elizabeth were two peas in a pod. Though close in age and appearance, Sarah knew her sister was softer, both in appearance and personality, and more graceful than she was. Sarah was more athletic and more outspoken. Elizabeth walked through life with a plan; Sarah bounced around like a pinball. "I'm Sarah. What's it like being a teacher?"

"Oh, it's great. Most of the time, anyway. Definitely a challenge these days." Rachel sipped her punch. "I think Meg won, don't you?"

"Won what?" Sarah asked as she filled a cup.

"The bet, silly! Remember the bet?"

Sarah shrugged and shook her head. "I don't have a clue what you're talking about."

"It was in the letter! James accepted Meg's bet. He agreed to take her to Paris if she managed to make him laugh during the ceremony."

"Oh, thank God."

"You didn't think she was serious about that alphabet of love thing, did you?" Rachel grinned widely. "Oh my gosh. Meg's going to—"

"Never hear about this, right?" Sarah said. "I didn't know about the bet, but Arthur and I had a hard time not laughing."

Rachel made a face. "I was so jealous when I saw you lined up with him. He's so cute, and Meg says he's really smart."

Sarah stared at Rachel in amazement. *Cute? Arthur?* "Looks like he's coming this way. You can find out for yourself," Sarah said as she stepped around the corner.

Chapter Two

After the wedding party filed out, the pastor indicated that Meg and James would join their guests shortly and encouraged everyone to explore the manor house in the interim. A string quartet played in the drawing room, while servers circulated with drinks and appetizers. The chairs in the main parlor were quickly and efficiently rearranged around small tables for casual seating.

The photographer posed the attendants behind Meg and James on the spiral staircase that dominated the front hall. Sarah was not the only one to tilt her head to see the stairs curving upward. She was happy for James and Meg, truly, but it was hard to be a bridesmaid—again—with no groom in sight, not even a boyfriend. *My choice. I was the one to declare a hiatus from men. Maybe six months is enough.* Sarah smiled, a real smile this time, at one of the groomsmen. *He's cute. What's his name, Mark? Martin?* He winked at her, brushing the hair from his brow.

Seeing the glint of his wedding ring, Sarah turned away. *Typical. I seem to always be attracted to either sleazy or self-absorbed men.*

"All right, everyone, thank you! Don't get too far away, but I want to get some family shots now. Let's start with the groom's family," the photographer said. "Meg and James, you stay put. Sisters on either side. Parents behind them. That's it. Grandparents next. Thank you."

Sarah sidled over to her mother and gave her a hug. "Beautiful wedding, Mom. Did you laugh or cry during their little speeches?"

Jillian smiled. "A little of both, honestly. They're so cute together. The look on James's face! It's wonderful to see them so in love."

"Okay, everyone. It's a bit chilly, but let's have the men outside for some fun shots, then we'll add Meg, then the bridesmaids alone and with the guys."

The men followed the photographer out the door, leaving the bridesmaids to chat. "I'll gather our wraps," one said, heading for the dressing rooms.

Sarah made her way to her sister. "Which one was that?"

"Oh, stop it!" said Elizabeth. "You know perfectly well that was Meg's sister, Trish. The blonde curls alone give it away. They look a lot alike."

"We all look alike in these matching dresses." Sarah laughed. "And those groomsmen. I can't tell them apart."

"There are some similarities," Elizabeth said. "Only your guy has dark hair."

"Don't call him that. He's definitely not my type," Sarah said, a bit sharper than she'd intended.

Any remark Elizabeth might have made was forgotten as the photographer's assistant requested their presence just as Trish returned, handing out the beautiful wraps Meg had given the bridesmaids. The ivory cashmere pashminas were embroidered with flowers of silver and the dusty rose of the girls' dresses. Sequins sparkled as the women took their wraps and headed out the door.

Although it was mid-February, Meg and James had been blessed with a sunny day, making the mid-forties temperature bearable. The wedding party posed on the double curves of the large staircase that led to the grand entry of the manor. "Now the bride and groom alone," the photographer said.

At the base of the steps, Sarah turned to watch Meg and James pose together. *It really is a lovely house. A beautiful place for a wedding.* The old red brick had faded over the years to a deep rose color. Bright white paint highlighted the half-circle window over the door and the narrow rectangular windows on either side. Freshly painted shutters complemented the windows of the two main floors. The exterior renovation of the manor appeared complete, but Sarah knew spring would bring more changes to the grounds, enhancing the natural beauty of the manor's setting and healing the scars from the renovation and construction efforts.

Maybe one day . . . Sarah sighed and joined the women in front of Blackwater Pond for a silly shot of them jumping in the air. "Groomsmen, join the bridesmaids, please. Spread out a bit. Now everyone, jump on my count, one, two, three! Make sure to kick up those heels. Once more." Sarah wasn't sure how or why these jumping shots had become de rigueur, but she tried to look as if she enjoyed them. "Okay, ladies, head over to the truck in front of the barn; we'll join you shortly. Men, stay put."

Sarah, with her typical competitiveness, reached the truck

before the other women, who picked their way through the sparse grass, mindful of their heels and hems. She couldn't resist climbing on the old truck's running board and watching the groomsmen repeat their jumping act. Arthur, she noticed, didn't jump, but put one leg in the air and raised his arms as if he had. Hadn't someone mentioned him being an athlete? Seemed pretty lazy to her. But then again, she was pretty sure Liam had mentioned a bike wreck. Maybe he was hurt. Sarah cheered for James as he raced the groomsmen to the truck. She noticed that Arthur stayed with Meg. *At least he's a gentleman.*

Meg had foregone the popular cowboy boots and barn wedding, but she couldn't resist the juxtaposition of rust and wedding finery. Meg wore a short white fur jacket over her gown as she stood beside the truck. James posed with one foot on the running board, jacket tossed over his shoulder, with a rose clenched between his teeth. The groomsmen looked under the hood as the bridesmaids pretended to push the truck.

Sarah watched in disbelief as James went along with all the silly poses. What had happened to her brother? Could love really change a person so much?

"That's a wrap for everyone but the bride and groom," the photographer said.

Everyone trooped toward the manor, but Arthur lagged behind the other men. She joined him and asked, "Why did the photographer have you guys come out early?"

Arthur scratched his head. "Apparently, the newlyweds wanted a picture of us being chased by a dinosaur. I'm not sure how that relates to a wedding, but it is what it is."

"I don't understand all these crazy shots either. James is surprising me with his willingness to be silly. Meg's been good for him."

"I would agree with that." Arthur smiled. "He's a lucky man." Nodding toward the mostly empty path ahead of them, he added, "You don't have to wait on me, I'm moving a bit slow."

"I noticed your gait is a little off on the left side. Are you injured?"

Arthur turned toward Sarah quickly and gave her a strange look. "'My gait is off?' Are you a doctor?"

"Physical therapist. Did you hurt your ankle jumping?"

Arthur eyes widened as he shook his head. "No, I definitely did not hurt my ankle. Bike wreck and an old injury, you might say." He gestured at his leg.

Josie and Rachel came running back down the stairs and surrounded Arthur, giggling at some private joke. Sarah murmured a quick "see you" and hurried inside.

She took a glass of champagne from a passing tray and turned to look for food but was intercepted by her grandmother.

"Sarah, darling, don't rush about so. You nearly knocked us down," her grandmother said with an imperious tone.

Sarah's maternal grandmother was not the sort of person who loved unconditionally. Sarah, like her mother, had always felt judged and not good enough for the woman standing beside her. Despite these feelings, Sarah greeted her grandparents warmly and asked what they'd thought of the service.

As usual, her grandmother did the talking. "The alphabet speech was too cutesy for us, but James certainly looks happy, and Meg is a beautiful girl. Now tell me about that young man of yours," her grandmother demanded. "Will we be attending another wedding this year?"

Sarah blushed. "Elizabeth is the one who's engaged, Grandmother. I'm not seeing anyone currently." She looked around the room, hoping someone, anyone, would rescue her.

"Whyever not? You're almost thirty. You shouldn't be wasting time at your age. Who was the young man with whom you behaved so badly during the service?"

Oh, Good Lord. Maybe I don't want to get married! Maybe I'll just find a sperm donor and forget about men. "Just a groomsman, Grandmother. We just met today. I don't know—oh hello," Sarah sputtered as Arthur appeared at her side.

"Good afternoon. Arthur King, at your service. Forgive me for intruding, but Sarah is needed across the hall." Arthur bowed slightly and spoke in a voice that brooked no argument.

He led Sarah away by the elbow as she waved over her shoulder at her grandparents. "Is your name really Arthur King?"

"What can I say? My parents have a weird sense of humor. It was okay as a kid, but you can imagine those classes where the teacher calls roll last name first: King, Arthur. Queen, Ann."

Sarah laughed. "Really?"

"No, not really," Arthur said, grinning. "Art Gladstone. I just use King for a laugh."

"It is pretty funny," Sarah admitted. "So, who needs me?"

"Uh, true confession, no one. I needed an excuse to get away from Josie and Rachel, and you looked like you needed a rescue, so . . ." Arthur folded his jacket over one arm, then tilted his head and looked at Sarah from behind a curtain of dark hair. "Seemed like a win-win to me."

She looked at him more closely. His large expressive eyes were a beautiful chocolate brown framed by impossibly long lashes. She hadn't noticed them before because she'd been focusing on his ridiculous black glasses taped together at the nose piece. His dark hair was wavy and a little wild. Sarah had to restrain herself from smoothing a flyaway curl. He was also taller than she'd originally thought, a few inches taller than her 5'7", and definitely not skinny. His ill-fitting shirt pulled at his broad shoulders. Perhaps she'd misjudged him. Well, obviously she had.

Realizing she'd been staring, Sarah blushed. "Thank you. I did need rescuing. Want to find a table and get some food? You can tell me the story of your bike wreck. I assume you fell into some poison ivy?"

"Oh, yes. Yes, I did," Arthur replied. They started toward the dining room, but stopped when the string quartet suddenly struck up a very familiar tune and Meg and James entered the hall. Arthur grabbed Sarah's hand and leaned toward her. "Oh, jeez. Here we go."

Josie popped up from a nearby table and began singing, "You've been to the ch-a-a-pel," changing the song to reflect James and Meg's newly married status. Rachel joined her on the second line, and Sarah could not have been more surprised when Arthur sang out the third line and spun her around. She laughed to find herself caught up in a flash mob as more and more of Meg's co-workers joined in from around the room, singing and dancing. Elizabeth and Liam ended the song by indicating that they too would be going to the chapel of love, in effect announcing their intentions to anyone who didn't know they were engaged.

Everyone laughed and clapped and put away cell phones as the song ended. Meg and James thanked everyone, then made their way around the room, speaking to their guests. Sarah turned to Arthur. "I think I was the only member of the wedding party surprised by that."

"That's why Rachel and Josie stopped me as we were walking in from outside," Arthur said. "I assumed you knew. Y'all didn't talk about it at rehearsal last night?"

"No, not that I remember. I'm kind of oblivious sometimes. Whose idea was it, anyway?"

Arthur scratched his chest on their way to the dining room. "Josie and Rachel came up with it. Meg's parents don't drink or dance—well, her dad doesn't drink—I think Meg's mom likes a little wine now and . . ." Arthur trailed off as Sarah's grin grew wider. "Sorry. Anyway, they wanted to do a little something extra to help everyone relax and have a good time."

"I think it worked. Things are definitely livelier than before. So, how long have you worked with Meg?" Sarah asked as they filled their plates with food.

Arthur looked at her curiously. "I don't work with Meg. I'm a landscape architect."

"Oh," Sarah said slowly. "So you're that friend, the guy Andy and Mom hired for the manor. You seemed to know Josie and Rachel, so I thought you might be a teacher too. Either that or a computer wiz like James."

Arthur laughed, setting his plate on a small table. "Ha! No, I just use computers. I sure don't fix them. Was it the glasses? Is that what gave you the idea? I thought they accessorized the suit quite nicely," Arthur said, striking a pose with his jacket over one shoulder.

Sarah pulled out the chair beside him and smiled as she sat down. "More the tape on the frames than the glasses themselves. Another casualty of the bike wreck?"

"Not exactly. I tore one of my contacts on Thursday, then wrecked my bike on Friday and didn't have time to get another pair." Arthur paused as he took a seat. "Jeez, was that just yesterday? Maybe I hit my head harder than I thought. Anyway, after the wreck, I got checked out at the hospital and ended up missing my plane, which caused me to miss the rehearsal dinner. I wasn't hurt exactly, no concussion anyway, but the abrasions just opened a passage for the poison ivy, which has caused all kinds of problems. Especially since I couldn't take anything while driving. Fortunately, there are quite a few flights between Orlando and Atlanta, so I was able to get on a later one and at least be here for the big event."

Sarah ate some fresh fruit while she watched Arthur, thinking of how badly past boyfriends would have reacted to missing a plane. Brandon would've pouted for a week.

"If you think I'm stylin' now, you should have seen me on the plane wearing my prescription racing goggles." Arthur grinned as

Sarah burst out laughing. "I found these old glasses in my glove compartment, or you'd have had to lead me down the aisle. Meg's lucky I love her, or I wouldn't have bothered."

Sarah had so many questions about this speech, but settled for "How do you know Meg?"

"Oh, we've been friends, close friends, forever. Hey, do you want a bite of this shrimp cocktail? It's really good."

"No, thanks," Sarah said, wrinkling her nose.

"I'm guessing by that face that you don't like shrimp." Arthur grinned. "Anyway, Meg and Trish lived next door. Trish and I are closer in age, but Meg's my buddy, like a baby sister."

"She's sweet. Elizabeth and I are really enjoying getting to know her. Of course, we've wondered about her sanity in choosing our brother. He can be prickly and clueless a lot of the time." Sarah laughed. "But don't worry, James absolutely adores Meg."

"Oh, I know, trust me. I heard the whole story. I've actually spent a good deal of time with them the past few months. Plus, I help James out with his chess club from time to time. When Meg got serious about James, she asked me what I thought about him."

"Whoa. Back up a minute. A chess club?"

"Yeah, at the elementary school. Meg's the official sponsor, but since she doesn't really play chess, she recruited James and then me. Eric helps sometimes too. I mean, you can never have too many adults when you've got a big group of kids trying to learn a new skill. It's just one afternoon a week for an hour or so. We came up with this team version of the game that's been real popular. I can't go very often, but the kids enjoy the club, especially on team days, and

I do too.

Sarah scrunched up her face. "I don't really get chess." She tilted her head slightly. "And Meg asked you to vet James?"

"In a sense, yeah. It means a lot to me to know she values my opinion."

"Sarah, Art, team chess downstairs in ten," Eric said, brushing by them on his way to find other members of the wedding party."

"All right! That's what I'm talking about! Literally!" Arthur said, as Sarah groaned. "Come on, Sarah, where's your competitive spirit?" Arthur took her hand and pulled her toward the stairs.

The basement housed the catering kitchen, a research and library area used by the local historical society, and a large open space for mixed use. Andy and Jillian had imagined it as a site for community meetings, but today it was called into service for a chess game. A large checked canvas was spread on the floor, and giant chess pieces stood in place as opposing forces.

As members of the wedding party surrounded the chessboard, Eric asked if they knew how to play. "I know how the pieces move," Sarah said, "but I don't really understand the strategy."

"Not a problem, Sarah. You can be on my team," Eric said. "Okay, everyone, this is a silent game—no verbal discussion among the teams as to strategy. No touching the chess pieces unless it's your turn to move. All team members play in sequence; no skipping players, passing moves, or going out of order. Once you let go of the piece, your turn is over. Okay?

"Team members communicate by miming, pointing, or signaling. Meg and James will judge, so no breaking rules. Take five minutes to number off and agree on signals. For example," Eric pretended to gallop, "this might indicate a knight. Okay, let's divide the teams."

The teams huddled together, determining their positions and indicators for moving pieces, which Sarah found confusing. *I'll just let Eric tell me what to do.*

When she saw Meg and James feeding one another hors d'oeuvres, Sarah thought chess might be better than watching a sappy display of newly wedded bliss.

James called out, "Time's up! White begins. Player number one advance. Everyone else stay behind the line."

Sarah followed Eric's mimed directions and moved a white pawn forward two squares. Liam moved a knight in response. While a spirited but silent interchange took place between Eric and Trish about the next move, Sarah's attention wandered.

Martin blew kisses to a pretty young woman holding a sleeping toddler. His wife, she hoped. *Maybe he's not sleazy, just friendly.* Liam and Elizabeth focused on each other more than the game. *Probably making wedding plans.* Sarah frowned. All around the room couples stood or sat. She hadn't seen Trish or Rachel with anyone, but Josie kept making goo-goo eyes at a guy who seemed to reciprocate her interest.

As the game progressed, Sarah's thoughts raced. What was she going to do when Liam and Elizabeth got married? When would they marry? What if they decided to move in together, like, right away? Could she afford the rent on their apartment by herself. Could she live with a roommate who wasn't her sister? Did she want to? Rents in Chattanooga were so high, it might be cheaper to buy a house. Not downtown but maybe in Redbank or Hixon. Her mother had said home prices in Tennessee were rising but still more affordable than in much of the country, especially for smaller homes and fixer-uppers. *Can I do that? Should I do that? Breathe!* Maybe she could. Maybe she would.

Only a few game pieces remained on the board. Sarah moved the bishop as directed to capture Black's only remaining knight. Arthur studied the board, followed directions from Eric, then stood behind Sarah and placed a hand on her shoulder as they waited for the black team to move. What the heck? Did Arthur think they were a couple because they'd walked in together and shared a few laughs? When her back stiffened, he removed his hand. Trish's next move put the black team in checkmate, and Arthur gently tapped Sarah's shoulder, reminding her to join the rest of the team in making a giant check mark in the air with their hands.

The game ended quickly with a sudden eruption of sound as the spectators cheered James's announcement that Eric's team had won. Arthur high-fived Sarah and the rest of the team, then disappeared back upstairs.

Meg and James had one more photo-op, cutting the cake, so they headed to the dining and conference room, where the white of Meg's dress just popped against the dark rose paint. Sarah saw her dad and Stacy, who hugged her, said they were getting in line for cake, then abandoned her with Pops and Granny, her grandparents on her dad's side.

Granny gave her a big hug and asked Sarah how her boyfriend

was, but Pops shushed her. "Now, Granny, Paul said not to ask about boys. So, tell me sweetheart, how's nursing?" Sarah long ago had accepted that Pops would never remember she was a physical therapist. She simply said everything was fine and let it go. She asked him if he'd been fishing lately, knowing he hadn't, and kept hoping Arthur would rescue her again.

When she finally got away from her grandparents, Sarah asked Josie if she'd seen Arthur. Josie gave her a pitying look and raised an eyebrow. "No, sugar, I believe he has left the building. I overheard Rachel asking him for a ride home."

Sarah was surprised by how dejected she felt. She had enjoyed Arthur's company a lot more than she would've believed possible. He was thoughtful and witty and, she huffed, rude enough to leave without saying good-bye. Angry at herself for caring, she wandered through the wide hall into the reception room, trailing her hand along the large sideboard looking idly at the collection of photographs of previous inhabitants displayed there.

"Sarah? I snagged you a piece of cake," Arthur said, handing her a plate. "I'm leaving early. It was great to meet you. Maybe I'll see you around," he continued in a rush. "Gotta take Rachel home. Wish me luck," he added, leaning in as if to kiss her cheek before seeming to think better of it, then patting her back and waving good-bye.

Sarah had been mute the whole time, unable to process anything Arthur was saying. Had he almost kissed her? Wait. He was leaving? With Rachel? Sarah watched Arthur as he took Rachel's cosmetic bag and dress from her as they approached the front door. Both had changed from their wedding finery into jeans. Arthur, Sarah had to admit, looked good in his jeans and woodsy green shirt with the sleeves casually rolled up to the elbow. Who knew forearms could be so sexy? Sarah's eyes narrowed as she noticed Rachel's skin-tight jeans and low-cut pink sweater. Oh, and look, she was still wearing her wedding heels. No doubt she'd "forgotten" more sensible shoes.

Oh, no freaking way. I'm not attracted to Arthur, am I? Am I actually jealous of Rachel? Wait, did 'wish me luck' mean Arthur is interested in Rachel?

Chapter Three

While many weddings among their contemporaries seemed to last all weekend, Meg and James had chosen the "wedding-lite" suggestion from Meg's father. Their simpler, less expensive service allowed them to use most of the money he'd set aside for a wedding as a down payment on a home. The couple had happily purchased a condo north of Atlanta in Acworth, where they both worked. This made perfect sense to Sarah, who'd often imagined a little house for herself but not a fairy-tale wedding.

Rather than a full meal with an open bar, Meg and James had served champagne and appetizers. They'd chosen a small wedding cake and cupcakes in lieu of a groom's cake. Guests could enjoy the ceremony, the games, music, food and company, but still have time to get home, or at least over the mountain, before dark.

After cutting the cake and feeding each other, Meg and James retreated to the dressing areas and changed into clothes more suited for travel. The Parisian holiday would come in the summer, but they'd honeymoon in a cabin at nearby Fall Creek Falls before going back to Georgia for the remainder of the school year.

Family and friends lined the outside stairs, showering the couple with rose petals as they ran for the vintage yellow taxi waiting in the drive. Andy's uncle, Randy Keith, a wiry older man, was quite dapper in a cabbie's jacket complete with brass buttons. He opened the rear door and ushered the newlyweds in before tipping his hat to the amused guests. As the car drove down the drive, everyone could see the large "Just Married" sign festooned with streamers.

"Where did that taxi come from?" Trish asked.

"Mom found it," Elizabeth explained. "Anyone who gets married here can use it. Randy Keith doesn't drive far, but it makes a nice getaway. For an extra fee, couples can use a horse and carriage. Liam and I might do that."

Sarah rolled her eyes. *Great, just great. Finish one wedding, dive into another.*

The guests started leaving rather quickly after Meg and James departed. Ready for this day to be over, Sarah said her good-byes and hurried into the dressing room to change her clothes for the hour-long trip back to Chattanooga, where she shared an apartment with Elizabeth.

Pulling earbuds from her backpack, Sarah settled in the backseat of Liam's car. She didn't want to rehash the wedding or listen to her sister's plans, but Elizabeth had other ideas.

"People are already sharing pics in the group chat on Instagram. Look at this one Josie posted." She showed Sarah a picture of her and Artie leaving the ceremony. "You both look really happy."

"Yeah, happy it was over," Sarah said, even though she agreed with her sister. She had enjoyed Arthur's company more than she wanted to admit.

Elizabeth's eyes widened. "Okay, so what did you think of Meg's alphabet speech?"

"Well, I didn't know it was a ploy to get a trip to France. Arthur and I were stunned, thinking it was the most inane piece of writing we'd ever heard."

Elizabeth grinned at Sarah, poked Liam, and said, "Told you so."

Liam glanced over at Elizabeth. "Yes, you did. I doubt she realizes it though."

Sarah eyed them quizzically and said, "Hey, I'm right here! What don't I realize?"

"That you like Arthur," Elizabeth said. "I never mentioned him. You did."

"Uh, that's because he was there when Meg was prattling on about 'T is for tummies'." Sarah huffed. "Don't be ridiculous. Arthur is funny, but I think he's lazy."

"What an interesting observation." Liam glanced at Sarah in the rearview mirror. "How did you arrive at that conclusion?"

Sarah leaned forward, arms over the seat, holding up fingers as she listed her reasons. "He didn't jump with the obligatory group jumping picture, he didn't race the other groomsmen to the truck, and," Sarah said triumphantly, "he did not have a hurt ankle. I asked."

"You did not!" Elizabeth sputtered.

"I did. I wanted him to realize that someone noticed his half-assed effort at jumping."

"You are so clueless sometimes," Elizabeth said. "Sarah, he—"

Liam interrupted. "You might cut the poor guy some slack. He wrecked his bike, missed his plane, the tailor brought the wrong suit, and he's covered in the worst case of poison ivy I've ever seen."

"And—" Elizabeth started.

"Oh, and he tripped and spilled coffee all over his shirt. Said it was the second time he'd done that today. I had an extra white shirt in my bag, so he ended up wearing it, despite it not fitting well."

"I noticed the clothes. Way to be prepared, Liam," Sarah added. "Arthur mentioned the wreck, and I couldn't help but notice the poison ivy. Okay, so he's not lazy. Just having an off day."

"More like week," Liam said. "Poor guy can't catch a break."

"I think Art—"

Sarah held up her hand. "Enough. Arthur's not lazy." She held up her earbuds and made a show of putting one in. "I just want to chill the rest of the way home."

"Okay, wait!" Elizabeth said. "Did you enjoy the flash mob?"

"Yeah, that was kind of fun. I was totally surprised. I told Ar— uh, someone that I was the only member of the wedding party who seemed uninformed about it." Sarah's voice grew thoughtful as she turned to the window. "Maybe I am a little clueless."

"I shouldn't have said that, sis. Honestly, I think you're just preoccupied. You seem to have a lot on your mind."

"Yeah. I guess I do." Sarah mentally listed her concerns: *loneliness, no boyfriend, housing, money, wanting kids, the rest of my life . . .*

Elizabeth glanced at Liam before turning to Sarah again. "Um, the reason I brought up the flash mob is that I wondered if you'd noticed that Liam and I sang the last couple of lines with the original pronouns?"

Sarah's brow furrowed. "Did I notice that you sang *we* are going to be married? Yeah, I noticed, but we all know that. Wait. Have you set a date?"

"Not for the wedding, but we've decided to live together for Liam's last year of residency," Elizabeth explained.

"I feel confident enough in my placement to be assured that I can handle the change," Liam said. "I don't want to call Elizabeth a distraction, but being with each other for extended periods of time during med school and the early parts of my residency would have been challenging."

"Gotcha," Sarah said, nodding. "So, when are you moving out?"

"Actually," Elizabeth began, "I know it's a lot to ask and would be a big change, but—"

"You want me to move?" Sarah guessed.

"You don't have to. You can get a new roommate. We can find—"

"No, it's okay, sis. I was actually thinking earlier today about buying a house."

Elizabeth clasped her hands together. "Really? That's amazing. Are you sure, Sarah? You love our apartment."

"Well, I did, but the residents are getting younger and younger. I think most of them are UTC students. Plus, the whole pool and clubhouse scene has gotten old. It was different when I was seeing Brandon, but lately, it's just made me feel old and lonely."

"But you don't have to be lonely, and you are not old!" Elizabeth objected."

"You should have heard Grandmother: 'You are almost thirty!

You're wasting time!'" Sarah mimicked her grandmother's strident voice, clapping her hands with each syllable.

"Well, you know Grandmother has a funny way of expressing her love. But she's got a point. Not that I think you need to rush into marriage or motherhood," Elizabeth added quickly at Sarah's protest. "I just think six months of not dating is plenty."

"Maybe, but I don't want to jump back in the dating scene and repeat the same story."

"If I may," Liam said, glancing at Sarah in the mirror. "Why don't you analyze past relationships and see what pattern exists. I feel sure you'd be enlightened by the process. There's bound to be either a 'type' of man or a pattern to the relationships, perhaps both, that you need to recognize in order to change the narrative."

Sarah thought about Liam's words. She was used to his somewhat pompous way of phrasing things, so none of that fazed her. "That actually makes sense, Liam. Thanks."

"You might also spend some time thinking about what you want out of life and out of a relationship. The house you mentioned suggests you've already started that process."

"Yeah. I do want a house. I just have to decide where, what kind, and how to pay for it. The relationship bit is easy. I want what you guys have."

"Oh, that's sweet, Sarah," Elizabeth said. "We want you to be happy too. You deserve that. But remember that every couple has their ups and downs. Liam and I have worked to make our relationship what you see.

"And we continue to do so," Liam added. "The work seems to

be where you fall short." He paused. "I'm truly sorry. I should not have offered that insight. You're not my patient."

"No, it's okay," Sarah said. "Just explain, please."

"It's like Mom told you last September." Elizabeth jumped in. "You like the flirtation, the chase, the falling-in-love bit, but real love isn't a race or a game." Elizabeth put a hand on Liam's shoulder. "Real love means you're home, you're safe, you're seen and accepted. It's real, and you know you can take what life throws at you because you're together and stronger because of it." She and Liam smiled at each other, then Elizabeth turned and looked at Sarah. "Honestly, you seem to get bored before you get to the good stuff, so you cut and run."

Sarah leaned forward. "I leave because they all turn out to be jerks."

"One more observation then, Sarah," Liam said. "Some men are jerks, but not all of us are. Could you purposefully be choosing the wrong men?"

Sarah sat back, stunned. *Why would I do that?*

Elizabeth turned and looked at her, but Sarah held up her hand and made a show of putting in her earbuds. She watched the scenery pass by but couldn't stop thinking about Liam's question. It didn't make any sense. She liked having a man in her life. Why would she deliberately choose an unsuitable one?

Liam helped them with their bags and dresses when they arrived at the apartment, then asked if Sarah wanted to join them for pizza. When Sarah declined, Liam said, "You'll figure it out, sis. Deep down, you know what you want. Don't settle for less. You're worth more than that, and you deserve happiness. Your time, your life, is too precious to waste on any more jerks."

Chapter Four

Left alone, Sarah wandered into the kitchen, fixed herself a snack, and thought about the apartment. Would she miss it? Truth be told, it was a bit sterile and industrial for her tastes. She preferred more color and patterns, wood floors over tile. Elizabeth, who was an interior decorator, had added little touches that made it a home, but she couldn't change the exposed ducts and concrete countertops. Still, Sarah knew she'd miss the familiarity and convenience. Within easy walking distance to their jobs and restaurants and bars, the apartment's location had definitely been a factor in paying the more expensive rent.

Why did I agree to move so quickly? I'm used to this place. Where will I go? Six months to find a new place? We've been here eight years. Sarah bit her lip. *I hate moving. It's so much work. Just the thought of boxing every-thing up. Ugh.* Procrastination was something Sarah had struggled with her whole life. Even when she was excited about a project, she took forever to get started. She'd really had to work on strategies to control her ADHD symptoms in school. Making a decision, moving, was not going to be easy.

If I move out of the city, I'll need a car. I'll have to drive to work, which means I'll have to get up early. Where will I shop? I need to stay downtown.

What apartments are nearby?

Currently, Sarah and Elizabeth only drove to work on the worst weather days. In fact, they rarely used the car, the same car they'd shared in college. Now they drove to the grocery store, their mom's house in Newton, and weekend outings. *Liam has a car. Maybe Elizabeth won't need one.* One thing at a time, Sarah reminded herself for the tenth time.

Finished with her snack, she pulled out her laptop and started looking at apartment complexes in the city. *Jeez, rent is higher in these new places than it is here. And the location isn't great. I'd still have to drive to work.* Sarah changed her search to homes for sale around Chattanooga but had no idea where to start. Everything sounded too expensive. She picked up her phone to call her mother. *Mom's a realtor. She'll know what I can afford.* Realizing that her mother was probably exhausted from all the wedding activities, Sarah's thoughts turned to what she wanted, both in a house and in a relationship.

Sarah tended to rush through life, either making impulsive decisions she later regretted or taking forever to decide things of import. Elizabeth made lists. Sarah thought she might try that, but even making a list was more difficult than it should have been. If she were to be the only one living there, then she could be happy with a small house. *But does it make sense to buy a small house if I want a man in my life? But what if I never find a man? I do want children someday.* Remembering her grandmother's comments, Sarah amended that thought. *Someday soon. Should I look for a house suited for kids?*

Frustrated with her lack of progress, Sarah thought she'd take Liam's suggestion and analyze her past relationships instead. So she put away the laptop, cleaned up her snack, and settled on the living room sofa with her journal in hand.

Liam and Elizabeth found her there a couple hours later.

"I took your advice, Liam," Sarah announced. "I've gone back in time and examined my relationships. Do you want to hear what I've discovered?"

"I do," Elizabeth said, pulling Liam down on the couch beside her.

"Okay, my longest relationship was with Blake. We dated most of college. I really thought we'd get married, and Blake acted like we would, but then his mother kind of blindsided me at graduation."

"I remember that," Elizabeth said. "She was rude, barely acknowledging any of us, after announcing that Blake would be much too busy in law school 'to fool with the likes of you!'"

"Right, she apparently convinced Blake that I wasn't good enough for him. He broke up with me about six weeks later." Sarah's voice deepened. "'You know it would never work, Sarah. I need to focus on law school and then my career. I'll need a different kind of wife, one more in touch with social mores.'"

"That rat! I didn't know he'd said all that. Well, I'm proud of you. You got right back out there," Elizabeth said. "You didn't seem that upset."

"I was though. I was embarrassed and ashamed. It really shook my confidence."

"It's good to recognize your feelings about the situation, Sarah," Liam said. "Have you identified how the end of that relationship affected others?"

"Well, no, I haven't thought that much about the whys, just the who and when," Sarah admitted. "After Blake was Brad, then Ethan, then Jerry, and most recently Brandon."

"Any similarities among these men?" Liam asked.

Sarah frowned at Liam. "I told you, I haven't got that far, but Elizabeth, remember when you said I was the constant factor in my relationships?"

Elizabeth nodded. "Yeah. Did you recognize a pattern?"

Sarah poked her journal. "My modus operandi is the same. Blake and I were together for over three years, but all my other relationships have been about eighteen months. I may have gone out with another guy or two in between, but in general, there's about three months between boyfriends."

"I've noticed that," Elizabeth said.

"Well, that breakup with Blake changed me for some reason. Ever since then, I've pretty much followed the same pattern. I meet someone and talk to them for a month or so, then enjoy the flirting, the buildup another month, seeing if I'm still interested, and if they care enough to hang around. Then I'm all head-over-heels in love for four or five months, before I get tired of them." Sarah yawned. "I don't break up, I just accept that while this guy is not perfect, he's good enough. That lasts about three months before I decide he's a jerk, but at least he's my jerk. I keep him around no matter how much he aggravates me just to have someone. The fighting, the spats, the threats of 'I'm so close to leaving' last a month or so, before I Am Done."

"So, you're the one pursuing and breaking up?" Elizabeth looked at Liam. "That seems important. Maybe you are picking the wrong men, Sarah."

"Good observation, Elizabeth, and excellent work, Sarah," Liam said. "You have more to do, of course. I'd recommend looking at the men and noting their commonalities and identifying what you want or definitely don't want." He stood, leaned down and kissed Elizabeth. "I'm exhausted. It's been a long day."

After Liam left the room, the sisters smiled at each other and shook their heads. "Dr. Shepherd is proud of you," Elizabeth said.

"Of you too. It's kind of nice having an almost-psychiatrist in the family."

"I'm proud of you too, Sarah. Maybe looking at your past will help you figure out what sort of guy you want."

"Someone I won't fight with all the time," Sarah said. "Love should be easy, right? I mean, you and Liam are always on the same page. I want someone who has my back, who's my best friend, and who always supports me."

"Whoa, whoa, whoa," Elizabeth said. "You can't seriously believe that. Yes, Liam has my back, but we've been together for ten years. Of course we've had fights. You've probably witnessed half of them."

"Those little squabbles you two call fights don't really resemble the raised voices and hurt feelings I'm talking about."

"Well, we do try to keep our emotions in check, but that doesn't mean we don't have serious disagreements. Don't you remember when we broke up?"

"You mean that time right after your high school graduation?

Ooh, real nasty breakup. It lasted, what? Twenty-seven minutes?"

"More like an hour and twenty-seven minutes," Elizabeth said, hiding a smile. "But it was tragic at the time."

"Seriously, how can you even call that a breakup? It was more like a power outage."

Elizabeth looked at Sarah with surprise. "That's actually a pretty good analogy. I seriously did not have any energy to figure out what to do. I was stumbling in the dark, panic-stricken." Elizabeth shrugged. "Okay, I know it didn't last a long time, but my heart hurt. I hurt. The thing is, Liam only broke up with me because his mother suggested that it would be more fair of him to 'set me free to date other people'." Elizabeth punctuated her statement with air quotes. "She was scared because we were getting serious and still so young. Liam thought he was doing the right thing."

"Yeah, right. He caved to his mother's demands," Sarah scoffed.

"Hmm. I think he considered her feelings and the reasons behind them. Liam's parents married really young. Perhaps his mother felt, and Liam intuited, that she might've chosen a different man had she waited. He wanted to be sure I wouldn't have the same regrets."

"Well, if that's so, why did he come crawling back before the evening was over?"

"Because he was hurting too. We talked about it and explored our options. Since I was going off to school, we agreed to see other people." Elizabeth smiled. "After six months, we knew we wanted to be together, even though we weren't anywhere near ready to get married or start a family. Liam has always had goals, and he's very in touch with his feelings. We're also both very rational, so it worked for us."

Sarah grimaced and shook her head, looking at her sister. "Yeah, it worked for you, but you see, the thing is, Elizabeth, you and Liam have no idea what it's like out there. You found each other so early, so easily, you've never struggled in the same way I have. You haven't ever been in the situation I'm in. Yes, you both went out with other people, but I don't think either of you was seriously looking for someone different. I remember you comparing every guy you went out with to Liam. You probably discussed your dates with him!"

Elizabeth blushed.

"You did, didn't you? God, you two are so analytical." Sarah laughed, then sobered. "You know I love Liam, and I'm glad you have each other, but please realize that your circumstances are unusual. Most people have a more difficult time finding their life partner.

"I do have other goals, Elizabeth, but I know I want a family." Sarah paused and bit her lip. "What if Grandmother's right? I'm twenty-nine, I don't have all the time in the world to find a guy and have babies. But I really don't want to use a sperm donor or marry the wrong guy just because I want a baby. I want a relationship that will last."

Elizabeth looked thoughtfully at Sarah. "Fair. Our situations are different, and you've made some good points, so maybe I'm not the best one to give dating advice. But the thing is, Sarah, I've been here while you've dated these different guys. Guys who pretty clearly demonstrated early on they weren't right for you."

Has it been obvious to everyone but me? Or did I know too? Sarah recalled swallowing her hurt, her pride, when boyfriends had disregarded her feelings, broken plans, or forgotten her birthday. She remembered the times she'd ignored rude, pushy remarks, tantrums, and caustic comments, just to avoid another fight. She realized how walking on eggshells around some of them had made her shrink into herself, hiding her talents, molding herself into what they wanted.

Elizabeth yawned. "It's been a long day. I'm going to bed."

They said good-night, but before Sarah left the room, she vowed not to let herself be mistreated ever again, to decide what she wanted and not rush into a relationship. She'd keep her options open, focus on other goals, and trust the universe to provide.

Chapter Five

Sarah thought about relationships and house-buying all day on Sunday before finally calling her mom to ask about down-payments and financing. "I know I'm not ready financially, but it makes sense to me to buy a house rather than rent if I can."

"It does," Jillian said, "but as a single income buyer, you'll need a larger down payment to keep the mortgage payments affordable. Your dad and I taught you to save at least ten percent of your allowance, but I don't know how well you've done with that as an adult."

"Believe it or not, Mom, I learned my lesson when Elizabeth had the money to buy Tuggles the Walking Dog and I didn't."

"Oh, honey, I remember how upset you were. It was so hard to stick to our rules and not buy it for you. At least Elizabeth shared him with you."

"Possibly only because a battery-operated dog wasn't as much fun as we thought it would be," Sarah said. "But regardless, I learned my lesson and started saving more, even after a salary replaced an allowance."

"That's good news, sweetheart. If you continue working to boost your savings and keep looking within your price range, I'm sure we can find you something, even if you have to compromise a bit on location or amenities."

After talking with her mom, Sarah decided to pursue her dream of home ownership. She could be impulsive but was good at following rules, especially those she set for herself. Sarah decided to discontinue online shopping and identified a few other places she could cut back a little. Knowing the fastest way to build up her savings would be to work more hours, she arrived at work early on Monday morning with a plan.

Sarah worked in the physical therapy department of a busy medical practice that was part of a large hospital syndicate. Stuck in a corner off the front lobby, the therapy room was small, with six tables usually staffed with two or three therapists. A tiny office was situated off to the side. Sarah knocked on her boss's open door. "Hannah, do you have a minute?"

"Sure, Sarah, come on in." In her late thirties, Hannah had managed the clinic for three of the four years Sarah had worked there. Somehow, she made balancing a demanding career while raising a family look easy, but her cluttered office testified to how busy she was. "How was the wedding?" Hannah asked from behind her desk.

"Oh, you know. It was really nice." Sarah perched on the edge of the guest chair, since a stack of mail was in its seat.

Hannah held out her hand. "You don't sound very enthused."

Sarah passed the mail across the desk. "Well, I've been to a ton of weddings over the last few years. They all tend to blend together after a while."

Hannah smiled. "I guess that's true. So, what can I do for you?"

"I wondered if you knew of anywhere that's hiring."

"Just about everywhere," Hannah said, raising her eyebrows. "You're not leaving us?"

"Oh, no, I'm very happy here. Just looking for extra hours. I'm thinking of buying a house, so I need to save for a downpayment."

Hannah looked at Sarah for a moment. "Hmm. Well, I'm surprised. It's certainly an admirable goal, but I thought you loved your apartment."

Sarah shrugged. "My sister's fiancé will be moving in soon, so——"

"Oh, so you need a new place pretty quickly." Hannah turned to her computer and pulled up her email. "Well, as you know, our clinic limits employee hours to forty-five per week. You're currently working forty. Physical therapists are in demand, so we can add an hour a day to your schedule if you like. Ah, here it is. There are also a couple openings for weekend shifts at Linwood and Elmtree Clinics, which are both in our network. Would you like that information?"

"Yes, and please add the extra hour to my daily schedule. I don't want anything to interfere with my hours here, of course, but I'll check with Linwood."

"One other option you might consider," Hannah continued, scrolling through her email. "I've been contacted by some of our rural clinics who need help staffing their offices. I'm only mentioning this because one is in Belford."

At Sarah's surprised look, Hannah continued. "You have some time saved up. You might consider taking vacation here and working at the Belford clinic for a week or two. Their pay is actually a bit more than you make now, so pulling two paychecks for a couple weeks could boost your savings account pretty quickly."

"They pay more?"

"Yes, positions in smaller communities are harder to fill, and there's a lot of political pressure to staff rural clinics."

Sarah nodded. "That makes sense." *PT helps with pain management, which means less medication, which is great because of addiction issues.* "Is the position grant funded?"

"Not that I know of. They have a therapist out on maternity leave. Do you want the information?"

"Yes, please," Sarah said. "I'd like to think about it."

Hannah forwarded the relevant emails and forms to increase Sarah's hours, then stood. "A word of caution, if I may. Don't overdo it. Working two jobs is really hard. While the extra money is great, your health is more important. Be sure to schedule downtime and take your vacation if your body needs it. And, of course, there are tax implications to consider as well."

"Thanks, Hannah. I'll be careful. It's a short-term solution, definitely not forever, and since I've sworn off men, I do seem to have more free time."

"No good-looking groomsmen then?" Hannah asked.

Sarah snorted. "Not really. Not that I noticed," she added, walking into the work room, thinking about Artie and how he'd left with Rachel.

"Oh well. When the time is right, the right man will come along." Hannah followed behind, coffee cup in hand.

"You sound like my new sister-in-law. Meg's always talking about 'speaking dreams into existence' and trusting the universe to provide."

"Well, there may be something to all that. Don't swear off men forever, Sarah. There truly are some good ones out there, and I think it's wise to remain open to what life has to offer." Hannah lifted her coffee cup. "For now, I think the universe is offering more coffee to get this day started."

HANNAH WAS A FRIEND AS WELL AS A BOSS, so Sarah considered everything she'd said but pursued all the options they'd discussed. Acclimating to the extra hour each day wasn't difficult, but adding a full eight-hour shift on Saturday took some getting used to. When her alarm went off that third Saturday, Sarah groaned. "It will all be worth it in the end," she muttered as she headed to the shower.

"It's raining," Elizabeth announced, handing Sarah a cup of coffee. "Do you want me to drive you to Linwood?"

"No, that's okay. If you can do without the car, I'll drive so you don't have to pick me up this evening. Don't you and Liam have plans?"

"Yeah, we're going to dinner with some people in his cohort. It'll likely be a late night. Are you sure you aren't too tired? I don't mind, and it's not a problem to get you home."

"I'll be okay, sis." Sarah yawned. "It's just the rain making me sleepy. It will all be worth it in the end."

At Linwood on this rainy Saturday morning, Sarah worked with three different clients who'd had knee surgeries. She guided them through exercises to strengthen and stretch their muscles, pushing and coaxing, sometimes through their tears, promising them it would all be worth it in the end. "My personal mantra for the duration," she thought each time.

The sun broke through the clouds midday, so Sarah ate her peanut butter sandwich sitting on a towel at the soggy picnic table behind the small clinic, enjoying the feel of sunshine on her back. In the afternoon, she worked both with a pediatric patient and a geriatric patient to improve balance, before giving a deep-tissue massage to a teenage pitcher's shoulder. The variety of treatments and diversity of patients was one of the things Sarah loved most about her job.

Leaving work, Sarah remembered she needed to stop for gas. She figured she could pick up some fast food without blowing her budget, so she stopped at a station near the interstate that had some restaurants attached. The cloudy skies made it seem later than it was. Sarah huddled in her yellow rain jacket, hood up to avoid the drips from the canopy above. She watched the numbers roll on the pump, not really noticing the cars coming and going around her.

"Sarah?"

"Yeah. Um, how are you?" she asked the guy on the other side of the pump, not entirely sure who he was.

"I'm terrific. What are you doing way out here? Don't you live downtown?"

Sarah recognized the voice, but Arthur definitely looked different from the last time she'd seen him. His hair was shorter, his face no longer ravaged by poison ivy, and his beautiful brown eyes were no longer obscured by dorky glasses. "I do, but what are you doing in Chattanooga? Don't you live in Acworth?"

"Crazy as it seems, I've actually just come from meeting with your, uh, with Andy Harrison at Blackwater Manor. Sorry, that was awkward. I don't know what you call him."

Sarah smiled. "Yeah, 'stepdad' feels weird to us, so we just call him 'Mom's husband'." She looked at the overhanging clouds. "Wasn't it a little wet to work on landscaping?"

"Eh, we were just talking, but it was wet," Arthur said. "That's why I'm running late. Thought I'd better fill up the car and my belly before driving the rest of the way home."

"Same," said Sarah. "Unfortunately I'm not as interested in the options here as I'd told myself I would be."

"There's a Mexican restaurant across the street. Care to join me?"

Sarah started to say no, as she had every time she'd been asked out the past seven months, but cheese enchiladas tempted her and she was pretty sure Arthur was dating that girl from Meg's wedding. Josie? No, Rachel. The one he'd taken home after the wedding. So, it wasn't a date. Just dinner with a friend.

"Meet you there." Sarah grinned.

The rain started again as Sarah and Arthur ran from their cars to the restaurant entrance. Arthur held the door for her and signaled for a table for two.

"Poison ivy all cleared up then?" Sarah asked as they sat down.

Arthur grimaced. "Yeah, thank God. It took weeks and a couple of cortisone shots to boot. I tell ya, I almost always have a little patch here or there—just a professional hazard—but that case was a whole new experience."

"You look different." Sarah grinned. "Without the glasses, I almost didn't recognize you."

"I thought there was a little hesitation. I hope I didn't scare you—at the gas station or at the wedding." He laughed. "This is my more normal appearance. You look a little different too." Arthur indicated her scrubs. "What are you doing out this way?"

"Ha, yeah, this is my typical workday attire. I've been working out at a clinic in Linwood on Saturdays for a few weeks now. Elizabeth usually drives me, so it's just a weird coincidence for us to be at the gas station at the same time."

The waiter appeared with a basket of tortilla chips and salsa and took their orders for cheese enchiladas and sweet tea.

"How was your meeting with Andy?"

"Good, good. He's a super nice guy, as you know. He was running late, but that old guy who drove the getaway car at Meg's wedding let me wait inside the manor. The one with the double name, you know who I mean?"

"Randy Keith. He's Andy's uncle, but they just found each other last year." Sarah waved her hand in dismissal. "Long story for another time. Can you make landscaping plans in the rain?"

"Well, yes and no. We'd talked some last fall, but I was too busy to do much then. I looked around a little at the wedding, so I shared some ideas, but a formal plan will have to wait until June when I'm able to make a true assessment of property, test the soil, see what's there, and so forth. The sun came out mid-afternoon, so we walked around in the mud a bit."

"Find any puddles to jump in?" Sarah asked.

"I did." Arthur grinned. "But, being the professional I am, I'm saving that for next time."

"Probably wise." Sarah laughed. "Can you imagine a formal garden with puddles for kids to jump in? Maybe you should add a splash pad."

"Andy's pretty much receptive to whatever I decide, but a splash pad might not fit the vibe I'm going for." Artie smiled. "The important thing with a Federal-style home is symmetry, so I'll probably add some arched arbors into a formal garden, some traditional hedges and so forth. I'm also planning a kitchen garden that I'm very excited about." Arthur grinned. "I could probably get away with an outdoor chessboard."

After the waiter delivered their meals, Sarah asked. "How would you make a chessboard?"

"I was joking, but it could be done with pavers or gravel and grass. Gotta stay within budget though. That's really important, especially since it's my first solo project."

"Well, that's exciting. Maybe a little scary too."

Arthur cocked his head. "Nah, I'm ready. I've been hoping for an opportunity like this for a while. Honestly, I'm a little bored, repeating the same residential landscape designs. I like variety."

"I do too," Sarah said, nodding. "I see a lot of different injuries in my job, which keeps it interesting."

"Is that why you're working at the clinic on the weekend? For the variety?" Arthur took a giant bite of enchilada.

"No. Liam's moving into the apartment Elizabeth and I currently share, so I need another place. I'm thinking of buying a house."

"That's a big goal." Artie swigged some tea. "Man, I was starving. How's your food? Will you stay in Chattanooga?"

"Food's good." Sarah smiled. "I'll stay in Chatty if I can find something affordable. If not, I'll look in the surrounding areas. Do you think you'll stay in Acworth?"

"For the short term. I mean, work is based there, but I don't particularly like the burgeoning suburban scene, ya know. I'd rather be in a small town or the country if I can figure out how to make a living there. Just seems more family friendly."

Sarah's eyebrows rose, but before she could say anything, the waiter was back.

"Can I get you anything else?"

"Just some more water, thanks," Arthur said, then looked at Sarah quizzically. "What?"

"Uhm, do you have a family?"

Arthur laughed. "I mean, I have a mom, dad, and brother, but I'm not secretly married with kids, if that's what you're asking." He set his empty plate aside. "I'm talking future family."

"Oh, okay. Sure. Then I agree. I really like where I live now, but I'd prefer raising kids somewhere with a yard." *Am I seriously talking about kids on a first date? Wait, is this a date?*

"Yards are good. Especially if you're going to have a dog, and every family should have a dog, right?"

"Right. Or a cat. Cats can be good pets too."

"I'll take that," Arthur said to the waiter, who had returned. He waved off Sarah's protests about splitting the check. "What're your feelings on fish?"

"Fish? As pets? Sure, okay. Fish, birds, hamsters. If the kids help take care of them, I'm good with just about any pet. Maybe not snakes or tarantulas."

"I'd rather the birds stay outside. There's something ineffably sad about a caged bird."

The waiter returned to ask if there was anything else, and Sarah forgot what she was going to say as Arthur stood and said, "I think they need this table. It's gotten crowded in here." He walked her to her car, adding, "Sarah, I really enjoyed talking to you. Maybe we can do this again sometime."

"Maybe," Sarah said, smiling and giving him a quick hug. "Thanks for dinner. It was great to see you again, Arthur. Drive carefully."

DRIVING THROUGH THE RAIN-SLICKED STREETS took a little longer than usual, but Sarah was too busy thinking about Arthur to realize it. He was a nice guy, interesting and easy to talk to. Maybe she could date him. *Am I ready? Is he available? Wonder if I can ask Meg if he's seeing Rachel without Meg throwing us an engagement party.* Sarah laughed out loud. She loved her new sister-in-law and knew she was really good for James, but good grief, that girl had love on the brain.

When Sarah was safely home, she changed into comfy pajamas and found her journal. Elizabeth's late night out with Liam was a good time to really dig into her past relationships and try to discern a pattern, a type among the men she'd dated. After ten minutes of sipping a mug of hot tea and staring at a blank page, all she'd managed was a list of their names. *Lists work for Elizabeth. Why won't they work for me?* Sarah covered her face in frustration. She could hear her mother's voice reminding her to start small, rather than trying to see the whole picture at once. *Pictures.*

Sarah turned her journal sideways and, without thinking too much about it, drew little images to represent past boyfriends in boxes down the side of the page. For Blake, a jacket and tie; for Brad, a sneering face; for Ethan, UPS in blocky letters topped with a bow; for Jerry, a muscular arm; and for Brandon, a martini glass. The sneering face gave her pause. But then she remembered finding Brad's sarcasm amusing at first. It had actually been what attracted her to him when they'd met. *Oh, okay, two columns: first what attracted me and second how we met. What else?*

Seeing the UPS logo, she added a column for their jobs and a column for things she'd enjoyed about dating them. *One final column for why I broke up with them.* Sarah returned to the first two columns. *Hmm, I met Blake in college when we were waiting on an elevator. I liked his smile. And I liked the way his smile made me feel. Brad, hmm. Brad I met through that girl Casey from my internship. Blake had just broken up with me and Brad was sarcastic. I thought he was funny. Until he wasn't.* Sarah skipped over to the final column and wrote MEAN. She added installing alarm systems for his job and moved to Ethan.

I really liked Ethan. Those muscular legs and cute shorts. He was funny and attentive. Maybe a little too attentive. Sarah remembered lots of presents at first. Before all the overtime started. And football season. Once she realized he was working overtime to pay gambling debts on football games, she was done. Still, she'd enjoyed his company. They'd had a lot of fun hiking and canoeing, playing Frisbee with his dog. *Aw, Smokey, such a sweet boy.*

Jerry, hmm. He'd had muscles too. He was a personal trainer in a gym with ambitions to open his own facility. Sarah was pretty sure he'd succeeded in that goal. They'd met on a dating app as had she and Ethan. Jerry had been nice; they'd gotten along, but he was pretty much obsessed with exercise and intense diets. Plus, he hadn't wanted a family. Sarah had tried CrossFit to please Jerry, but it just wasn't her jam. *Wait, did I change to please each guy?* Not wanting to get distracted, Sarah jotted a note about changing at the top of page and turned her attention to Brandon.

She'd met Brandon in a bar. Out with a group of friends celebrating an engagement, she'd gone to the bar for a round of drinks. While he prepared them, they'd flirted a bit. Brandon had a really nice, seductive kind of smile. Even though she knew he had to be younger than she was, Sarah returned to the bar the following week just to see him. It hadn't been long before they were a couple.

Elizabeth said he was immature and too stuck on himself, but Sarah thought he was fun. She soon realized Elizabeth was right. He was immature and flaky, and Sarah was embarrassed to think about how many chances she'd given him to choose her over video games or his buds. Brandon obviously hadn't known how to be in a real relationship, but then, Sarah wasn't sure she did either. Maybe all this soul searching would help her to figure it out.

Chapter Six

Over the next three weeks, if Sarah wasn't working or sleeping, she was trying to figure out what she wanted in a relationship and in a house. She'd added a sense of humor and good conversationalist to her wish list for a partner but was still iffy about specifics for a house.

In late March, when Hannah asked her to help staff a booth at a student recruitment event the university was hosting, Sarah was happy to revisit her alma mater, promote her profession, and have a break from a grinding routine.

She and another PT gave a slide presentation to high school and early college students, discussing physical therapy as a great career path in which job openings outstripped the availability of qualified applicants. Afterward, they set up in the hall to answer questions and distribute fliers.

A couple of pharmaceutical reps stood behind a neighboring table. Sarah stared at a man with a shaved head and muscular build. He looked familiar, but she couldn't place him. "Phil?"

"Yeah? Oh, hey, uh, Sarah, right? Remind me where I know you from," the man said. "No, hang on." He snapped his fingers and pointed at her. "At Cross Chatty, with Jerry."

"Oh, that's right. I remember now." They'd been on the same workout schedule a couple of years ago during Sarah's short-lived foray into CrossFit. Phil asked if she was still seeing Jerry. Sarah said no, that he'd moved to Florida. As students converged on the tables, Sarah wondered if the universe had sent Phil her way.

Sometime later, a group of women passed by.

"Sarah?"

Sarah looked up from a box of brochures and noticed a familiar face from her brother's wedding. Thankfully, the woman was wearing a name tag. "Rachel? I'm surprised to see you in Chattanooga."

"We've had professional development meetings here today."

"Oh, is Meg here as well?"

"No, just the fourth-grade social studies teachers. I didn't realize you were a physical therapist," Rachel said, picking up a brochure. "What are you doing here?" she asked, eyeing Sarah's scrubs.

"Oh, a recruitment presentation." Sarah struggled for something to say. She wanted to find out if Rachel was dating Arthur without asking directly. "Uh, is this your first time at UTC?"

"Yeah, it's a nice campus. Does your sister work in the medical field too?"

"No, Elizabeth's an interior designer," Sarah said. "Work going okay?"

"Yeah, sure. It's nice to have a day out of the classroom though. How have you been?"

"Great," Sarah replied, then threw caution to the wind. "I had dinner with Arthur the other night."

Rachel's eyes narrowed, and she put down the brochure. "Yes, I know. Art mentioned that when we were having lunch Monday. I see him all the time, you know."

"Yeah, well, great to see you. I need to get back to the office." Sarah added the box to the wagon they'd brought to transport supplies. She suspected that Rachel wasn't being completely honest, but if Arthur wasn't available . . . Sarah turned to Phil and asked if he'd like to get dinner and catch up.

March rolled into April as the increasing balance in Sarah's bank account battled with her increasing exhaustion. Working two jobs was super tiring. She'd been out with Phil a couple of times, but no longer willing to endure habits that annoyed her, Sarah ended things when he started mansplaining musculature to her. Sarah added a note to her journal: *must respect my opinions and not discount my knowledge.* The universe might be taking its sweet time meeting her romantic goals, but accepting Hannah's suggestion of working through her vacation at the Belford Clinic meant her financial goals were within reach.

Sarah had three weeks of vacation and a week's worth of personal days saved, so she planned to double-dip for a month. That and her increased savings would give her the money she needed for a down payment if she stayed within the housing budget she and her mother had worked out. She was grateful her parents had emphasized saving and giving as a regular part of money management. That learned frugality meant she had a head start on her goal.

Sarah recognized her position of privilege. Her parents had not only paid for her college education but also bought the car she still shared with Elizabeth. So now, she wanted to do this on her own. Just a couple more months. Not that she'd had time to actually look at houses, but she did scroll through the listings nightly just in case. She could do this.

By the end of April, Sarah had identified more traits she'd like to see in a partner. He'd need to be reliable but not overbearing. Shared interests would be nice, but she was too independent to need to do everything together.

One weekend, Sarah swapped her Saturday shift at Linwood for a Sunday shift with one of the other therapists who begged and bartered. The clinic was open fewer hours on Sunday, but Sarah felt she could stand the loss of a couple hours income. Peggy's carrot cake definitely sweetened the deal.

Sarah decided to spend her Saturday morning browsing at the River Market. Lots of local vendors set up booths with jewelry, crafts, candles, and food. She'd missed browsing and talking to the artists and treating herself to culinary delights from various food trucks while she'd been working so hard. The weather was nice but a bit cool, so Sarah wore jeans and a light sweater. She brushed her curly hair, secured it with a big clip at the back of her head, added a bit of lip gloss, then grabbed her sunglasses and headed out the door.

The River Market was set up near the Chattanooga Aquarium, about a fifteen-minute walk from her apartment. Sarah loved living in the small city. The people were friendly and the streets were clean. She waved at tourists in a horse-drawn carriage. Soon she spotted the brightly colored vendor tents lining the brick courtyard area. She wandered slowly, smiling as she looked, but did not buy.

For once, she wasn't going to give in to temptation. She'd wait, save her money, and buy something for her house—when she found her house.

On a whim, she strolled through an offering of outdoor plants. If she had a house, she'd have a yard. Maybe she should learn a little something about gardening and plants.

"That's a good choice. It's a re-bloomer."

Sarah turned her head, wondering if the vendor was speaking to her. Seeing that the man was addressing someone else, she started to walk away.

"Oh, yeah, I know. I was checking the color. I've got a client looking for the Autumn Royalty."

Recognizing Arthur's voice, Sarah spun around and said, "As I live and breathe, it's Arthur King. Even his house plants are royal." She curtsied.

Arthur grinned, bowed, and said, "At your service, my lady."

Sarah laughed and hugged him. "Arthur Gladstone. Are you sure you live in Acworth?"

"Pretty sure.

Sarah stepped back, saying, "Then you must be stalking me. How do you even know about the River Market?"

"Oh, I follow one of the gardeners here on Facebook and saw he had some native species I'm interested in cultivating, so I made the drive."

"Native species of azaleas?" Sarah put her sunglasses on top of her head.

"Yeah, and other plants. I particularly want a native azalea though."

"How are they different?" Sarah asked, genuinely interested, following Arthur as he walked among the plants.

"Well, they're generally taller with smaller flowers that have a great scent. The flowers resemble honeysuckle. They lose their leaves in the winter, so you won't see them lining the front of a house, but man, they are spectacular in bloom."

"And you drove all this way for just a native azalea?"

"Eh, it's not that far, but I'm also interested in a lot of the wildflowers they've got: columbine, cone flower, fire pinks, that sort of thing. Most of my garden is shady, so that's what I'm looking for today." Arthur motioned to the small plants displayed on a table.

"You have a garden? That must mean you have a house."

"I chose my house because it has a garden and a greenhouse. It's a rental, but the landlord doesn't care what I grow. Well, as long as it's legal." Arthur explained. "I also need the garage to store my tools, so my truck has to stay in the driveway."

"I'm jealous."

"You're jealous of my truck? You can hang out in my driveway anytime." Arthur laughed as Sarah bumped his shoulder. "You want to grab some lunch?"

"That sounds great, but to be clear, I'm jealous that you have a yard. I'm still searching."

"Yeah? How's that going?" Arthur asked as they walked over to the food trucks.

"Not great," Sarah admitted. They made their selections and found a brick wall that made a good seat. "I've been spoiled living downtown."

"I can understand that. Chattanooga seems nice," Arthur said.

"It is," Sarah agreed. "Back in the day, it was one of the dirtiest cities around, with a lot of water and air pollution, but the revitalization effort really worked. Of course, the traffic is crazy, so I usually walk to work. Elizabeth and I both went to college here and decided to stay." Sarah continued speaking, watching Arthur's reaction. "Speaking of college, I was doing a presentation at UTC last month and ran into Rachel."

Arthur nodded. "Yeah, she mentioned running into you." He laughed. "In fact, she mentioned it about a dozen times the last time I saw her."

"Do you see her often?"

"Often enough," Arthur said. "It seems like every time I visit Meg and James, she's there." He tossed his trash in a nearby can. "Want to go pick out plants with me?"

"No, I'm glad I ran into you, but I think I'm going to take advantage of my day off and take a nap." Sarah gave him a quick hug.

"Well, okay. Next time you're in Acworth, give me a call. I'll give you a tour of my garden."

Sarah smiled and walked off, calling over her shoulder, "Say hi to your truck for me!"

By the time Sarah reached her apartment, she'd decided to look at Arthur's social media. He was cute and interesting. If he was available, maybe they could go out. His Facebook account didn't show many posts, mostly birthday greetings, so she assumed his privacy status was set pretty high. Seeing a greeting from Rachel, Sarah opened her page and scrolled down. No relationship status, but there, nestled among photographs of Rachel's admittedly cute apartment, her cat, and lots of group friend pics, were pictures of Arthur, several taken at James and Meg's condo and some at restaurants. Were they dating after all?

That evening, Arthur texted a photo of his truck sitting in his driveway. Sarah wanted to respond but didn't know what to say, especially after having seen Rachel's pictures of the two of them together. She deleted the text.

Chapter Seven

Over the next few weeks, as Sarah worked extra hours at the Linwood Clinic, she thought about characteristics and habits of an ideal partner. Perhaps because she'd been so busy, leisure time activities came to mind. She enjoyed physical activities but wasn't a gym rat or CrossFit fanatic as Jerry had been. She liked variety and a sense of play rather than routine or prescribed exercises in her workouts. *I like being outdoors, appreciating nature.*

As the weather warmed, Meg called with an invitation Sarah was delighted to accept. "Our new neighbor Craig has a boat and wants to take us all out on Lake Allatoona this Sunday. He doesn't know many people yet, so he wants us to invite our friends. Liam and Elizabeth are coming, and I've asked Tom from work and another neighbor, Gail. I don't think you've met them. Please say you'll come. It's supposed to be almost eighty degrees and sunny! I'm not planning on swimming, but we'll have lots of fun."

"That's a lot of people. It must be a big boat."

"Oh, it is. Seating for twelve, I think. Craig grew up on the water and knew what he wanted. James said it's fantastic."

"Wow, okay. Well, thanks for asking, Meg," Sarah said. "I've been pulling lots of hours, and a day in the sun sounds fabulous."

When her alarm went off the following Sunday, Sarah wanted nothing more than to go back to sleep, but she'd promised Meg and knew a day at the lake would do her good. Liam and Elizabeth had driven to Acworth on Friday, so Sarah was alone for the ninety-minute drive to the lake. James had warned her to watch for the unnamed road that led to the Stamp Creek day use area where they planned to put in, but Sarah still managed to get lost. When the road ended at a small cemetery, she turned around. Before long, she saw a hand-painted sign pointing to the day use area.

Sarah squeezed her car between two SUVs in the crowded parking area and called Elizabeth as she walked toward the lake. "Hey, I'm here. Where is everyone?"

"Hey, sis. Glad you made it. We had to put the boat in because a line was forming, but we're in a narrow cove to the right. Face the boat ramp and walk up the hill from the little dock. You'll have to swim for it, but we've got towels."

"Oh, ha ha. See you soon." As Sarah crested the hill, she realized Elizabeth hadn't been kidding. The three women were on board Craig's boat about fifty feet from shore. In the lake, James was playing some sort of aquatic volleyball with Liam and a couple of other guys.

James spotted her immediately. "About time! Glad you could join us."

"Sorry, I missed a turn," she yelled back. Shading her eyes, Sarah waved to Liam, then watched as Arthur's broad shoulders rose out of the water as he pounded the volleyball toward Liam. In an exaggerated Southern voice, she simpered, "Why, I de-clar-ah, it's King Arthur."

"At your service, Lady Sa-rah," Arthur said, shaking his wet dark curls from his face.

Sarah held a corner of the brightly colored knit sun dress she wore over her royal blue one-piece bathing suit and curtsied. "I hope that service includes portage to the boat."

"Nah, but I'll race you. C'mon in, the water's fine."

"Right," Sarah laughed, taking off her shoes and wading a bit into the lake. "It's cold!"

James met her at the shore and pretended he was going to give her a bear hug. "Eek, no, you're wet!" Sarah squealed, surprised at her brother's goofy display of affection.

"You will be too in a minute," James said. "It's chilly, but actually feels pretty good. I'll get your bag to the boat, maybe even without getting it wet, but no promises."

Sarah added her dress, hat, and sunglasses to the bag, along with her shoes. She waded up to her knees, splashing water on herself, then ducked under the water and swam toward Arthur, who was treading water about twenty feet from the boat. Craig had already made his way aboard.

"Ready to race?" Arthur asked, grinning at her.

"You're on," Sarah replied. "On the count of three."

His chocolate brown eyes challenged her as they chanted together before swimming furiously. Sarah was a good swimmer, but Arthur was better. His powerful arms propelled him past her, and he reached the boat first.

"Good race!" Arthur high-fived her and waved her aboard. "Ladies first."

Sarah climbed the ladder and gratefully took the towel Elizabeth offered. She dried her face and arms, then wrapped the towel around her waist, turning just in time to see Arthur hauling himself aboard. He dropped to a seat near the ladder while calling out encouragement to James, who was swimming side stroke, holding Sarah's bag above the water.

Elizabeth poked Sarah in the back. Sarah realized she'd been staring and closed her mouth. Arthur was a below-the-knee amputee. His left leg ended about four inches below his knee. Sarah's mind was reeling with memories of Arthur not jumping in the wedding photos, of his gait being off, of thinking he was lazy. *Gah, how could I have been so clueless? I was so judgy.*

Sarah turned and greeted Liam and noticed the other woman aboard was Rachel. *Is Rachel with Arthur? Wait. Am I being fixed up with Craig?* "Hey, Meg, thanks for including me today." She gave her new sister-in-law a hug. "Careful, I'm wet, and that water is cold! Are your neighbors here?"

"They couldn't make it, but Rachel was free, and Artie said he'd love to come, so we're all here now," Meg said, speaking above the music suddenly blaring from surround sound speakers.

"Yeah, it's got a great sound system. Bluetooth connectivity," Craig said as he lowered the volume.

Craig continued to point out features of his new boat to Liam and Rachel. "Obsidian windshield with walk through to the stretch out lounge . . ."

"Here ya go, Sarah." James held her bag out after climbing aboard.

"Thanks, bro. Do you want this towel, Arthur?"

"Nah, I've got one in my bag behind you there. The green one. Hand it to me, will ya?"

"Yikes! That's heavier than I expected," Sarah said. "You must have bricks in there."

"Nah, just my leg."

Sarah grinned, then noticed Rachel glaring at her before turning to Craig.

Laying her hand on his beefy arm, Rachel cooed, "Craig, thank you so much for inviting us aboard your boat. Now that Sarah's *finally* here, you can really show us what you've got."

Craig was a big guy with sandy blond hair. His florid face deepened with a blush at being directly addressed by Rachel, a vision in a tiny hot-pink bikini. "Uh, yeah, all right, everyone hold on to your drinks. We'll take 'er for a spin."

James stepped toward the bow of the boat to pull up the anchor. Rachel flashed Sarah a triumphant look before she and Meg joined him.

"Speaking of drinks, shall we?" Arthur asked, motioning toward the back of the boat.

Sarah followed as Arthur leaned forward, using his arm to balance himself on the left side of the boat as he hopped toward the back. Cushy bench seating lined both sides of the boat behind the helm. Arthur bent down and opened a compartment, revealing a built-in cooler.

"What's your pleasure? Beer, Coke, water?"

"Water, please," Sarah said.

Arthur handed her a bottle and grabbed a beer for himself before sitting down abruptly as Craig gunned the engine and maneuvered the boat from the cove into the lake.

"What's that all about? Rachel, I mean," Arthur asked quietly.

"I don't know. You know her better than I do," Sarah said. *Duh. She likes you.*

"Maybe she likes Craig," Arthur said, looking pleased.

Sarah frowned. She'd been surprised to see Arthur, then angry that maybe she was being set up, then happy because she enjoyed Arthur's company, and now she was just confused. She wanted a day off, not a day in the middle of a soap opera. "Maybe so. Thanks for the water, Arthur. Should we join the others now?"

Sarah was still frowning when she plopped down in the seat next to her sister.

"Somebody's grumpy," Elizabeth teased. "What's going on?"

"I'm just moody. And exhausted." Sarah sighed deeply and looked out over the sparkling lake, enjoying the breeze.

"Are you still working all those extra hours?" Arthur asked, joining them under the canopy in the middle of the boat.

"Yep," Sarah replied, turning toward him. "So I intend to enjoy every minute of this day."

"So, when do you move?"

"Oh, she hasn't found the house yet. She's just being proactive, since Liam and I are kicking her out," Elizabeth joked as she went to join Liam, who was sitting near the helm.

Sarah watched Elizabeth put her arm around Liam's shoulders and his come around her waist.

"When's their wedding?" Arthur asked, leaning close to Sarah so she could hear him over the wind and roar of the engine.

"No clue," Sarah answered gloomily. "I'd like to be out by August though, when Liam starts his final year of residency."

"Meg said they've been together forever."

"Meg talks a lot." Sarah wondered why Arthur's comment irritated her, then wondered what Meg had said about her.

"Hey, now, that's my best buddy you're talking about." Arthur grinned at her. "Maybe once Craig stops showing off, he'll moor this rig and we can go for another swim. Want a rematch?"

"Ordinarily, I would, but today I just want to be that girl soaking up the sun. I really am tired." Sarah yawned as the noise from the boat's engine changed. "I'm glad Meg invited me though. This is a nice break from work on top of work."

"I think you may get your wish," Arthur said. "Looks like Craig's found us a quiet place to hang out for a while."

Craig had slowed the boat, pulling into a narrow channel that widened into a hidden cove. He spun the boat around in a gentle arc before signaling James to drop the anchor. Standing and stretching, he smiled at his passengers.

"How'd you find this place, Craig?" James asked. "It's perfect." He looked out over the broad expanse of calm water. Birds flitted in and out of a border of reeds along the shore.

"I spent many a summer on this lake. My grandparents owned a house just around the bend." Craig pointed. "We fished all over. This channel's the perfect spot for a little fun but dead ends about a hundred yards from here, so we should be alone except for a canoe or a jon boat or two." He rubbed his hands together. "So, do we want to eat, swim, organize some water volleyball? What's your pleasure?"

"Let's wait awhile to eat," Meg suggested. "I'd like to sit in the sun and catch up on girl-talk."

The men took that as their cue to leave. James kissed Meg with a loud smack, calling out, "I shall return," as he picked up the volleyball and jumped overboard. Liam shook his head, kissed Elizabeth softly, and dove overboard. Craig hung the ladder on the side of the boat and climbed down. Arthur hobbled to the swim platform at the rear and slid into the water. Before long, Craig and Liam were teamed up against Arthur and James. Meg and Elizabeth huddled together on the swim platform, legs dangling in the water while they discussed wedding plans, so Sarah stretched out on one of the bow lounges next to Rachel. She was just getting warm and drowsy, when Rachel spoke.

"It's not going to work, you know."

"I'm sorry, what?"

"You're not going to get Art by racing him. He needs a more nurturing woman."

"What makes you think I'm trying to get anyone?" Sarah asked, not opening her eyes.

"Just give up, Sarah. You're not right for him."

And you are? Hmm. If she's warning me off, maybe he's not as interested in her as she'd like. Sarah raised her head and looked at Rachel. "Well, thanks for the warning. Now, if you'll excuse me, I'll just lie here quietly not pursuing anyone."

Rachel sat up and started calling encouragement to Arthur and James.

Is she trying to make Craig jealous now? Oh, who cares? I'm going to enjoy my day. The sun warmed Sarah's back as she listened to sounds of the game, laughter, and bird calls carrying over the water. The boat rocked gently, and the lake worked its magic as she dozed off, wondering what a relationship with Arthur would be like.

A sudden movement of the boat shifting to one side woke Sarah as Craig climbed aboard. She wasn't sure how much time had passed.

Rachel immediately started praising Craig's volleyball prowess. "You were great. Way to smash that ball! Can I get you a beer?"

Even with her eyes closed, Sarah could imagine the scene. A little disgusted by Rachel's fawning, she sat up and stretched, then stood and jumped into the water, nearly colliding with Arthur when she resurfaced. She wiped the water from her face and opened her eyes. "Oh, hi. Guess I should watch where I'm going." Sarah shivered from the sudden change in temperature.

"Always a good strategy," Arthur said. "How was your nap?"

Sarah rolled her eyes. "Well, someone kept talking, but I did finally doze off for a while."

"Rachel's like that. Like a pretty little pink bird chirping away."

Sarah laughed at the image. "You know, I think she's worn pink every time I've seen her. Most girls outgrow that."

"There's still time. She's even younger than Meg."

"I meant they outgrow it by middle school." Sarah paused, then splashed Arthur. "Wait. Are you saying I'm old?"

"Well, if the shoe fits." He splashed her back and swam off.

Sarah gave chase, dove under the water, grabbed Arthur's leg, and pulled him under. He retaliated by dunking her. When she surfaced, Arthur trapped her in the circle of his arms. To get away, she'd have to duck under them. Sarah stared into Arthur's eyes and waited, daring him to dunk her again. Or maybe kiss her. *Whoa, where did that come from?*

"Lunch time, guys!" Meg called from the boat.

Neither moved for a moment. Then Arthur flashed a grin and put his hands in the air and backed away. Sarah turned and swam. On board, she quickly toweled off, slipped her dress over her bathing suit, and watched as Arthur hoisted himself aboard at the swim platform.

"Meg, are you playing hide and seek with my bag again?" Arthur asked.

"Oh, Artie, I'm sorry," Meg said. "I may have moved it when Elizabeth and I were talking. I'll get it." She attempted to scoot around Craig, who was fixing himself a plate.

"No worries, Meg. I'm just giving you a hard time. Sarah, hand me my bag, will ya," he said pointing. "Need to get my leg on."

"Your sea leg?" Sarah teased.

Arthur burst out laughing. "No, matey, I've only got the land leg today.

Sarah complied, noticing that James looked horrified, Meg delighted, and Rachel angry.

Arthur took the bag, nodding his thanks as he moved to the back of the boat to dry his leg and replace the prosthesis.

"Wow, this looks amazing," Sarah said eyeing the charcuterie board Meg and Elizabeth had prepared. She quickly fixed a plate of cheese cubes, crackers, fruit, olives, sliced tomatoes of various colors, and other raw vegetables. "Is that sangria?" She pointed to the pitcher. "I will gladly have a glass of that."

Meg poured her a glass, opened herself a water bottle, and patted the seat beside her. "Are you having fun, Sarah?"

"Yeah, this day's just what I needed," Sarah said, taking a bite of tomato. "Oh. My. God. This is the best tomato I've ever eaten. Where did you get this?"

"It's one of Artie's," Meg said. "Some heirloom variety."

Rachel sat across from them. "Art always brings such interesting food to our get-togethers."

Sarah ignored that. "Arthur! I need you," she called.

"Whoa," Arthur said, sitting beside Rachel. "I'm feeling a little cognitive dissonance here."

"What?" Sarah stared at him in confusion.

"Just, you know, words you never expect to hear together." Arthur laughed. "I'm teasing you, Sarah. What do you need?"

"I need to know about these tomatoes." She held up the remains of her slice.

"Oh, okay. Well, that one is an Ox-heart Pink. It's one of my favorites, looks like a giant strawberry without the seeds."

"That's my favorite too," Rachel squealed.

Arthur's eyes met Sarah's as he pointed at her plate. "That one is a Black Russian. It's a little smoky. The little one is a Black Cherry tomato. Very sweet." He paused. "Like you."

"Why, thank you, kind sir," Sarah said with an exaggerated southern accent. "Tell me more."

Arthur laughed. "They're all heirloom varieties, grown from saved seeds. I've got some that date back fifty to a hundred years."

"And you grew these?" Sarah asked. "At your house?"

"In my greenhouse, yes."

"OMG. These are out of this world." Sarah laughed. "Will you marry me?"

Artie grinned, but when Meg clapped her hands and squealed with delight, Sarah blushed bright red.

"I think you need some sunscreen," Meg said, smiling. "You're a little red."

Sarah was glad for the excuse to walk away from the group to retrieve her bag. She'd obviously been joking, but Meg had acted like she'd been serious.

"Art, can I get you some Sangria?" Rachel asked.

"I'm good, thanks," he replied.

Sarah sighed as she removed her cover-up and applied sunscreen to her face and arms, not realizing Arthur was behind her.

"Want me to do your back?"

"Okay," Sarah said quietly.

Arthur squeezed some sunscreen in his hands, warming it slightly before applying it to Sarah's shoulders, gently lifting each strap to rub the lotion under the fabric. As he rubbed lower on her back, Sarah moaned a little. It had been a long time since anyone had touched her.

Arthur's hand stilled. "My turn," he said, turning so she could put lotion on his back. To cover her embarrassment, or perhaps to avoid thinking about his broad shoulders, Sarah started naming muscles as she touched them, rubbing a bit harder than was necessary to apply sunscreen. "Trapezius, Deltoid, Rhomboid minor, Rhomboid major, Latissimus dorsi."

"Solanum lycopersicum," Arthur replied.

"What?" Sarah asked, hands paused on his back.

"You were showing off your knowledge of muscle names; thought I'd share my knowledge of tomatoes," he said, turning toward her.

"I wasn't showing off," Sarah said defensively. "I was distracting myself."

"Oh, yeah?" Arthur grinned, taking the sunscreen from her. "Why is that?"

"Ask Meg!" Sarah sputtered and returned to the group.

Chapter Eight

The afternoon passed quickly as the crew of eight enjoyed a beautiful day at the lake. After lunch, and an impromptu game of cards, Craig asked if they'd like to do a little tubing. Meg immediately said no, as Arthur blurted out, "Oh, man, I should have waited about my leg."

"You in, man?" Craig asked Arthur.

"Oh, hell yes."

"Artie's addicted to physical activity," Meg said. "Sort of like Sarah."

"Oh, yeah? What sort of physical activity? Extreme sports or a little softball on the weekends?" Arthur asked.

"Mostly just running or hiking—"

"And white water rafting," James said.

"And rock climbing," Elizabeth added.

"I can't do the white water, but I'm up for the rest of it," Arthur said as he stood up.

Sarah noticed Rachel's glare, smiled at her, then asked Arthur where he climbed.

"Boat Rock, mostly. It's about an hour from home."

"Oh, I thought maybe Rocktown. It's not far from Chattanooga."

When Craig asked if Sarah had ever done any sky diving, Arthur moved away to remove his prosthesis.

"That's big nope from me," Sarah said. "I'm not really into extreme sports. I just enjoy new things and need to burn off excess energy."

"Usually, anyway." Elizabeth laughed. "I hardly know the Sarah of the last couple months."

Craig had a two-person tube which he unhooked from the canopy and tossed into the lake behind the boat. Liam and Elizabeth dove in and hoisted themselves onto the tube. Craig was a good driver, gently pulling forward until the tow rope was exposed, then waiting for their ready signal. James watched to see when they'd had enough.

When Arthur rejoined them, Rachel turned to him, hands folded as if in prayer. "Art, will you please, pretty-please ride with me? I've never tubed before. I really want to try it, but I'm a little scared. Will you hold my hand?"

"Uh, sure, okay," Arthur said, as Liam and Elizabeth climbed back on board.

Arthur and Rachel made their way out to the tube. Sarah could see Arthur demonstrating how to get on the tube, but Rachel seemed to lack the necessary arm strength.

James had been watching closely. "Hang on to the tube, Rachel. I'll pull you in." He towed the tube back to the ladder, while Arthur swam to the back of the boat.

"Climb aboard, Rachel. We'll help you get on from the swim platform," Liam said.

Once Rachel was situated, with most of the tow rope sitting on the tube, Arthur pulled the tube a short distance away from the boat before pulling himself up. Sarah could hear Rachel talking nonstop as the boat picked up speed. When the tube crossed the wake, Rachel let out a squeal.

"It does look fun," Meg admitted. "Do you think it would be okay, James?"

"If Rachel can do it, you certainly can," Sarah said, as James assured Meg it would be fine.

When their ride was over, Rachel slid off the tube and dog-paddled toward the boat, jabbering the whole way, assuming Arthur was right behind her. Sarah dove off the swim platform and joined Arthur at the inner tube.

"Need a hand?"

"Nope." Sarah easily pulled herself forward on the tube.

"Mind if I join you?" Arthur asked.

Sarah answered by patting the spot beside her. When she reached for the center handholds, Arthur's hand brushed hers and their eyes met.

"Are you ready?" he asked smiling.

"I think so." Sarah shifted closer to him.

Craig seemed to know they were more confident riders and whipped them back and forth across the wake, delighted by their whoops of laughter.

When they got back on board, Meg was still considering whether to give it a try. Rachel chimed in, "It's not too scary, and James will look out for you."

"I know, but I really don't like to be cold."

"You'll be having so much fun you won't notice," Elizabeth said.

"Just a short ride, Craig," James instructed. "We don't want to bounce Meg too badly."

James and Meg climbed on the tube and signaled for Craig to start. Everyone's cheers quickly turned to calls to halt when the tube hopped a little and Meg slid right off into the water. James immediately swam to his wife's side.

Craig circled around, and the couple climbed back on board.

"Short enough, man?" Craig asked. "Seriously, I'm sorry about that. Do you want to go again?"

"No, thank you," Meg called. "That's enough fun for one day. I'm going to sit up front with Rachel and dry off a bit."

Everyone agreed that the day had been lovely, but it was time to head back. Sarah stood and stretched. "This day was just what I needed," she announced to anyone listening before joining Arthur at the rear of the boat. Sarah smiled and grabbed a Coke. "I need the caffeine. Do you want anything?"

"Just water, thanks," Arthur said as he reached for a dry towel.

Sarah sat down beside Arthur. "Can I ask you a question?"

"Lawn mower. I was twelve."

"Okay," she said slowly. "I had wondered, but I'm actually asking about Rachel."

"Rachel? Well, that's different. Usually the first thing people ask is how and when I lost my leg." Arthur took a swig of his water and looked at Sarah, as he dried his leg and fitted his prosthesis. "What about Rachel?"

"Oh. Well, I'd like to hear the leg story sometime, if you want tell me, but—" Sarah toweled her hair. "I just wondered, um, are you sure you're not . . ."

"Interested in Rachel? No," Arthur stated. "She asked me for an early ride home from the wedding, then insisted we go out to dinner to thank me and got a little huffy when I declined." Arthur rubbed the back of his neck. "I'm trying to keep my distance because I don't want to encourage her, but you heard her, wanting me to ride with her. It would have been churlish to refuse, but no, I'm not interested in Rachel."

"Churlish," Sarah repeated, with a little laugh. "Who uses words like that?"

"We do," Arthur said, grinning. "You know, me and my knights."

Sarah smiled, "So, you don't have a girlfriend?"

"I'm not seeing anyone currently, no. Are you?" Arthur asked, looking at Sarah.

"No, I've sort of been on a break from men."

"So Meg said, but I thought maybe things had changed."

"Again with the talking about me!"

"I asked," Arthur said. "Maybe that was out of line, but I was curious, you know. At the wedding I got mixed vibes. We'd be having fun, and then you'd get pretty tense. I thought maybe I was imagining it." Arthur shrugged. "I mean, I was pretty spaced out on antihistamines. Then I had a nice time at the Mexican restaurant and the River Market, but you didn't respond to my text, so I needed to know."

Sarah looked toward the front of the boat and shrugged. Elizabeth had joined Meg and Rachel on the bow. Liam and James were watching Craig drive the boat. "Yeah. The truck picture. Sorry. Sometimes I don't know what to say and then forget that I haven't responded."

Arthur nodded and took Sarah's hand. "I don't like to play games, Sarah. I like you. Maybe Meg's right and the universe is aligning for us. Maybe that's why we keep running into each other." Arthur squeezed her hand. "What do you think? When you're ready, can we go out on a real date, get to know one another better?"

"What do you like about me?"

"Wow." Arthur's eyes widened in surprise. "Okay, well, you're direct. You've got a great sense of humor, you're not pretentious, you're honest, and you speak from your heart, even if you're a bit blunt at times." He smiled. "You're very pretty. And you've got great legs. Two great legs. I like legs."

Sarah laughed. "Okay, I admit to being blunt. You forgot quick to judge. I totally misjudged you. I thought you were lazy, but you're not." Sarah touched Arthur's forearm. "I'm sorry about the mixed vibes. I was definitely feeling sorry for myself at the wedding, but I'm better now. I like you too, Arthur."

"My friends call me Art or Artie." Arthur booped her nose. "Your turn."

"Well, Arthur, um Art, Artie, you're kind and funny and easy to talk to. I love that you're active and smart and not at all pushy. You seem very comfortable and confident, and that's quite sexy. You're excited by your work, and I like that." She touched his arm again, smoothing the fine black hairs. "This sounds crazy, but you have sexy forearms. I noticed them as you were leaving the wedding," she said, raising her eyebrows.

Arthur held his arms out in front of him, looking them over. "I think maybe you've been away from men too long, Sarah." Arthur placed his hand on Sarah's forehead. "Or maybe out in the sun too long. Are you sure you're okay?"

Sarah put her drink down, stood up, and pointed a finger at him. "I'm being honest. You are a sexy man, and those shoulders, yum."

Arthur backed away from Sarah's finger but smiled. "Damn. I like hearing that."

"Arthur, can I kiss you?" she asked, leaning close to him.

"Yeah?"

She moved closer. "Wait. Is that a question?"

"Well, everyone is staring." Looking toward the front of the boat, Arthur yelled, "What?"

"Can you tie us up?" Liam called. "I can do it if you're too busy." He walked to the back of the boat, waving his hand in front of his face. "You two look pretty intense back here. Everything good?"

"Everything's great," Arthur said, just as Sarah shrieked in agony.

Chapter Nine

"Sarah, what's wrong?" Arthur and Liam asked as she dropped her Coke can, muttering curses and sounds of pain.

"Ow, ow, ow!" Sarah put her hand to her lip. "Something stung me!"

Arthur looked at the can rolling on the deck. "Yep. Yellow jacket. Maybe more than one. Let's get you some ice." He took the roll of paper towels Elizabeth handed him, gave Sarah some ice for her lip, then wiped up the spilled drink while Liam tied up the boat.

"Let me look." Arthur put his arm around Sarah's shoulders.

"I'm sorry to be a baby, but it hurts." Sarah sniffed as she pulled the towel away from her mouth. "How bad is it?"

"It's pretty swollen. Hold still now," Arthur said as he gently pulled out a stinger. "Are you allergic to stings?" he asked calmly but looked at Elizabeth in concern.

"No," Sarah said. "I just hate being stung."

"And they always seem to find you, don't they, sis? Let's get out now." Elizabeth retrieved Sarah's bag and her own, handing them to Liam, who had tied the boat to the small dock. "James and Craig need to get the boat on the trailer before the ramp gets any busier." Liam helped them out of the boat, as Arthur joined them on the dock.

"I only found one stinger, but yellow jackets can sting multiple times, and I'm guessing your guy was a little angry. I have some antihistamine in my truck." Arthur motioned toward the parking lot.

"I can't take anything now." Sarah knew she was whining but couldn't stop. "I have to drive home. I've got to work tomorrow."

"Don't be silly, Sarah. Liam can drive his car, and I'll drive ours. Go with Art, take the medicine, and then get changed," Elizabeth said firmly.

Still holding the ice to her lip with one hand, Sarah allowed Arthur to take her other hand and lead her to his truck. He opened the glove compartment, rifled among some papers and withdrew a package of Benadryl, then handed her a pill and his bottle of water.

"I'm lucky you had some antihistamine, Arthur. Thank you." Sarah winced as the swelling pinched.

"Between stinging insects and poisonous plants, I should probably invest in the stuff." He retrieved a bag from the floorboard. "Let's get changed and find your car so you and Elizabeth can get started before you pass out."

"I'm not going to pass out," Sarah insisted. "Benadryl doesn't work that quickly."

"You're obviously exhausted, Sarah. It's not my place to say so, but maybe the house isn't worth this," Arthur said, putting his arm around her waist. "Where's your car parked?"

Sarah's eyes sparked, but she was too tired for an argument. "Stupid yellow jacket. I really wanted to kiss you."

Arthur leaned close. "We'll get there, Sarah, but now's not the time. Where's your car?"

"It could be," Sarah insisted.

Arthur looked at her, both exasperated and amused. "Quit being a brat. With that lip, you wouldn't enjoy a kiss right now." He pulled her close and whispered in her ear. "And kisses should be enjoyable. Especially first kisses."

Sarah's lopsided smile grew larger, but her lip hurt. *I probably look ridiculous.* She put the ice back on her mouth and followed him to the bathhouse, where Elizabeth was waiting.

"Let me see your lip," Elizabeth said. "Yikes, that's really swollen."

After the sisters changed, they met everyone in the parking lot to say their goodbyes. "Thanks for the ice," Sarah said when Craig handed her a cup, "and for including me. I had a great time. Sorry for worrying everyone." Sarah climbed in the passenger seat of their car, barely noticing everyone's concerned looks. Everyone except Rachel, that is. Rachel, still wearing the hot pink bikini, was hugging Arthur!

Between her work exhaustion and the Benadryl, it wasn't long before Sarah was asleep. Once home, Sarah roused herself enough to get out of the car.

"Don't worry about the bags, sis," Elizabeth said. "Just get into bed."

When she stumbled into the bathroom about 2:00 AM, Sarah noticed her swimsuit had been rinsed and was hanging over the shower rod. "Good old Elizabeth," she thought, before seeing her reflection in the bathroom mirror. "OMG!" she whispered seeing her hugely swollen lips. "I must've been stung more than once. Wait, I think Arthur said that." Thinking fondly of him, she muttered, "Stupid yellow jackets." Sarah rummaged in the cabinet for more antihistamines, then slept until her alarm went off the next morning.

"SLEEP OKAY?" Elizabeth handed Sarah a cup of strong black coffee sweetened with brown sugar and a touch of ginger and cinnamon.

"Oh, yeah. Definitely. I really needed yesterday," Sarah said. "Remind me tonight to tell you all about Arthur. I've decided I really like him."

"Score another one for Meg. When you were tubing, she said she felt the universe was aligning for you."

"We almost kissed. Would have except for that stupid yellow jacket. I tried to get him to kiss me anyway, but he said something that made me mad." Sarah frowned.

"What did he say?"

"Well, it's kind of fuzzy but something about me working too hard." Sarah backed away from the table and fixed a bagel with cream cheese for her breakfast, wincing as she bit into it. She patted her lip gently. "I definitely wanted to kiss him. I hope I didn't make a fool of myself." Giving up on the bagel, Sarah pulled a protein drink from the refrigerator and asked, "Why didn't you guys tell me about his amputation?"

Elizabeth cleaned up her own breakfast dishes while answering. "Well, I tried to tell you on the way home from the wedding, but you kept interrupting me, and then Liam said it wasn't our story to tell. I mean, Art's not just an amputee. He's intelligent, hard working, a good friend—"

"Super nice, funny, and sexy as all get out. I completely misjudged him at the wedding. Did you see the man's shoulders?" Sarah sighed. "I guess I understand, but I think I deserve a little credit. I've seen all kinds of injuries and been through the sensitivity training about not identifying patients by their injuries. You know, we can't say 'meniscus tear at ten'. We have to say 'forty-year-old male with meniscus tear at ten'. Arthur's been an amputee since he was twelve, so I'm sure he's used to all kinds of reactions, but I'm not bothered by amputations. I've helped several people fit their prostheses and helped in rehab after the surgeries. It's an important part of recovery."

"Hmm, I guess I didn't know that. I thought there would be specialists for that."

"Well, sure, but we get patients with all kinds of needs at the clinic. The only thing that bothers me about Arthur is Rachel. He says he's not interested, but she's always there!"

The sisters spent a happy fifteen minutes discussing Rachel's clinginess, wondering what Meg saw in her, before leaving for work.

Before they parted ways at the end of the block, Elizabeth asked, "So, when are you seeing Art again?"

"I'm not sure. He may not even have my number. If he doesn't call, I'll risk enduring Meg's 'told-you-so's to get his. Oh, wait. He

sent me a text after I ran into him a few weeks back. Maybe Meg—
oh, it doesn't matter. Chances are pretty good we'll be in Belford at
the same time, which makes me a tiny bit regretful that I asked Beth
Ann if I could stay with them. I mean, things could get awkward
while I'm staying with my mother's husband's grandmother."

"Sarah," Elizabeth cautioned. "You said you weren't going to
rush into things!"

"I'm not, but still."

Chapter Ten

Sarah's phone chirped with an incoming text before she reached the clinic.

"How are you feeling? Still swollen?"

"It's Art, btw."

Sarah smiled, pleased to know that Arthur was thinking about her. "Walking to work now. Bit puffy and sore, but okay."

"Can I call you tonight? I'd like to see you again. This weekend?"

"Yes! Talk soon."

Sarah saved his number in her contacts before waltzing into the office, her smile broad, if a little lopsided.

"Sarah? You're awfully chipper for someone with a bruised lip. What on earth happened to you?" Hannah asked.

"Well, yesterday was great, right until I got stung." Sarah explained the whole bee-sting saga as they prepared for their day.

"SARAH, IT'S ART. Er, you sound out of breath. Is this a bad time?"

"Arthur, hi, just lugging my laundry to the basement. Can I call you back in five minutes?" Sarah loaded her laundry into the community machines, then opened the door to a tiny walled courtyard with a few chairs scattered about. Pulling two chairs close together, she propped her feet in one, and returned Arthur's call.

"Hey, you. Thanks for calling."

"I said I would. I meant what I told you over the weekend, Sarah. I'd like to get to know you better."

Sarah smiled. "That's really nice to hear, and I feel the same way, but you should know I'm a little scared and a little scarred."

There was a pause before Arthur said, "I think that applies to most people, Sarah, but if this weekend is too soon, we can—"

"No, no, Arthur, this weekend sounds good. I just thought I should warn you. It's been a while. So, do you have anything particular in mind?"

"Oh, I've got a few ideas. What's your preference? Indoors or out?"

"Out, unless you'd prefer indoors. I mean, you're outside a lot, right?"

"If I didn't like being outside, I'd have a different job, Sarah, but there's a lot of desk work too. So, hiking? River Market? Picnic? Outdoor dining? I hear there are good restaurants in Chattanooga."

"Well, if you don't have to rush back home—"

"I don't. I've set aside the whole day, Sarah. How about we start at the River Market, then go on a picnic?"

"I'd like that, Arthur. Maybe we could take a short hike too. Then we can have dinner with Liam and Elizabeth. How does that sound?"

Although they were both super busy, they texted every day trading information about hiking trails and dinner options. Sarah accepted his friend request and looked at his photographs, most of which were flowers. A few featured people she assumed were family, and two showed the chess club at Meg's school with the children's faces blurred out. Since they'd made a date for Saturday, it was Sarah's turn to beg Peggy to swap shifts with her. She couldn't barter a homemade carrot cake but did buy a gift card to thank her.

To save Arthur from having to loop around Chattanooga's many one-way streets, Sarah suggested they meet opposite her apartment building. On Saturday morning, her heart was racing as she paced up and down the sidewalk, watching for his forest green truck. *Gah! Stand still! Am I nervous? Maybe just excited.* Sarah combed her fingers through her hair and pulled it back in a ponytail. *Oh, there he is!* She waved and Arthur pulled to the curb.

"Hey you," she said, climbing into the cab.

"Lady Sarah." Arthur grinned and kissed her hand in an exaggerated show of chivalry before pulling back out into the traffic. "How are you this fine morning?"

"I'm good. It's the first right. Right here," Sarah said, thinking she could, well, count on one hand the number of times anyone had kissed her hand. "The parking lot's a couple blocks down," she added, squeezing his hand."

Arthur parked and hurried around to Sarah's door. She'd already opened it but reached for him as she stepped out. Arthur drew her into a hug. She kissed his cheek. "It's so good to see you."

"Let me look at you. How's the lip?"

"Lips are good," Sarah said, smiling. "Ready and waiting."

"Maybe we'll test that out later." He laughed. "Coffee first."

They paid for parking, then crossed the busy street and headed to the food trucks. The air was still cool, and Sarah was glad she'd worn a jacket. "Hey, we're twins." Sarah slipped her arm underneath his jeans jacket and around his waist. "Even our shirts are the same buttery yellow. What does yours say?" She smiled at the block letters as she read aloud: "'Seed, Sow, Water, Grow.' Let me guess, Meg?"

"Yep. What does yours say?"

Sarah opened her jacket so Arthur could see her T-shirt, which pictured a row of flowers with 'Physical Therapy' scripted above it. "You've got to admit, Meg carries a theme well," Arthur said.

"That she does," Sarah agreed, stopping at a food truck. "This place has good coffee." After they placed their orders, she asked, "So, what was the design of the blanket Meg gave you year before last?"

"Is this a test?" Arthur laughed. "Pretty sure it had dogs on it."

"Same," Sarah said, smiling before stopping a runaway quarter. "Here you go, sweetheart." She handed a little girl the coin she'd dropped.

"Where should we go first?" Arthur asked once they had their coffees.

"Oh, I don't know. Somewhere less crowded," Sarah suggested, hugging his waist.

Arthur laughed. "Right? There are a ton more people here than last time. Honey."

Sarah stared. *Did he just call me 'honey'?*

But, no, Arthur led Sarah to a booth selling local honey. He chatted with the people running the booth about flowers and bees, while Sarah picked up soaps and smelled them. She loved the look and smell of some small soaps molded into the shape of honeycomb cells, some with imprinted bees. Her boss Hannah had a birthday coming up, so she decided to purchase a set. Arthur was reaching for his wallet when Sarah said, "I'll get that," and took the jar of honey from his hand. "You drove all the way up here to see me, and you bought the coffees," she added as she handed the soaps to the vendor.

"Well, thank you, Sarah," Arthur said frowning a little.

"What's that look for?" Sarah asked. "Do you object to a woman paying her own way?"

"No, I just don't want you spending your money on me. You've been working so hard."

"It's ten dollars, Arthur. I think my budget can handle it."

"Is this our first fight?" He asked, then laughed at Sarah's look. "C'mon, let's look at these pots."

Sarah wasn't too interested in the pots, but Arthur seemed to find them fascinating. She watched as he talked with the sellers, asking about colors and prices of various styles. Her mind wandered as he started asking about bulk rates and availability. *Will we fight over money? Or is it really about control?*

Sarah knew her independent streak had caused problems in past relationships. Perhaps she was overly sensitive about socially dictated male and female roles and expectations. Brandon hadn't minded splitting tabs and even let her pay his way quite often. She made more money than he did, so it had seemed fair to her. But Jerry, or was it Ethan, had made it plain that he would pay. She could cook for him, buy him gifts and so on, but Jerry, it had definitely been Jerry, the trainer, had basically said he felt emasculated when she paid. Well, that wasn't the word he used. Sarah doubted he knew that word, but that had been his meaning. Ethan had been the one who wanted to be her hero. Life wasn't a fairy tale. Why would an independent woman need a hero? She'd rather have a partner.

"I'm sorry, Sarah. I shouldn't have taken so long," Arthur said. "You look pissed."

"Do I? I'm not. I didn't mind, I was just lost in thought," Sarah said. "Did you not buy any pots?"

"No, but we exchanged information. I think I'd like to carry their pots someday," Arthur said as they continued browsing among the booths.

Sarah looked at him blankly. "Carry their pots? I don't understand."

"Sorry, if and when I open my own business, I think their pots would be great to stock in the shop."

"Landscape architects have shops?" Sarah asked, still confused.

"No." Arthur grinned. "My dream is to own a full-service gardening center, one that offers landscape design and features a lot of native plants. I might work a commercial job or two a year to keep my license and skills current, but my passion is for smaller, more intimate spaces and heirloom plants."

"Oh. Wow," Sarah said. "I had no idea. Based in Acworth?"

"I doubt it. I moved to Acworth for the job. Meg moving there a few years later was an added bonus, but I think she and James like it better than I do. Cobb County has really grown since I moved there, and it's still growing. I was promised the opportunity to design spaces for some of the office complexes going in."

Arthur frowned and paused for a second at a vendor selling sand art. "I used to do these as a kid," he said, putting the small jar back down. "More and more though, we're designing back yards of some of the McMansions around town. And they all seem to want the same things—patios, fire pits, tiny turf grass yards, a few nandinas and a crepe myrtle, or a freaking Bradford pear. They *want* to look like everybody else." Arthur sighed. "It drives me crazy. Sorry, didn't mean to rant. It's just frustrating."

"I'm sure. So, how long until you can open your own business?"

"No idea. If the Blackwater Manor job goes the way I want, it could happen pretty soon. That's why it's so important to me to do a good job." Arthur steered her around a couple with a baby stroller. "What about you? Is there a dream job in your future?"

"Oh, I'm happy where I am. I may pursue some sort of specialization some day, like geriatrics or sports medicine, but I like variety."

"Right?" Arthur stopped. "Yum, smell that? I'm going to grab us some of those cookies for later. I'll meet you here in just a minute, okay?

"Sure," Sarah said, as she paused at a booth selling T-shirts. "T-shirts are always fun to look at." She quickly realized they were all plant related. *Arthur's obviously passionate about his job, but does he even have time for a relationship with all his plans?*

When he rejoined her, she held up a T-shirt and said, "Look, Arthur. This is perfect for you: 'That's what I do. I grow stuff and I know things.'"

"I actually have one of those. In fact, pretty much every T-shirt I own has plant slogans. Look at these: 'Powered by Plants' and 'Hoardiculturist'. Which do you like best?"

"This one," Sarah said, holding out a long-sleeved forest green shirt that said 'Plant Native' in large orange letters.

"I like it," Arthur said. "Hey, I bought that native azalea I was telling you about last time. Okay, I'm getting it and this one," he said as he picked up an ivory-colored shirt. Arthur quickly paid and suggested they head out for their hike.

They started walking toward the truck, passing by a large fountain surrounded by small tables. A little boy danced in front a street musician. Sarah clapped and cheered him on, then turned to Arthur. "So, have you chosen a name for your dream business?"

"No, I keep tossing around ideas, but anything I like has already been taken a dozen times."

"Like what?" Sarah asked.

"Oh, you know, things that play with my name. Like Garden Art or Artscapes. I thought about using something King Arthur related, but Camelot Gardens is taken."

"What about Heirloom Gardens?" Sarah remembered those heirloom tomatoes and Arthur's fondness for native plants.

"Taken."

"Midsummer Gardens or, I know, Gladstone Gardens."

"Taken and very taken. You wouldn't believe how many

businesses are named Gladstone Gardens. Many of them are rock suppliers."

"I know!" Sarah turned toward him as they stopped at the curb waiting on the traffic light to change. "Bees Needs! It's kind of a play on the bee's knees. You know that saying?"

"Yeah, I've heard it, and I like puns," Arthur said, "but I think it might be a bit misleading. Frankly, I'm surprised you'd think of anything to do with stinging creatures," he added quietly, brushing a finger softly across her mouth.

Sarah thought she'd never felt anything so exquisite as that finger on her lips.

Arthur moved his packages and took Sarah's hand in his as they waited for a bus to rumble past.

"I'm still thinking." Sarah squeezed his hand.

"No rush," Arthur said, as they started across the street to the parking lot. "I've been working on a business plan for years."

Noticing a car looking for a parking space, Sarah motioned to the driver that they were leaving.

He opened the truck door and helped Sarah in. "I got you a present," he said, handing her a white paper sack.

Sarah looked at him in confusion. "A present? For what?"

"Just for being you," he said, looking intently in her eyes.

Sarah put the sack in the floor and turned in her seat to face him, hoping he would kiss her. She leaned toward him and placed a hand on his tanned forearm.

Artie cupped her face, gazing into her eyes, thumbs brushing gently over her cheeks. When a car horn sounded, he grinned as

Sarah huffed in frustration. "Patience, Sarah. First kisses are special. You only get one, and a parking lot really shouldn't be the place for ours." He walked around the truck, waving to the impatient driver before climbing in. "Open your present."

Sarah's heart had fluttered as Arthur talked about first kisses. The anticipation was nice, different, but nice. And frustrating! *Okay, fine, I won't rush things.* As he backed out of the parking space, Sarah pulled out the ivory-colored shirt he'd bought. It pictured a row of vegetables, including a turnip, carrot, and beet. At the top it said, "Let's root for each other."

"You didn't have to buy me a present, Arthur." *I really wish you hadn't.*

"I know, but I wanted to. It's not a big deal."

Maybe not to you. "It's nice, Arthur. Thank you. But you really didn't have to buy me anything."

"I thought you might appreciate the sentiment. I get the sense that despite being competitive in some areas, you're a great cheerleader for humanity. I'm just sorry they didn't have it in pink. That is your favorite color, right?" Arthur laughed as Sarah poked him.

Chapter Eleven

arah directed Arthur out of the parking lot, then asked why he thought she was a cheerleader for humanity.

"Just an observation. It's little things, like signaling that couple that our parking spot would be vacant soon."

"But that was after you bought the shirt," Sarah objected, "and if I'd known they were going to interfere with our first kiss, I wouldn't have helped them!"

Arthur burst out laughing. "Okay, bad example, but you helped that girl find the quarter she'd dropped." He patted her hand. "You're a good human."

"Well, thanks, Arthur, but it wasn't a big deal. Turn right here." Sarah pointed at the road to Signal Mountain.

"Maybe not, but you noticed them. Everyone wants to be noticed." Arthur smiled at her but drummed the steering wheel impatiently as traffic slowed after the turn. "Jeez, this is as bad as Acworth traffic. Which trail did you decide on, anyway?"

"The Bee Branch Trail. It's about twenty minutes away but may take longer with all this traffic."

"Again with the bees; I'm going to start calling you honey." He grinned at her. "It's probably just construction. I noticed some signs and cones on the interstate when I was driving back from Belford. What's the trail like?"

"It's the loop trail I sent you. Gah, I hope there aren't bees. Elizabeth and Liam recommended this trail. They hiked it last fall and said it took an hour or so." Sarah pulled up the trail guide on her phone. "No big views, but it has creeks and some beautiful cascades. Ooh, and wild flowers."

"Can't have wildflowers without bees," Arthur said. "Bridges over the creek, right?"

"Yeah, there are pictures of bridges," Sarah said, suddenly realizing that he was asking because of his prosthesis. She felt awkward and wondered if they should hike a different trail. A minute or so passed in silence.

"I would love to design a garden with a bridge over a creek, but arbors and gates are more common features."

"Oh my gosh, Artie! That's it!" Sarah cried. "The name for your business. Arbor Gate!"

"Hmm. Arbor Gate Landscapes. Arbor Gate Landscaping Service. I like it." He smiled. "Art Gladstone, Arbor Gate, same initials. I could probably do a logo with the A and G intertwined. Maybe one day have an actual gate with the logo. I really like it, Sarah. Thank you."

Sarah smiled and leaned back in her seat, happy to have come up with a name. "So, how did you get interested in plants, anyway?"

"Meg's grandfather, actually. Did she ever tell you about her dad?" Artie asked, looking at Sarah as the cars in front of them slowed once again.

"No, but I met him at the wedding. He seemed pretty remote, not like Meg at all."

"That's her stepfather. Meg's dad died when she was just six years old." Artie paused. "Our stories are intertwined. Truthfully, I'm not surprised she hasn't talked about all this. Meg focuses on the sunny side of life, which is one of the things I love about her." He glanced at Sarah, then continued. "Her dad died in a car wreck about a week before my accident. He was driving drunk. No one else was killed, but three people were severely injured." Artie paused again as he seemed to relive the moment. "Trish, Meg, my brother Rob, and I were playing outside when the police came to tell her mother."

Sarah was quiet, thinking about how quickly things could change. Meg's father's decision to drive drunk had irreparably changed numerous lives. Even Sarah's innocent question had changed the tenor of their date, and now, Sarah realized, her understanding, both of Artie and of Meg, would change as a result of hearing this story.

"Trish went to investigate and came running out screaming for my mother. I can still hear her: 'Miz Riz Glad-stone, Miz Riz Glad-stone.' It was hours before we kids learned what had happened." Artie rubbed the back of his neck. "Meg and Trish stayed at our house that night, and my mother stayed with Meg's mom. I remember Dad grilling hot dogs, then turning on the TV, making popcorn, and all of us just sitting there staring blindly at the television. Not talking. Like I said, Meg was only six. She sat beside me, tears streaming down her face until she fell asleep." Artie blew out an audible breath.

"The next day, Meg's grandparents arrived. Her dad's parents.

We barely saw the grandmother that first trip, but Doc stayed outside with us a good bit." Artie looked at Sarah as he stopped at another traffic light. "Doc, that's what Meg called him, so I did too. Rob was fourteen, Trish was almost thirteen, and I was twelve. Rob and Trish got, um, close that week. They kept wandering off. I wasn't welcome, so I just hung out with Meg." Artie braked for the slowing traffic and looked at Sarah again. "I didn't mind. I've loved Meg from the first time I saw her as a newborn baby. Anyway, Doc worked in the yard every day, and he gave us jobs to do. Weeding and things." Artie merged onto the interstate before continuing. "Looking back, I can see he was distracting himself from the loss of his son, and I'm pretty sure Doc had fought his own battle with the bottle earlier in life. He needed to keep busy.

"He was a good man and a good friend all during my teenage years. He helped me so much after I lost my leg." Artie was quiet again. He changed lanes, then glanced at Sarah. "I hadn't intended to go into all this today, but it's hard to tell one story without the other. Do you want me to stop?"

"Only if you want to. I want to hear your story, Artie," Sarah said, rubbing his arm.

Artie nodded. "Okay. A day or so after the funeral, Rob was supposed to be cutting our grass. He and Trish wanted to go swimming, so he asked my dad if he could pay me to do it instead. My dad said okay, but then Trish and Rob had an argument, so Robbie tried to back out of our deal. Dad wouldn't let him, said he had to honor his word."

"Artie," Sarah interrupted. "You need to move over. This lane is going to end soon."

"Okay." He put on the turn signal. "Am I scaring you?"

Sarah shook her head. "No, but if now's not the best time, that's okay too."

"It's easier to tell when I'm not watching you, Sarah. But don't worry, I'm almost there." Artie changed lanes. "I didn't have a lot of opportunities to earn money, since Robbie usually claimed the chores first. So when I saw him cutting the grass after what Dad had said, I just lost it. I mean I had plans for that money. I let out a yell, went running across the yard and jumped on Robbie, which tilted the mower just enough for the blade to snag my foot. Blood squirted everywhere." He finished in a rush, then breathed deeply again.

"I'm sure I screamed, but mostly I remember Meg's scream, which brought her mother running. Then she screamed and apparently passed out and chaos erupted. I woke up in the hospital in excruciating pain. When I came home a few days later with my foot in a cast, Meg sat with me while I cried."

Sarah reached for his hand. "Wait, your foot was in a cast?"

"Yeah, the doctors thought they could save it. But the pain would not stop. The doctor told my parents that amputation was the best option, but my dad and Rob were very outspoken in opposition. My mother couldn't bear to see me in pain and cried every time she came near me. My dad, well, I wouldn't want you to think badly of him. He just believed the doctors when they said the pain medicine would help, that the pain would lessen with time. Dad felt like I should hang in there, you know. He believed he was doing the right thing, but I just wanted the pain gone. If the foot had to go, so be it.

After the longest damn week of my life, my dad agreed."

"So, how did Meg's grandfather help?" Sarah prompted when Artie paused.

"Lots of ways. Doc saved my sanity and maybe even my life. Like I said, I was going nuts with pain, about ready to chop my foot off myself. I mean it was agony. Every time I moved my foot, all those nerve endings were just on fire. I remember sitting in the living room watching TV with Doc and Meg after lunch one day. My parents were arguing in the kitchen. I kept bumping the sound up, but I heard Dad say he didn't want a cripple for a son and Mom burst into tears again. I wanted to block it all out. I reached for my pain pills."

Sarah gasped. "They left pain pills where you could get to them? But they're addictive!"

Artie held his hand up to stop her protest. "My parents aren't terrible people. They believed the doctor who said the pills weren't addictive, and they believed the therapist who said not to baby me, to let me control what I could."

"I can see the wisdom in that," Sarah said, "but still—"

"Yeah. Luckily, Doc intervened. He stopped me, looked at the label, and walked into the kitchen. I muted the TV and heard him ask my parents if they'd rather have an addict or a cripple for a son." Artie glanced at Sarah. "You can imagine how well that went over. My dad said it wasn't any of Doc's business, but that the doctors had promised the meds weren't addictive. Doc called bullshit on that. He'd been a pharmacist and knew what could happen." Looking at Sarah again, Artie continued. "Then Dad started yelling about what he wanted and didn't want, and I'd had enough. First and last time I ever cursed at my dad. I believe my exact words were, 'You should fucking ask me what I want. It's my damn leg.'"

Sarah pointed to the right. "This is our exit."

Artie exited the expressway and stopped at the light, looking at Sarah. "Long story short, I had the surgery." He sighed and ran his hand down his face. "The thing about being twelve is that you don't realize the consequences of your actions, your decisions. Even though I knew they would take my leg, I somehow thought I'd be able walk and run and swim again immediately. Talks about the 'long road to recovery' and my options didn't prepare me for the reality. So while Rob and Trish and my friends were getting on with their lives that summer, I was stuck with lots of doctor visits, swelling, phantom pain, learning to use a wheelchair and crutches, meetings about a prosthesis, and on and on. Don't even get me started on how those 'friends' reacted. And Mom's friends. Jeez. I can't stand being pitied.

"The worst thing was needing help with everything. Can you imagine being a twelve-year-old boy needing help to pee? To shower?" He was quiet for a minute. "No, I take that back. The loneliness, the isolation was the worst thing. I had a rough couple of years." When the light changed, Artie asked, "Right or left?"

"Right."

Artie continued, "Rob was no help. He was embarrassed to be seen with a cripple. And my dad, well, I didn't know what was going on with him. He wasn't around much. Turns out he was picking up extra hours to pay the medical bills. Anyway, Robbie barely talked to me. Wouldn't look at me half the time. We'd shared a room before the accident, but after, I was moved downstairs to the guest room. Mom thought it would be easier, and it was, but it kind of felt like I wasn't part of the family anymore."

"Oh, Artie."

He waved his hand. "I know they didn't mean it that way, but that's how it felt. Rob and I still have a tense relationship."

"I'm so sorry."

"Don't be. It's not your fault. It's not anyone's fault. Well, maybe mine. I was the fool who rushed in."

"You were twelve." Sarah squeezed his hand.

"Yeah, and I've forgiven myself for being an idiot. I just wish Rob wasn't so weird about it," Artie said gloomily. "At least Doc was there. He kind of forced me to acknowledge my feelings, but then he'd offer a way out, you know. He'd say things like, 'Man, it sucks that you can't go swimming with your friends today.' Then later he'd kind of casually mention the Paralympic swimming competition. Show me an article or something. Kind of let me know I wouldn't be sitting in a chair the rest of my life.

"He helped my mom a lot too, riding to appointments with us, getting me in and out of the car and so forth." Artie barked a short laugh. "He even convinced her to let him paint the guest room so I didn't have to live in a peach and teal nightmare. What's the road name again?"

"Odum Farm Road. It's probably another half mile or so," Sarah said following the directions on her phone.

"The biggest thing? Doc kept me busy, you know, which helped keep my mind off all the things I couldn't do that summer. He showed me how to start azaleas from cuttings. I could do that from the wheelchair. He pushed me around the yard and talked about the plants, using the Latin and common names."

"Turn right here, Artie."

He turned and kept talking. "Doc asked my opinion about which plants to put where and gave me the books where I'd find the answers. He gave me a way to be useful in planning a garden for Meg's playhouse. We planted flowers and vegetables." Artie slowed the truck. "Is this the place?"

At Sarah's nod, Artie pulled into the crowded lot and parked the truck. He took Sarah's hand but stared out the windshield as he continued. "Doc talked to me about patience and careful tending of plants. He showed me that we needed to remove the weaker seedlings if the others were to make it, and when he taught me about pruning dead branches from the bushes, I realized he'd been talking about my leg all along."

Finally finished with his story, Artie looked at Sarah and noticed her tears. "Come here," he said, pulling her close.

With his arms still around her and his chin resting on her head, Artie said, "Doc came to my high school graduation. Trish was a year ahead of me, so it was me he'd come to see. He'd brought Meg, of course, but he told me how proud he was. When I told Doc I planned to major in horticulture, he had tears in his eyes. He died that next spring. I cried like a baby when Meg told me."

Sarah sniffed, sat back, and smiled through her tears. "That's a beautiful story, Artie. I'm just sorry you had to deal with all the emotional fallout on top of the amputation.”

“Yeah, life sucks sometimes, but mostly it’s beautiful. Meg would start singing about rainbows and clouds about now. I think I’d rather go for a hike.” Artie added the cookies from the market to his pack.

“Hang on. Doc helped you, right? But, Artie, I think you helped him too, by giving him a purpose when he needed one. Keeping you busy kept him busy. And in helping you accept your loss, your new reality, I imagine he had to do the same. Does that make sense? I think you saved him as much as he saved you.”

Artie looked at her, considering. “I never thought about it that way. Thank you, Sarah.”

Sarah easily pulled on her boots while Artie fully loosened his laces. Because his prosthetic ankle did not bend, he had to work to get his foot in. After adding water bottles to their day packs, they crossed the gravel lot to a short paved trail leading to an overlook where several visitors stood, admiring the view.

“This right here’s worth the price of admission,” a man staring off in the distance said.

Artie leaned close to Sarah and whispered. “Is that even a compliment since it’s free?”

“Be nice.” Sarah giggled. “Do you think the trail goes all the way down to the river?”

“Nah.” Artie read from a nearby sign. “Elevation change of less than four hundred feet.” They gazed over the rock wall at the Tennessee River winding its way through the gorge below them. “It’s kind of strange to get the view right at the first part of the hike.”

Sarah wrinkled her nose. "Right? I don't think I've ever walked down a mountain I hadn't walked up first. Are you ready to start?"

"Yeah," Artie said, as they moved from the view to a staircase leading to the trail down the mountain. "I hate to think about climbing these on the way out."

"I didn't know there were stairs, Artie. Is that going to be—"

"Nah, I'll be okay." The stairs were narrow, so Artie led the way. At the base, he turned and said, "Sorry for all the trauma dumping earlier. It kinda put a damper on my mood."

"I'm glad you told me, Artie. It's a part of you. I'm not bothered by your amputation. I admire you for coping so well." The rutted and rocky trail widened a bit as it meandered through immature hardwoods and brushy undergrowth on its way down to a creek.

"I don't really have a choice, do I?" Artie was quiet a moment. "I have noticed that you seem perfectly comfortable seeing the prosthesis. Joking about it, even." He held out his hand to help Sarah down a steep step on the trail.

"Artie, if my jokes bother you—"

"They don't. I like laughing with you. Most people are a bit more uncomfortable, you know, but still, it's not exactly first date conversation."

"Your math is wrong. If we count the Mexican dinner and lunch at the River Market last month, this would be our third date," Sarah teased. They both turned, hearing voices behind them.

"Third date? Well, damn, come here, woman. We should definitely be kissing by now. What are we waiting for?" Artie held his arms wide as a troop of scouts walked between them.

"Too many kids," Sarah called over their heads. "Guess you'll have to wait for something more special."

They followed the scouts down the hill as the trail narrowed and grew shady. The ground was riddled with tree roots. "Liam and Elizabeth didn't mention any of this," Sarah grumbled. "If it weren't for those kids, I'd wonder if we were actually on the trail."

"I see the first bridge." Artie pointed. "That dried mud suggests the root exposure is from erosion, probably from all that winter rain. Hiking here last Fall was probably a very different experience. See how the creek bank is washed out? I'd guess it floods frequently. We'll just have to be careful."

Both watched their footing on the roots, sometimes holding on to tree trunks or branches as an aid to balance when stepping down. The going became easier as they crossed a short suspension bridge over the creek and followed the trail through a sunnier patch of blooming wildflowers. "Ooh, buttercups," Sarah said, pointing out the dainty yellow blooms.

"And Spring Beauty." Artie pointed to a low-lying pink flower. "Native Americans used to eat the tubers of those. Yellow trillium." He indicated a stand of the distinctive three-leafed flowers.

Continuing up the trail, Sarah heard Artie behind her naming different plants he saw: foam flower, rue anemone, dogwood, Mayflowers. She turned. "Did you just say Mayflower? Like the ship?"

"Yeah. Well, related, anyway. Supposedly, it was the first flower the Pilgrims saw blooming in the new world, but I think it's just a story. The plants are also called May-apple, Podophyllum peltatum."

Artie pointed to the small white blossoms.

"I never thought about where the ship name came from. Isn't that weird? I should've been curious, but I accepted what I was told and never thought to ask. But names have to originate somewhere. What about dogwood? Why are dogwoods called dogwood?"

Artie grinned. "Some people say it's because the fruit is edible but not fit for dogs."

"Wait. Dogwoods have fruit?"

"Yeah, the red berries in the fall. That's their fruit. That story is likely apocryphal though. There are tons of stories about dogwoods." Noticing Sarah's questioning look, he continued. "One story says that the cross, you know, *the* cross, was made of dogwood, which supposedly was a big tree until it was cursed to be forever small after the crucifixion."

"I've never heard that," Sarah said. "Aren't the blooms supposed to look like a cross?"

"Yeah, they're always four petals, with indentations for the nails, supposedly. Makes for a good story, anyway."

"Look at this one, Artie. It has heart-shaped leaves!"

"Oh, cool. You found Little Brown Jug, Hexastylis arifolia." Artie lifted a few leaves and showed her some of the jug-shaped flowers. "It's also called wild ginger or heart leaf. Native Americans used it as a medicine, but modern scientists believe it's toxic."

A passing couple paused to see what they were looking at, so Artie went back through his story about the wildflower, ending with a warning about its toxicity.

"I think we started down the trail in the wrong direction," the man confided. "Everyone we meet is heading the other way. But here's a warning for you. The bridges are not in good shape!"

Sarah wondered if they should turn back, but Artie thanked the couple and walked on ahead of her. When they reached the bridge, he stopped before each missing board to be sure Sarah saw them. The trail started back up the hillside and quickly became rocky. "I swear, Liam did not say one word about rocks. He's usually the first to complain if the trail is not in good shape or is too steep. I'm beginning to think they didn't actually hike this trail," Sarah complained.

Artie waited by a particularly large rock, then said cheerfully, "No worries, looks like we're heading back down toward the creek in a few minutes." About ten steps later, his left foot landed on a pebble, which slid off the rock, causing him to stumble and fall sideways into a large bush to the side of the trail.

Sarah's heart pounded as she rushed to his side. "Artie, oh my gosh. Are you okay? Let me pull you up."

"I can get up by myself, thanks." He grumbled, rolling to his hands and knees. "Ouch."

"Are you all right? Is anything broken?"

"No. Stop hovering, it was just a little fall. Argh! These dang thorns keep sticking me."

Not wanting to get stuck, Sarah backed up and let Artie extricate himself from the flowering bush. She understood his reluctance to let her help because she would've been the same way—too embarrassed to want any more attention. But she did not understand his anger, and he definitely sounded angry.

Once he was upright, she asked, "Do you want me to carry your pack? It may be throwing you off balance."

"I'm fine, let's just walk."

"Do you want a walking stick?"

"No! And I don't need a damn nursemaid. I can do this. Let me do this."

"Fine, do it by yourself then. I let you help me over rocks. I don't see the difference." Sarah stormed off down the trail but cried out in pain as she rounded the corner.

"Sarah?" Artie quickly followed and found her trying to pull a vine with briars from her T-shirt.

"Ouch!" Every time she moved, it seemed to grab her. "Dammit." Sarah pulled at the vine again.

Artie stepped over the downed tree branch that had caused Sarah to step off the path. "Let me help."

"No! I can do it," she said, freeing one part of the vine from her shirt, then crying out again as another ricocheted and hit her face.

"Sarah," he said quietly. "Stand still, please. I want to help, and you're making it worse."

Sarah stood, tears streaming, with one hand over her cheek while Artie carefully pulled the rest of the briars from her shirt.

"Let me see." He gently tugged her hand down. "It's bleeding a bit but doesn't look too bad. It's just a little boo boo." He paused. "Honey."

Sarah's mouth quirked up on one side. "If you call me Honey Boo Boo, I swear I will throw you into that briar patch." She scrubbed the tears from her face with the hem of her shirt and noticed a tinge of blood. "It's still bleeding."

"A little. It got you pretty good." Artie reached in his backpack and pulled a napkin from the bag of cookies. "Here you go. I'm sorry, Sarah. This is my fault."

"What? No, it's okay," Sarah protested.

"No, it's not. If I'd let you help me when I fell, you wouldn't have stormed off." Artie rubbed his eyes. "I've let my pride get in my way more than once today, and I'm sorry. I just, you just treat me like I'm normal, Sarah, and I like that, so despite my better judgment, I chose to not use the hiking poles in my bag. I was showing off a bit, thinking I could hike this trail without them.

"Most of the time I'm fine with being an amputee. I've lived this way for two decades after all. It's who I am." Artie rubbed Sarah's arm. "But on a date, first, third, thirtieth, I just want to be a guy with the woman he finds attractive. And instead, I've made a fool of myself, let you get hurt, and made you cry. I really am sorry, Sarah."

"I cry when I get mad, Artie. And I get mad when I don't understand things. If it's okay for you to help me, why can't I help you? Shouldn't we help each other?"

Artie looked at her, then looked up into the trees. He took a deep breath, looked back at her. "Yeah, of course. What you said makes perfect sense. Unfortunately, the male brain, or at least my brain, is not always rational." He tilted her chin to look into her eyes. "I have this idea that I should help you, watch out for you, protect you."

"Because I'm a woman and weaker than you?" Sarah grew angry and stepped back.

"No, I'm not stuck in the Dark Ages." He took her hand. "Walk with me, please." Where the trail allowed, they walked side by side as Artie explained. "It's not because I see you as weak, but because I'm seriously attracted to you. I probably shouldn't say it, and I know you want to take things slow, and that's great and all, but every time I see you, the more I feel like we could have a future together." Artie stopped and shrugged, brushing a curl behind her ear. "I know it's early days, but I can't help it. I want to watch out for you because I care so damn much about you and what you think of me," Artie said. "I don't want you to perceive me as weak."

Sarah had to remind herself to breathe as she tried to process Artie's comment about a future together. *Nope, not going there. I'll think about that one later.* "We all need help sometimes, Artie. That doesn't make us weak."

"Again, rationally, I know that, and I agree with you. It's just that recent events have reminded me that I'm different, that I'm vulnerable, and I don't like it." Artie paused in the middle of the trail. "I mean I'm successful, I'm generally happy, I'm healthier than a lot of whole-bodied guys my age. But I'm competitive by nature. I see myself in competition with them. I'm also an amputee, and I can never forget that, whether I'm walking in the woods or competing in races." He shrugged ruefully, then continued walking. "I should've broken my PR in that race in February, and I didn't even make it out of the second leg."

"Boy, you are competitive. That was weeks ago. Wait. Second leg? Do you mean it was a triathlon?" Sarah asked. "Whoa, no wonder you're in such good shape. So, what happened?"

"Pretty much the same story as today. I hit a loose rock and went down. Since I can't feel if my foot is on the pedal, I use clips to hold it in place. When the bike started falling, I couldn't get my foot loose in time. The poison ivy cushioned my fall, but because the bike fell on top of me, all the scratches just opened a pathway for the urushiol, which is what causes the rash. I guess I should be grateful it was a blackberry bush today, despite the thorns."

"Was that what got me?" Sarah asked, touching her cheek.

"Oh, no. You met up with the dreaded saw briar, Smilax glauca. It's nasty stuff. Very sharp thorns." Artie pointed to a fallen log in a small clearing. "There's a pretty good seat if you're ready to take a break. Are you hungry?"

"Yeah, I am, actually." Sarah removed her backpack and sat down. "So, do you often compete in triathlons?"

"I've done the triathlon in Orlando for the last ten years. They're very supportive of para athletes, including amputees. I trained hard through the fall and winter and did well in the swimming, so I'm disappointed. I don't expect to win, but I do expect to finish."

He turned to Sarah. "Hey, you run and swim. Do you race competitively?"

"Not really. I mean, a 5K now and then, especially if it's a fundraiser. But swimming is just fun exercise." Sarah paused. "Artie, we don't have to talk about this if you don't want to, but I'm curious. With the prosthesis, I mean. I've seen the special running ones, but when you swim, do you have, is there . . .?"

"A sea leg? There are swimming prostheses, but they're not al-lowed in racing, so no sea legs for the swimming leg." Artie grinned, then looked at the ground, speaking more seriously. "What you need to know, Sarah, is that I do have to talk about it, or at least think about it, all the time. I have to prepare, know which prosthesis I'll need for the day's activities. I have to be sure that my shoes aren't too heavy and that the heels don't vary in height so that my gait isn't different."

He looked at Sarah. "I have to budget both time and money for new legs, which I end up buying about every three years. I have to be very aware of the condition of my residual leg and how the prosthesis fits. And air travel? I can't just go through the x-ray machine. I always, always get pulled from line, patted down, and swabbed for explosives."

Artie put his hand on Sarah's arm. "Please understand that I'm not complaining, Sarah. I'm just explaining that life is different for me. Some women can't handle it. They think they can, but the first time they feel my stump rub up against them in the bed or see me hop to the bathroom, they're done." He drank some water and shrugged. "Unless they're oddly turned on by amputees, and I've heard of that situation as well. Then there are the ones who want to mother me, make me an invalid so they can take care of me."

"Like Rachel," Sarah interrupted, as her mind immediately jumped to the conversation they'd had on the boat.

"Rachel?

"Yeah, you know she's interested in you. At the lake, she warned me off and said I wasn't right for you. She intimated that she was and that you needed someone who would look after you, not compete with you."

"Well, she's wrong. I don't want somebody to fetch and carry for me. I'm touchy about my limitations. That's why I got mad earlier. I want to carry my own weight, literally and meta-phorically." Artie looked into Sarah's eyes. "I meant what I said earlier, Sarah. I like you. I sure as hell don't want to scare you away, but these are just things you need to know."

Sarah pulled some sandwiches from her pack and silently handed one to him. She opened a bag of chips to share and took a swig of water before speaking. "Okay." They ate their lunch in relative silence, listening to the birds and the leaves rustling in the breeze.

"Okay?" Artie asked, handing her broken pieces of one of the oatmeal cookies he'd bought that morning, wrapped in a napkin. "Sorry. They're a little worse for wear."

Sarah took the napkin and looked at the broken pieces. "Like us." She grinned. "Okay. Thanks for telling me. You're right that I never considered what it's like to be you. I mean, some of it, sure. Like using a prosthesis, going to fittings and all that. Yeah." Sarah nodded. "Bathing. Getting around the house. Sure. I've helped a few patients adjust to a prosthesis. But I'd never thought about flying or swim-ming or how much more energy and thought and preplanning you have to do." Sarah bumped his shoulder. "But I'm not scared off, Artie. I'm not grossed out or weirdly attracted either. I like you, and I generally have a good time with you. This hike, well, it's had its ups and downs, but I'm rooting for us."

Artie smiled a little sadly and said, "Yeah, I see what you did there. Good to know you're not scared off." He stood and held out his hand. "Ready to see if we can finish this hike without any more tears or true confessions?"

Sarah decided to take the lead rather than risk making Artie uncomfortable by watching his every step. She was grateful he'd taken out his hiking poles and was using them for extra balance. Lots of people use hiking poles. She decided to get a pair for herself. At the very least, they might help her avoid running into any more saw briar.

As they approached the third bridge, they heard shrieks of laughter from the scout troop playing in a small pool in front of the falls. With a sinking feeling, Sarah noticed the third bridge was out. Apparently, the water in this area had risen enough to shift the bridge parallel to the shore. Other hikers were stepping from one rock to another to ford the elevated water level of the creek.

"Well, damn," Artie said as he caught up with her.

"What should we do?" Sarah asked. "We're not that far from where the trail loops back to the beginning, but we could go back."

"Oh, hell no. We're not going back. You lead. I'll follow. Just let me know if the rocks are wobbly or slippery."

Sarah frowned. "Are you sure, Artie? I don't mind."

"I'm using the poles, so we should be okay, but if I fall, I fall. To be honest, I think going back would be hard on my leg."

Sarah nodded and started across the creek, testing each rock carefully. She could hear Artie behind her, and every once in a while, she'd glimpse his hiking stick as he positioned it in the creek.

About two thirds of the way across, someone yelled: "Heads up!" Sarah saw a flash of orange as she dodged a Frisbee. She teetered on the rock. At first she thought she'd manage to stay upright, but then fell backward. Artie tried to catch her, but they both fell in the knee-deep water.

Sarah realized she had fallen on top of Artie. She rolled onto her hands and knees. A torrent of water splashed her in the face as the boys raced to retrieve their Frisbee. Sarah closed her eyes and wiped the water from her face with an angry hand. She opened her eyes to see Artie's face shift from concern to laughter. He leaned forward and removed a wet leaf from her face and stuck it on his own. Suddenly, they were both laughing, slipping and sliding as they climbed out of the creek.

One of the scout leaders apologized profusely and handed Sarah a towel. She dried off as best she could before handing the sodden towel to Artie.

He raised his eyebrows and they both started laughing again as he wrung out the towel. "Are you hurt?" he asked her.

"No, I'll probably be sore, but I'm fine. Are you okay? Are your boots waterproof?"

"Yeah, but I need to change the liner sock. We should get back to the truck," Artie said.

Pretty soon the trail merged with the part they'd hiked in on. The sun shone through the leafy treetops, dappling the trail. Sarah was again in the lead when she suddenly shrieked, "Bees!" Dozens of small bees were flying around Sarah's bare legs. "I can feel them crawling on me! Do something!"

"You're okay. You're okay. I'm pretty sure they're sweat bees, honey," Artie said quietly. "I'll brush them off. Keep walking." So Sarah walked quickly, almost dancing, as Artie chased after her, brushing at her legs.

When a passing group of teenagers approached them, Sarah became aware of how ridiculous they must look and stopped in the middle of the trail, hiding her face. Artie hugged her and they both started laughing again.

Chapter Twelve

They were both out of breath by the time they reached the top of the stairs at the overlook. They squeezed through cars and trucks jammed close together in the unpaved lot. "Some poor sucker's day is about to get worse." Artie pointed at a car with a flat tire. After a few more steps, he stopped suddenly and swore. "Oh, come on!" He pounded the silver contraption angled behind his truck in frustration. "Some jerk blocked us in. There's no way to get around this trailer."

Sarah came closer, noticing two propane tanks behind a large silver box. "What do you suppose this is?"

"Don't know, don't care." Artie laid his hand on the truck's hood. "The engine's still warm. Jeez, this could take a while." He pointed to a sign on the truck's door, which pictured a meditating Buddha. "Vin's Pots of Zen," he read, taking out his phone. "It might be a kiln. Great. No answer and the mailbox is full."

Artie lowered the tailgate of his truck, unlocked the cab, placed his day pack and poles inside, and pulled out another bag and wool blanket from the backseat. Holding its corners, he flung the blanket up and let it settle in the truck bed. Retrieving a couple of water bottles from a small cooler, he hopped on the tailgate and patted the space beside him. "Might as well get comfortable. We could be here a while."

He drank his water. "I'd almost rather have the flat tire. At least that way, I could do something. I hate being at the mercy of other people. This guy, he could take hours."

Sarah stood by the tailgate and drank her water, watching him. Sure, he was angry and irritated, but he wasn't dwelling on the situation.

He removed one boot and untied the other. "Give it a tug?" Sarah helped pull the boot off and continued to watch as Artie pulled a towel and spare leg sock from the familiar canvas bag. He removed the wet sock and pressed the tab on his prosthesis which allowed him to remove it. She climbed up beside him and took off her own boots and socks and lay down as she watched him carefully dry his stump and wipe down the prosthesis. "You okay if I leave this off awhile? My leg's a little swollen."

Sarah nodded. "Sure."

Artie lay back on the blanket beside her. He sighed, then turned toward her, tracing her cheek. "So, what's the story behind your fear of bees?"

"I just don't like them. I hate being stung."

"At the lake, Elizabeth said they always seem to find you. Have you been stung a lot?"

Sarah pointed at a half-inch scar on her left hand. "One time we were at my grandparents' playing tag while running through the sprinklers. I was probably four or five. James was chasing me. I ran through this cluster of pine trees, stepped in a hole, and fell on one of Grandmother's ceramic cats, which broke." Sarah closed her eyes and shuddered. "All these yellow jackets just erupted around me. I got stung so much I didn't even know I was cut. James turned the sprinkler on me to scare away the bees, then carried me inside. My mother saw blood on my shirt and thought I'd sliced open my abdomen. Four stitches and some Benadryl fixed me up. I mean, it wasn't life-changing or anything. I rarely think about it."

Artie kissed her scar. "I think all our scars change us. Your fear of bees makes more sense after hearing that story." He rolled onto his back and closed his eyes.

Sarah leaned up on one elbow. "'To live is to be marked.'"

Artie opened one eye. "What?"

"I remember reading that in one of Barbara Kingsolver's books. *The Poisonwood Bible,* I think, in a part about changing and getting a story." She lay back down and was quiet awhile. "Poisonwood, now there's a plant I wouldn't want any part of. It apparently causes a horrible reaction, worse than poison ivy. Good thing we're not in the African Congo."

"Hate to break it to you, but there's a poisonwood tree in the Florida Keys—Metopium toxiferum." Artie laughed at Sarah's outraged face. "I don't think it's there to personally attack you, honey," he joked.

Artie closed his eyes, and Sarah watched him. Meg hadn't exaggerated. He was smart and kind and good-looking. Funny and thoughtful. His yellow T-shirt stretched taut across the broad chest and shoulder muscles developed by swimming and gardening and living. *How could I have ever thought he wasn't worth noticing?* Sarah lay back down and looked at the sky. Despite all the things that had gone wrong, she had enjoyed being with Artie today. *Is this what a real relationship is like? Am I ready for a relationship with him? How can I be sure?*

A while later, a cacophony of voices rang out from across the parking lot. "Here come the boy scouts." Artie sat up and stretched before beginning the process of putting his prosthesis back on. He rolled on a dry sock, stuck his stump in the prosthesis and stood, clicking it back in place. Artie took a few steps before leaning back against the tailgate beside Sarah.

"Prego, prego, mi scusi," a voice echoed, interrupting the boys' laughter.

"This must be the guy," Artie said as the man hurried toward them.

"Oops, my bad," a handsome young man said in a heavy accent. "So sorry, I no ree-lize my trailer, how you say, block you."

"You had to realize it, man," Artie said. "You had to walk past it to get to the trail. You were just too inconsiderate to move it elsewhere."

Sarah wondered about Artie's wisdom in confronting a man who outweighed him by a good twenty pounds of muscle, despite being a little shorter. She hopped down and went to his side, wondering if she'd have to try to defuse the situation before things got out of hand.

The guy grinned and pushed his dark curly hair behind his ears. He held his hand out in placation, then placed it on his chest, saying, "Si, si, mi dispiace. The lot is so full. I think, it take little time to run, but the bridge, he is gone. Mi scusi, signore, bellissima. I go now, yes?"

Artie frowned as the guy walked quickly to his truck, backed out, and pulled off. Turning to Sarah, he shook his head and pulled his keys from his pocket. "Feel like driving a truck? I'm 'all done in' as my grandmother used to say."

Sarah was surprised but readily agreed. Once they were out of the parking lot, he leaned his head back and appeared to nap. As they neared her apartment, she spoke quietly. "Hey, Artie?"

"Yeah?"

"I've been thinking about all the stories from today. Our scar stories and the flower stories and Meg's story and just life and everything. When I started high school, I had a lot of trouble focusing long enough to finish assignments, and I kept getting in trouble for blurting things out, so Mom and Dad sent me to counseling. Sometimes it was just me, but once a month or so, a group of us would meet and talk."

"Okay?"

"Well, in one of the group sessions, the counselor told us a story about a rich lady who thought she was all that." Sarah laughed. "Remember saying 'all that and a bag of chips?' Anyway, the rich lady had a bug crawling in her hair."

"Are you trying to tell me I have bugs in my hair, Sarah? Because I'm sure not rich."

"Eww! No! I hope not anyway." Sarah shook her head. "It's just that the lady thought she was so fine, but everyone else could see she had lice. The counselor said it could go the other way too. We see our faults, real or imagined, but others don't, or at least don't see the things we obsess over. You know?" Sarah paused, waiting for Artie to reply. When he didn't, she continued. "She had us write nice things about each other on a paper with a mirror drawn on it. It was labeled something like 'seeing ourselves as others see us'."

"Okay? I'm not sure where you're going with this, Sarah."

"It's just like those flower stories you told me. I think the stories we tell ourselves are sometimes more fiction than fact. I won't ever think you're weak, Artie. I promise you that. No one who knows you would. You are stronger for your scars."

"Okay."

"Okay?"

"Okay, Sarah. Thanks."

Sarah smiled to herself. She loved the way Artie said her name. She found it very comforting, like being hugged.

Artie opened his eyes and asked, "What was written on your mirror, Sarah?"

"Oh. Well, some of the comments were just one word or two words, you know, like smart, pretty, nice. But a few surprised me: 'stands up for the underdog,' 'good listener,' and 'fearless soccer player.' I kept that paper for a long time." Sarah pulled to the curb outside her apartment building and turned to Artie. "Coming in?"

"Nah, I don't think so, Sarah." He scrubbed the back of his head. "It's been a physically and emotionally tiring day. We're later than we'd thought we be, and I need to get back to Acworth and put the finishing touches on a presentation I'm doing Monday."

"Okay, another time then," she said, climbing out the truck.

Sarah was disappointed but not surprised. Artie was clearly exhausted.

Artie walked around to the driver's side and took the keys from her. He leaned against the truck, pulled her into a hug, and spoke quietly. "I'm sorry so many things went wrong today. I will make it up to you. I promise you that, Sarah," he added, kissing her hair.

Sarah pulled back from the embrace. "Maybe it wasn't the first date we imagined, Artie, but I've had worse. Maybe next time we'll share dating horror stories rather than scar stories."

"You sure you still want a next time?" he asked.

"Of course, Artie. I still like you. A lot." Sarah put both arms around his neck.

Artie moved a strand of hair behind Sarah's ear and looked at the scratch on her face, rubbing his thumb across it. "I don't think it will scar, but it will always be part of our story, Boo-Boo," he said, kissing it softly.

"As will Yogi," Sarah snickered.

"God, I hope not." Artie laughed. "Vin's Pots of Zen. Jeez. That guy's not worth thinking about."

"Oh, I don't know," Sarah teased. "He was pretty cute."

"You're cuter." Artie pulled her close again. "Sorry we didn't get our first kiss."

"There's still time," Sarah said, then sighed. "But I guess a street in Chattanooga isn't the place for it either," she added as a passing car blew its horn. "We'll wait. It'll be worth it in the end."

Chapter Thirteen

"Why are you so late? Where's Art?" Elizabeth asked from the sofa when Sarah banged open the apartment door. "I thought we were all eating spaghetti together."

"It's a long story, sis. Artie's headed back to Acworth."

"Uh oh, that sounds like the date didn't go well. Do you not want to talk about it?" Elizabeth asked, muting the television.

In the past, Sarah had pouted or raged in private and refused to discuss her relationship problems. This time, she replied, "I *do* want to talk about it. Is Liam still here?"

"Yeah, he's looking over some case notes in the bedroom. Should I ask him to leave?"

"No, I want to talk with both of you," Sarah said, "after I shower."

Sarah towel-dried her hair and dressed in comfy leggings and a T-shirt before putting a tiny Band-Aid over the scratch on her cheek, which had started bleeding again. Over a spaghetti dinner, she told Liam and Elizabeth the whole saga.

"So, you still haven't kissed?" Elizabeth asked in disbelief.

"Oh, he's kissed me—my hair, my cheek, my forehead, my hand. A lot of hand kisses. I've kissed him too, in the same way. But he says first kisses—real kisses, you know—the first shared kisses are rare and special and deserve a special place, a special atmosphere. I'm both frustrated and intrigued," Sarah admitted.

"Do you think you'll go out again?"

"Yeah, but I'm freaking out a little," Sarah admitted. "I really like Artie, but I don't want to mess things up by moving too fast. That's what I've always done, so I shouldn't do the same thing. I think I should see other guys, don't you?" Sarah spoke faster now. "I mean, I just met him three months ago, and we've seen each other a total of, what, five times?"

Elizabeth got up to retrieve some cookies from the cabinet. "It seems to me that you're trying to convince yourself not to fall for Art."

"Maybe I am, and that scares me too. I know it seems weird to plan to see other guys when I like him so much, but being exclusive right away seems risky too. Plus, we're both super busy and live in different states, so it's not like I can see him every day or even every week. I think we should maybe not be exclusive right away."

"That is different," Elizabeth said.

"I know, but if I follow the same pattern, then I'm more likely to make the same mistakes. Right?" Turning, Sarah asked, "What do you think, Liam? Should I go out with other guys or tell Artie I want him to be my boyfriend? I mean, he's really sweet and I'm very attracted to him, but his intensity scares me a little."

"I'm not going to tell you or Art how to manage this relationship," Liam said, "but I suggest that you figure out what it is about his intensity that scares you."

"Maybe just the fact that he said he could already envision a future between us. I mean, that's gotta be a red flag, right? It's far too soon."

"Envisioning a future early in a relationship isn't necessarily a cause for concern. If he were asking you to move in with him, yes, we'd be worried. If you believe he's sincere, then his honesty about his feelings might be considered commendable, but you aren't responsible for his feelings. How do you feel about what he said?" Liam asked.

"I don't trust it."

"His feelings or his words?"

"I don't know, maybe both. Why would he feel that way? We barely know each other. I should definitely see other guys."

"Sarah?" Elizabeth objected. "Does that really make sense to you? You've been saying since the wedding that you want to find someone to build a life with. Why are you running away now?"

"I'm not running away. I want to keep seeing Artie, but I'm afraid to get too serious too soon. That's what I've done my whole life, and we all know where that's gotten me. Why would it be different with Artie?"

"That's a very good question, Sarah. What are your thoughts?" Liam asked.

"I think that for once someone should just tell me what to do!" Sarah said. "Life would be so much easier." She ate a piece of garlic toast, glaring at Liam. Getting no response, she continued. "When we were having the whole discussion about helping and not helping, Artie said he felt a need to protect me—"

Elizabeth and Liam burst out laughing. Liam said, "I'm sure that went over well."

"Oh, ha ha," Sarah said. "I'll admit I was mad. I don't think women particularly need a hero or a protector, but Artie," Sarah paused and bit her lip. "Artie said he felt that way not because I was a woman but because he cares about me so much. That's when he said he thought we could have a future together. I mean he admitted he didn't have a right to feel that way, but insisted he did."

Liam and Elizabeth exchanged glances.

"What?" Sarah demanded.

"How did him wanting to watch out for you make you feel, Sarah?" Liam asked.

"Mad at first, then scared, confused, uncertain." Sarah ticked each emotion on her fingers.

"And?" Liam prompted.

Sarah ran her hands through her hair and smiled ruefully. "I'm not saying it always has to be a man protecting a woman, but I like the feeling, the idea at least, of someone watching out for me. I want to watch out for him too."

"Do you feel protective of him because he's an amputee?" Liam asked.

"Maybe. Partly. But truthfully, the amputation is not something I've thought a lot about until today. I mean, when he fell in the blackberry bush, I didn't think about the reason he fell; I just wanted him to not be hurt." Sarah considered. "It's honestly not surprising that he got mad when I told him to give me his bag and find a walking pole. I'd have been insulted if he treated me that way.

"Everybody falls now and then, but people with lower-limb amputations are at greater risk. Artie is very capable of taking care of himself. I overreacted out of concern and then got upset that I'd made him mad. It was a crazy hike—a real bonding experience.

"Amputees face a lot of challenges on a daily basis that most of us never think about," Sarah said. "It's kind of like that saying about walking a mile in another man's moccasins."

"I think it's another man's shoes," Elizabeth interrupted.

"Pretty sure it's moccasins," Sarah insisted. "But the point is, Artie's experience is different from mine and yours because he is an amputee. We don't think about the difficulty of buying shoes or walking on the beach or hopping to the bathroom in the middle of the night because it doesn't affect us. People sometimes fuss about accommodations for people with disabilities, maybe thinking they're unnecessary because they personally don't need them. They should walk a mile in Artie's shoes."

Liam held up his phone. "The quote comes from a poem called "Judge Softly" written by Mary T. Lathrap in 1895. There are several lines in the poem about walking in moccasins, but here's the thing. The poet wasn't Native American. She was Scots-Irish from Michigan and a licensed preacher. Most of her work was about the Temperance movement."

Thereupon followed a conversation and friendly debate about cultural appropriation and language sensitivity. "Why shouldn't the saying be 'another person's shoes'," Elizabeth demanded. "Women walk just as much as men."

"But can you not see that if the original was about a man's moccasins, it might also be wrong to change it to shoes?" Liam suggested.

"Should Lathrap have been writing about the indigenous experience when she wasn't Native American?" Elizabeth asked.

"If she was validating their experience, why shouldn't she?" Liam countered. "It would be different if she were making fun of their truth or getting the facts wrong. Perhaps there's nothing wrong with giving voice to their plight in a way that permits it to be heard by a larger audience."

Growing tired of their debate, Sarah stood and put away the cookies. "Would a blind person feel insulted by Liam's comment about seeing? Is it insensitive to say 'stand on your own two feet' when Artie's around? I honestly don't think he would care, but we should just ask. We shouldn't assume that every amputee feels the same way. Artie appreciates my jokes, but some people probably wouldn't, and he might not if I made them too often. We shouldn't assume every woman or Native American or amputee represents every other person with the same characteristics. People are complex. Everyone's story is different. We're all vulnerable about some things, and we should respect that."

Liam stood and gave Sarah a big hug. "Well, sis, you've certainly traveled miles on your journey toward true empathy today. I'm really happy for you. One more question, which I know Elizabeth is dying to ask: What was your favorite part of this first date?"

Sarah remembered Artie kissing her hand, brushing his finger across her lip, and holding her in his arms. She remembered him helping her around obstacles on the trail, how he held her hand, and shared his knowledge of plants. She thought about their shared laughter in ridiculous situations, and finally, she thought about the scar stories they'd shared.

"Honestly, his openness and vulnerability, the way he trusted me with his story and how comfortable I felt hearing it was really special. The things he told me today were more intimate than any kiss I've ever had. As bad as some parts of our hike were, it may have been the best first date I've ever had."

"So, when's the second date?" Elizabeth asked.

Sarah had to admit they hadn't arranged one. When she finally heard from Artie that evening, his text was only eight letters: Home ttyl. She replied with a heart and pulled out her journal. She wanted to remember all her feelings and misgivings about Artie. *I like him so much. Is he too good to be true?* Sharing their truths had been a different sort of experience for her. It required a level of vulnerability and trust she hadn't had with any previous boyfriend. *It felt nice but scary. What if I'm wrong again?*

When she woke the next morning, Sarah stretched and smiled, remembering their date. She texted Artie saying she'd had a nice time and hoped to see him soon. His reply was again terse—okay, talk soon. Now Sarah was filled with uncertainty. Was the okay a reference to the times they'd answered each other with "Okay" and the other had questioned, "Okay?" Or was something else going on?

THE RIDICULOUSNESS of her 'teenage angst' prompted her to call Artie on her walk home on Monday evening. The phone rang several times before he picked up, somewhat out of breath.

"Sarah, hi."

Sarah smiled, hearing him say her name. She may have curled her hair around a finger and danced a little. "Bad time? You sound out of breath."

"I am a little. I left my phone on the kitchen table and had to hop."

"Oh, um, I don't quite know what to say about that. Is everything okay?"

"Yeah. My leg's still a bit swollen from Saturday, so I'm taking an early break from the prosthesis and didn't grab the crutch. How are you feeling?"

Sarah pictured Artie hopping across a room and wondered briefly how she felt about that. She decided rather quickly that she didn't care, but she was uncertain whether she should reassure him of that or ignore it. "I'm okay. I definitely had a few twinges yesterday and this morning, but I've been on my feet all day, so I worked all the kinks out." *Crap. Should I have said I was on my feet? Was that insulting? Why am I feeling so awkward?* "Hey, Artie, hang on a second, okay? I've got to cross this busy street and need to pay attention to what I'm doing." Sarah hoped she could relax and return to their normal repartee.

She crossed the street and found a bench to sit on. "I'm just going to sit here while we're talking. I don't seem to be capable of doing two things at once today. So, are you bruised? Inquiring minds want to know." She winced.

"Inquiring minds?" Artie snickered. "You sound like my—"

"Don't say it, Artie." Sarah was more relaxed now, focusing on Artie and not his leg. Laughing, she said, "I know, I know, it's ancient. My gosh, my mom says that all the time. I don't know why I said it. But are you bruised? I seem to remember falling on you in the creek."

"I don't really have a mirror low enough to see my backside, but I'd say there's a good possibility bruising exists. I'm glad we can laugh about it. Did you eat spaghetti and snuggle on the sofa without me?"

"I did. Well, the spaghetti part. Liam, Elizabeth, and I had a good talk over dinner. I entertained them with all our hiking woes. Elizabeth always says the bad stuff makes good stories, and I think she's right. But you know what, Artie? Liam asked me what my favorite part of our date was, and I had a hard time deciding."

"That little to choose from, huh?"

"No, I had a lot of good moments, Artie. That's what I wanted to say. My favorite thing though was sharing our stories. I felt seen and heard." Sarah smiled to herself. "I can't tell you how rare that's been for me."

Artie didn't say anything for a moment.

"Are you there?"

"I'm here, Sarah. I'm here. I hear you."

Such simple words, Sarah thought, intuitively sensing all of Artie's meanings. "Artie, I want to see you again. I want to continue getting to know you. I want that first kiss, but I've got something else to say. Sharing our truths feels more intimate than any kiss I've ever had."

"Okay."

"Okay?

"Yeah."

Somehow, Sarah could tell Artie was smiling. "So, what's your schedule like?"

"Unfortunately, I've got to go up to Lexington tomorrow for work. I'm sort of mentoring a new hire. Bruce and I will be up there for several days, but I should be back for the weekend. How about you?"

"I should be free on Sunday. Want me to drive to Acworth? It's my turn to travel."

"Well, as much as my truck is pining for your company in the driveway, maybe we can meet in the middle and avoid the long drives."

Sarah was quiet for a moment.

"Sarah, you there?"

"Oh, yeah, just lost in thought. I don't know where the middle would be. Do you?"

"Somewhere around Resaca," Artie said.

"Resaca? Sounds like some place accessed through a wardrobe."

"Nope, not a lion or witch in sight. They do, however, have Civil War battlefields, so more like a time machine, I guess."

"Hmm. That is different. Is that something you want to do? Visit a battlefield, I mean?" Sarah asked, glad for once that Artie could not see her face.

"Oh, yeah, I'd love to." Artie paused, then laughed. "Nope, can't do it. I'm teasing you, Sarah. Resaca is a real place, a tiny little town almost exactly halfway between us, but I don't want to walk around old battlefields this weekend, not that there's anything wrong with that. There's a better option if you don't mind combining my work with our date."

"Oh, thank goodness. You had me worried for a while there, Seinfeld. What's behind door number two?"

"You sound like my grandmother again," Artie said.

Sarah laughed. "I know, I know. I had no idea so many TV and tabloid phrases had ingrained themselves in my mind. I must've spent more time with my grandparents than I realized!"

"Maybe so. Well, the other option is to visit Barnsley Gardens, which is just a few miles off I-75. This guy Barnsley moved up from Savannah before the Civil War and built a big house, even bigger than Blackwater Manor. He had a ton of acreage and created crazy amazing gardens with lots of rare trees and roses. The house fell to ruins after the war, but there's been quite a bit of restoration done on the gardens."

"I think I've been there," Sarah said, "years ago when I was a kid. I have vague memories of daffodils and logs. I think we sat on the logs or climbed on them while looking at the daffodils. There were ruins, brick walls, and wood floors but no ceilings. I remember that. And there was an artist painting in the middle of a sort of courtyard near a huge fountain. I remember telling her I wanted to be an artist too, because I wanted her to like me. The only other thing I remember is my dad fussing about how much it cost to get in. I think the restoration must have just started because there wasn't much to see back then. Anyway, it sounds fun. Are they open on Sunday?"

"I think so. I'll double check before I send you the link. And Sarah, I'm really looking forward to seeing you. It's too late in the season for daffodils, but I'll pay the admission, especially since it's work related. I want to check out some things in relation to my plans for Blackwater Manor."

"Okay, but I'll pay for lunch," Sarah said, smiling. "Can't wait to see you Sunday, Artie."

Chapter Fourteen

As luck would have it, Artie and Sarah were not able to meet that Sunday. Artie called to reschedule because of "work problems," but he wouldn't be more specific. Sarah wasn't heartbroken, knowing she needed the time to prepare for her rapidly approaching month-long stay in Belford, but still, it was disappointing. Instead of holding Artie's hand and waltzing through the gardens, she was doing laundry and planning what to pack.

On Monday, she darted into the apartment lobby out of a sudden rainstorm and noticed a guy about her age who was just as drenched as she was. She nodded hello and started up the stairs. He followed. By the time they'd reached the third floor, it had turned into a race and they were laughing.

"Hi, I'm Charles," he said, once he caught his breath. "Do you always run up the stairs?"

Sarah noticed his chiseled jaw, nice smile, and blond hair as she took his proffered hand. "Sarah. Only when I have competition. I assume you just moved in."

"I sure did. How did you guess?"

"I have amazing powers of deduction," Sarah said, smiling. "One, there's been an empty apartment across the hall. Two, I saw a moving van on the street Saturday morning, and three, I don't recognize you."

Charles grinned. "Across the hall, huh. Maybe you can show me around the city sometime then. Have you lived here long?"

"Oh, awhile. Where are you from?"

"Virginia, actually. Moved here for work, not knowing a soul." Charles motioned to his rain-streaked suit. "I should change and scrounge up some dinner. Maybe find that umbrella I'm sure I packed. It was nice meeting you."

"Yeah. See you around." *Is the universe trying to tell me something? I mean, this guy is literally right outside my door. Maybe it's a sign.* Sarah unlocked her door, then turned and said, "Hey, my sister and her fiancé and I are going out to dinner tonight. Would you like to join us? Nothing fancy, just some barbecue at a place down the street."

"Wow, that's a really nice offer." Charles grinned. "I shouldn't be surprised. Everyone I've met in this building has been great, so yeah, sure."

"Great," Sarah said. "We'll meet you here at seven."

Smiling to herself, Sarah stepped into her apartment, calling for Elizabeth. "Sis, I just met our new neighbor. He's really cute, and he's coming to eat with us tonight."

"What?" Elizabeth came out of her room toweling her hair and followed Sarah into her room. "You invited a cute guy to dinner? What are you thinking? What about Art?"

"This isn't about Artie, Elizabeth. I just invited a new neighbor to join us for dinner. Charles practically fell into my lap, so I thought

I'd take the opportunity to get to know him," Sarah said. "I'm just being open to what the universe offers."

Elizabeth put a hand to her forehead. "This makes no sense. Liam keeps telling me to let you figure things out by yourself, but if you like Art, why are you tempting fate?"

"Tempting fate, how?" Sarah asked. "It's just dinner with a new neighbor. If I like him and he likes me, maybe we'll go out. I've had one real planned date with Artie. One. I do like him, but we're not exclusive. Plus, he's too busy to see me."

"So, is this a retaliation thing?"

"No! Of course not," Sarah said, pulling on a dry shirt. "This is me, staying true to what I resolved to do after your fiancé told me to analyze my dating history. You were both in favor of me breaking my pattern, so why are you giving me grief now?"

Elizabeth sighed. "I don't mean to be. I'm just worried that Art is going to be hurt or mad, and then Meg will be mad, and maybe you won't even like Charles." Elizabeth turned toward the door. "Liam was right. I should've kept my mouth shut. Do what you want. I just hope it's not something you regret."

"I get it, Elizabeth. I do," Sarah said, throwing her wet scrubs in the hamper. "But I think I need to keep my options open. I like Artie a lot, but he's not here. We've only seen each other sporadically because things keep getting in the way." Sarah followed Elizabeth into the living room. "Am I just supposed to sit home and wait for the stars to align?" She paused until Elizabeth shook her head. "I'm not pursuing Charles, or anyone else for that matter. Look at me, no lip gloss, no special clothes. If I like him, I'll see where it goes; if

I don't, I won't. And that goes for any other guy that I happen to meet. It's just a friendly dinner."

It soon became apparent that Liam had more interest in Charles than Sarah did. There wasn't anything particularly objectionable about him. Tall and blond, he worked for a bank and seemed nice enough. He joked about running only when someone was chasing him as he told the story of how he and Sarah met earlier. When Sarah replied that if she'd been chasing him, she wouldn't have been in front of him, he'd laughed and conceded the point, patting her on the back. Sarah caught Elizabeth watching this exchange as Charles and Liam moved on to a discussion of different restaurants within walking distance of their apartment. Elizabeth raised her eyebrows, and Sarah gave a tiny shake of her head. No, she wasn't interested. Not even a little bit.

Thoughts of Artie dominated her mind after they returned home that evening. As Sarah packed her lunch for the next day, she wondered if and when he would call. Should she call him? Ethan, Jerry, and Brandon had all texted frequently, which had seemed proof that she was constantly on their minds. Did Artie not think of her as often? *I should call him. But what if he's busy? I could text. No, he hasn't responded to the last one I sent. I don't want to bug him.*

She rounded the counter of their open concept kitchen into the living room, where her sister was sitting on the floor surrounded by fabric swatches and decorating magazines. "Elizabeth? Do you and Liam text back and forth throughout the day?"

Looking up from her work, Elizabeth said, "Well, sometimes. I mean, we're both pretty busy, so it's not constant, but we'll usually reach out a few times. Why?"

"Just wondering," Sarah said and was quiet for a minute. "Past boyfriends have been more communicative than Artie, and I was wondering why."

"Figured as much. Look, maybe Art is busier than they were. He's not sitting at home playing video games before his evening shift at a bar like Brandon."

"True. But he could text first thing in the morning to let me know he's thinking about me," Sarah said.

"Do you send him good morning messages?" Elizabeth asked.

"No." Sarah walked into the kitchen and wiped down the counter after putting her lunch in the refrigerator. She came back in the room and sat on the sofa. "I'm generally rushing around trying to get myself out of the door on time. It's not like I'm worried or anything, just thinking."

"Well, as you said, you've only been on one planned date. But since you shared a real connection with him at the lake and on that one date, I wouldn't worry about it. Maybe Art's just not a great texter. If it bothers you, talk to him about it."

Sarah shook her head. "No, I don't want to do that."

"Whyever not?" Elizabeth asked, holding up two swatches and laying one aside.

"He might think I'm just sitting around waiting to hear from him. I don't want to be smothered. Or come across as needy. I'll just wait and see how things go."

"Sarah! You said Art doesn't like games. Don't play one!" Elizabeth shook her head in exasperation. "Here I go again offering unsolicited advice, but listen, if you ignore things that bother you, they tend to blow up. And half the time the other person doesn't even realize you're bothered by those things. If you want more communication, talk to him about it."

Sarah got up and walked to her room. "I will. Eventually." She closed her door.

"You keep saying you're avoiding old patterns. You should avoid old behaviors too. Tell the man what you want!" Elizabeth shouted in exasperation.

"Good point," Sarah yelled back.

A few minutes later, she walked back into the living room. "To be honest, all the constant texting annoyed me sometimes. I'd be at work, hear a text come in, and get stressed when I couldn't look at my phone. It would prey on my mind until I could check, and then it would be some stupid video or 'sup' message from Brandon, which put the pressure to carry the conversation on me. He'd get irritated if I didn't immediately respond, and then I'd apologize to him when he was the one interrupting my work!"

"Did you ever tell him it irritated you?"

Sarah looked at Elizabeth like she was crazy. "Of course not. I didn't want to be rude to my boyfriend." She paused. "Which was dumb. Why would he stop irritating me if I didn't tell him he was?" Sarah picked up a book from the side table and started back to her bedroom.

"Exactly."

"I'm such an idiot," Sarah said. "Okay, add 'no games' and 'better communication skills' to the lengthening list of how to stay in a long-term relationship."

When Artie called an hour or so later, they set a date for the following Saturday to go to Barnsley Gardens. "I have officially resigned from temporary hours at the Linden Clinic," Sarah said, "so I'll be free as a bird that weekend."

"Except for packing and moving to Belford," Artie reminded her.

"Well, yes, except for that. Actually, I'm going to put you on speaker so I can fold these clothes. You know I'm not leaving until Sunday, but I still feel like a kid on summer vacation! I'm on target to finish all my case files and say my see-you-laters at my real job too. Working in Belford for a month is a change of pace, if not a true vacation. I'm excited about working forty hours a week instead of fifty-three like I've done for the past however many weeks."

"Starting a new job can be tricky. Are you nervous?"

"Uhm, no, not really. I'm kind of excited about it. I like meeting new people, and I've talked to my boss, and she seems great. It's going to be weird not to be in Chatty for a month though."

"I'm sure. I really liked that area though. Are you sure you want to drive to Adairsville on Saturday?" Artie asked. "I mean, I can come help you pack instead."

"No, I've been looking forward to this awhile, Artie. I don't want to be distracted by a to-do list. I just want to be with you," Sarah said. "Mom's been talking with a real estate agent in Chatty, so I may be looking at houses the next weekend! Besides, Chattanooga is not that far away from Belford, and Acworth is not that far from Chattanooga. I can and likely will be driving over the mountain more than once this coming month."

"Even if I'm in Belford?" Artie asked.

Sarah moved the basket of clothes to the floor and sat down on the bed. "What? Wait. Did you get your schedule cleared? Are you going to be working on the Blackwater grounds in June?" Sarah asked.

"Maybe. If the universe cooperates, I'll be taking my vacation more or less at the same time. I should have at least three weeks, anyway. Of course, this thing with Bruce has to be settled first."

Hearing a shift in Artie's tone, Sarah took him off speaker. The first time he'd mentioned Bruce, Artie had seemed a little excited about mentoring a new hire. Then he'd been cautious, but lately, Artie's voice hardened when he spoke about the intern working with him on the project in Kentucky. "Artie, will you tell me what's going on with Bruce?"

"Just work stuff," he said tersely. When Sarah didn't respond, he sighed. "All right, so my boss Jason asked me to mentor Bruce, right? The guy's fresh out of college and thinks he knows more, a lot more, about designing outdoor spaces in an office complex than I do. Truth is, his ideas are a bit passe. The client wants something different, a little edgier. Jason thought I'd be able to teach him a few things, but Bruce, although he seemed willing enough in the beginning, has dug in his heels and objects to everything I say."

Sarah lay back against her pillows, murmuring appropriate words of support without offering an opinion, and just let Artie talk. She recognized that he truly was frustrated and uncertain how to proceed but knew he would not appreciate her interference any more than he'd appreciated her offers of assistance on the trail.

"Then the client started questioning my opinion and wondering if I had 'actually been able to canvas the site given my condition'."

Sarah sat up. "What? That's ridiculous. Where did he get that idea?"

"My 'condition' can sometimes be a factor in extreme terrains but definitely not in greater Lexington." Artie sighed. "I'm worried the client may pull out if he feels it's an issue. And a tiny part of me wonders if that's why Jason sent Bruce along to begin with."

"But Artie, that's discrimination. It's illegal. You should file a complaint with your HR department." Sarah forgot her resolve to listen without offering solutions as she paced the room.

"Laws don't stop discrimination, unfortunately," Artie said. "But before I take any formal action, I'm going to talk to Jason. He's always been fair, and I've never felt like a token disability hire. Our office may not be a shining example of diversity, but it's far from discriminatory. I don't want to burn bridges unnecessarily."

"That makes sense, but Artie, if the client is discriminating against you for being an amputee, how does he even know?" Sarah sat back down on the bed. "I mean, seriously, it's not obvious when you're wearing long pants."

"Eh, if someone's looking, they'd probably notice, but I haven't been running around in shorts on the worksite or anything. I think Bruce probably said something. His attitude toward me changed completely mid-week when he showed up at the hotel pool. I was sitting on the edge of the pool after a swim, and we were just shooting the breeze as normal. But when I got up, his eyes got big and he made a quick departure. That sort of reaction happens, so I didn't think much about it until the client's comment."

Sarah took a deep breath. "So, I guess talking to Jason is your next step."

Artie agreed that it was and changed the subject to their upcoming date. After working out the details, Artie ended the call. "Can't wait to see you on Saturday."

Chapter Fifteen

Sarah awoke early on Saturday morning. Excited about her date, she considered a pink sundress but remembered Rachel's penchant for pink and chose a blue one instead. Silly, she knew, but she didn't want to remind Artie of Rachel, even though he'd assured her he wasn't interested. Best to forget about her.

Dressed and ready to go long before her planned departure time, Sarah decided to leave rather than pace the floor. *Always good to allow time to get lost, which I seem to do pretty often.* The website's directions were clear though, and she drove right to the gardens with no mishaps.

Spotting Artie casually leaning against his truck, his blue shirt pulled taut across his pecs, Sarah's eyes lit up. She whispered, "Wow." She parked quickly and was barely out of the car before Artie was embracing her. She hugged him tightly, thinking of how much she'd missed him. "You're here early."

"I couldn't wait to see you, so it's great you're early too. I've missed hugging you. I've missed you, Sarah." Still half-hugging her, Artie leaned back and looked at her. "You are beautiful. I don't think I've ever seen you with your hair down. I like your dark curls."

"Aah, thanks. You clean up pretty good yourself," Sarah said, rubbing her hand along his shoulder. "I like your curls too." *And that mouth. Stop drooling, Sarah. Gah, I want to kiss him. Not in a parking lot though. Not for our first kiss.*

"Shall we?" Artie offered her his arm as they walked toward the admission gate. He paid and handed Sarah some brochures about the gardens and resort. "Here you go. I think I've probably read most of this online already."

Sarah skimmed the brochures as she walked. "Hmm, Godfrey Barnsley built an Italianate villa—wow, 6000 acres, that's a lot of land—in the 1840s as a gift for his wife Julia, but she died before the house was finished. Oh, that's sad."

"Yeah, Barnsley was heartbroken. Construction wasn't restarted until her spirit appeared to him and told him to finish the house and gardens as a legacy to their six children."

Sarah stopped suddenly. "Wait, her spirit? As in ghost?"

"So they say. The resort offers ghost tours, if you're interested." Artie took her hand as they resumed walking.

"No, thank you. I haven't made my mind up about ghosts yet."

"Well, if there are ghosts, some of them may be soldiers. This area really does have battlefields." Artie shook his head. "Barnsley had seriously bad timing. He finished construction just before the war started, but Union troops occupied it and did a lot of damage."

Sarah read from the brochure. "Union troops stole or destroyed valuables estimated at $150,000."

"In today's terms, that would be millions," Artie said, speeding up a little. "Look, here's the boxwood parterre garden."

"Par-what?"

"Parterre. It literally means 'on the ground', but to fully appreciate a parterre garden, you need to view it from above. See those the red and yellow flowers? They're planted in the middle of the hedges, see?" Artie pointed, then made a diamond shape with his hands. "The English boxwood is planted in interlocking diamond shapes. From higher up, we'd see the full design. It's a neat feature."

They walked along the pathways between the hedgerows. Then Artie paused. "Do you hear water?"

Rounding a bend, they saw a three-tiered fountain with ruins of the villa in the background. "Oh, I remember this," Sarah said. "The gardens are more developed now, but the fountain is the same. The ruins too, of course. I didn't appreciate then how beautiful it all is. It's really nice."

"It is," Artie agreed. "That element of surprise is something I'd like to capture in my design. The designer here used the rolling hills to keep some features hidden until you turn a corner." Artie paused considering the parterre garden from in front of the ruins. Turning back, he said, "I'm not sure how I could incorporate surprise for the property at Blackwater Pond, since it's so low in the valley with much flatter land, but I like a challenge. These ruins are spectacular."

They circled the fountain and walked closer to the ruins, where a large corner portion of the old red brick villa stood, its arched window openings draped with ivy. Walking across the original wood floors, now open to the elements, Sarah asked, "Was the house destroyed in the war, Artie?"

"Nah, a tornado took the roof off about a hundred years ago, and by that point the Barnsley offspring who'd inherited the property weren't interested in sinking money into a garden restoration. Some German guy bought the property." Artie nodded toward a group of workers pushing carts with folding tables and chairs. "I expect we're about to get kicked out of this section. It looks like they're setting up for some event."

The workers pointed the way to the next garden as they cordoned off the ruins. "Oh well," Sarah said, smiling, "I guess that's our cue to stop and smell the roses."

Artie touched her waist as they walked through an arbor covered with pink climbing roses. "I'm glad we're here early in the day and early in the season. I have a feeling the bees love this place, but no worries, Sarah. Pretty as you are, you can't compete with the aroma of two hundred varieties of roses."

Sarah grinned. "No joke. That smell—it's enticing but kind of overwhelming, honestly."

"Right? It's hard to distinguish one smell from another. Pink and red roses generally smell like you'd expect, but yellow ones? Take a whiff."

Artie's so cute, all excited about the flowers. She sniffed. "Oh, it's citrusy. Almost lemon. Do all yellow roses smell that way?"

"Nah, some are sweeter but still fruity, like Just Joey." Artie pointed to a plant with a few five-inch apricot-colored blooms. "It's hard to choose a favorite." As they continued walking among the roses, Artie noted particular varieties he thought would do well at Blackwater Manor, including a very fragrant rose with a deep raspberry color.

"The petals are so dense," Sarah said. "It's not like a rose you'd get from a florist."

"No," Artie agreed. "It's a very old rose—Madame Isaac Pereire," he read from a sign.

As they continued exploring the rose garden, Sarah and Artie noted some flowers with more spicy scents. "Clove? Cinnamon? Kind of surprising."

"I like it." Sarah sniffed again and touched a petal. "Aren't roses a lot of work?"

"Well, they certainly can be, but all garden plants need regular maintenance, pruning, watering, fertilizing. Roses are no different. I'm no expert, but I imagine that if they're planted in good, well-drained soil with lots of sunshine and watched carefully for disease, they would do pretty well," Artie said.

Sarah's mind flitted to an earlier conversation with Elizabeth and Liam. It seemed roses had a lot in common with relationships. She would like a few rose bushes at her house one day, but how would she ever choose?

They wandered among the garden, reading signs if a plant was not yet blooming, smelling the flowers if they were. "Chestnut Rose, Chinese variables." Sarah put her arm around Artie's waist and snuggled close as he examined a bush with lots of buds, wondering if the rose garden would be the location of their long-awaited first kiss.

Artie's arm came around her shoulders. "This one's called Old Blush. It blooms from June until early December, so we're a little early." He turned to Sarah and brushed a strand of hair back behind her ear. His eyes softened, and his mouth widened in a slow smile as he moved closer. His face approached hers but stopped as a sudden movement caught his attention.

Sarah huffed in frustration at seeing a group of photographers descend upon the garden, a bride and her maids in tow. "You would think that with thousands of acres in this place, we could find a tiny patch of ground without a crowd of people around."

"I know, right?" Artie laughed and began whistling as he led Sarah along another path lined with rose bushes. "There's one plant I particularly want to see," he said, moving on down the path. "Ah, here we are."

"It's green!" Sarah said. "Almost the same green as its leaves. How bizarre. Is it a succulent, like a cactus or something?"

Artie pointed to the sign. "Rosa chinensis 'Viridiflora'. It's a really interesting plant but not a true flower. The sepals repeat forming a flower shape, but there aren't any petals. Even in nature, things aren't always what they seem." He leaned close to the plant and sniffed. "It's also peppery."

Sarah inhaled. "Oh, wow. It sure is."

"Another interesting thing about this plant is that it's sterile. Without gardeners taking cuttings to grow new plants, there wouldn't be another generation. Pretty amazing it's been around since the 1800s."

"That is amazing," Sarah said as they walked. "Do all roses have cowlicks?"

Artie stifled a laugh. "What?"

"The sign said the cowlicks hold the petal things."

"Oh, you're talking about the 'kay-lix'." Artie emphasized the long vowel sound, as he stopped at another rose bush. "See this little cup? That's the calyx. It holds the sepals which protect the bud, then the petals form the flower."

Sarah smiled. "Thanks for clearing that up, Professor Gladstone. Do you want a green rose for Blackwater Manor?"

"Nah. I don't want to copy another garden's design. It's an interesting variety though. The only thing I know for sure is that I will include a kitchen garden." Artie consulted the garden map. "We'll go there soon. One little stop along the way." He squeezed her hand. "I think you'll like it."

They walked through a gap in a tall hedge and found an open courtyard paved with bricks of different colors. Wrought iron benches stood in the center at intervals beside large tiered pots filled with petunias, marigolds, and vines. Artie led Sarah into a little niche in the surrounding hedge where a strong, sweet scent emanated from pots of cream and pink roses. "It was kind of the designer to include these private alcoves," Artie said. "Our own little patch of ground."

He turned toward Sarah running his hands along her bare arms as he stepped nearer to her. Sarah's arms encircled his waist, and she gazed into his eyes. Artie bent and brushed his lips softly across hers, then with more pressure as he pulled her closer, opening his mouth slightly and teasing her lips with his tongue. Artie was playful and gentle at first but unrelenting as his hands held her face captive. When Sarah moaned softly, Artie smoothed her curls and backed away slowly.

"Don't go away," Sarah demanded, eyes barely open, but aware now of the sounds of a large group of people walking through the courtyard.

Artie enclosed her in his arms and spoke softly in her ear. "If we keep kissing, someone is going tell us to get a room, and the resort prices are a bit out of my budget." He hugged her tightly, tilted her chin, and kissed her softly once more. "Definitely worth waiting for."

Sarah could only smile in response as they returned to the courtyard. She felt like dancing or bursting into song. If this had been a movie, she would have.

"What's that grin for?" Artie asked looking at her. After Sarah confessed her thoughts, he asked what song she had in mind.

"Oh, "Shut Up and Kiss Me" pretty much sums it up," Sarah said, thinking of Mary Chapin Carpenter's song.

"A girl after my own heart." Artie stopped their progression to steal a quick kiss, his hand at her waist. "Do you listen to a lot of country music?"

"I'm from Tennessee. It kind of comes with the territory." On their way to the kitchen garden, Sarah said that she had eclectic taste in music, listening to a bit of everything. "I honestly don't know a lot about music, but if I like it, I like it."

Sarah followed along as Artie walked through the kitchen garden, making lots of notes in his precise, all-caps handwriting, sketching designs and ideas in his ever-present notebook.

"I hope I'm not boring you too badly," Artie said. "I want to get a few more pictures, then we can eat.

"I'm not bored, but I'll wait over there." Sarah meandered among rows of beans and peas on her way to a bench. She leaned back and closed her eyes, luxuriating in the sunshine, smiling at the memory of their kiss. A moment later, she looked up and Artie was there, smiling back. He leaned down, kissed her softly and held out his hand.

"Ready for lunch?"

"I haven't heard about any plans for a restaurant at Blackwater," Sarah said later as they enjoyed their farm to table salads. "Why do they want a kitchen garden?"

"I'm not entirely sure. Andy mentioned the importance of community buy-in. Maybe they intend to provide locally sourced produce to existing restaurants or food banks." Artie reached across the table and caressed her hand. "Is there anything else you want to see in the gardens or should we check out the gift shop?"

They separated in the gift shop, with Artie looking at plants while Sarah browsed idly among the kitchen towels and T-shirts. Before long, he walked over holding a small rose bush with large creamy blooms tinged with pink at the center. "Hey, I'm ready to pay for this. Did you want anything?"

Sarah said no and joined him in line where she picked up a bottle of floral syrup. "Does this actually have lavender in it?"

Artie looked at the display. "Yeah, I'd guess so. A lot of flowers are edible. Hibiscus would be good. Or Strawberry, of course. Some of those roses we smelled might be pretty tasty. If they have a sampler set, I'll get you one."

"No," Sarah said sharply. "You don't have to buy me something every time we go out."

Artie nodded his head as his eyebrows rose in surprise. "Just the rose then."

Oh, jeez, Sarah. Overreact, much?

Sarah took Artie's hand in mute apology as they left the shop. "They have such pretty roses. How did you decide on this one?"

Artie tilted his head and looked at her. "It was pretty easy, actually. I'm attracted to beauty and complexity. My new favorite rose has both. It smells wonderful, blooms repeatedly, and has great disease resistance. And look at the flower. See all those layers of petals and how the color changes from inside to out."

They walked in silence for a few minutes, then Artie squeezed her hand and said, "Sarah, I don't want to ignore your feelings. I like giving gifts, but I'm sorry I upset you."

"It just made me uncomfortable."

"I did notice that," Artie said with a grin. "Maybe one day you can tell me why."

Sarah frowned. "I'm not sure I know why. I am sorry I overreacted though."

"Okay."

"Okay?"

"Okay, I can respect that."

They walked in comfortable silence until they neared the parking area. "Sarah, I had a really nice time today. I hope I didn't bore you too much talking about plants and planning gardens. I'll be busy, but I'm excited about spending more time with you in Belford."

Sarah smiled and swung their linked hands. "I'm excited about that too, Artie, and I think your plant passion and knowledge is kind of sexy. We should love what we do. Where are you staying?"

"Andy suggested the Crabtree Inn, which is apparently pretty much the only game in town. I need to know my exact dates before I make reservations, but I should see you soon."

"I can't wait, Artie. It'll be so great to see you more often."

They parted with another soulful kiss before heading back to the reality of their separate and changing lives.

Chapter Sixteen

The next morning, Sarah loaded her car with two suitcases packed full. She packed scrubs for work and a few dresses and casual clothes for evenings and weekends. Hoping to do some exploring around Belford, she added hiking clothes to her bag. At the last minute, Sarah added a bathing suit in case she decided to take a dip in the river or at least play in the creek that ran behind Beth Ann's house.

As she wedged her hiking books between a box of books and a suitcase, Sarah wished she had bought the Raffertys a gift to thank them for letting her stay in their house for a month. *If I hadn't flipped out about Artie buying me a gift, that floral syrup would've been nice. Maybe I'll stop and get a box of candy. It's not much, but I doubt they'd accept more.*

Beth Ann Rafferty wasn't kin to Sarah, but she was family. She was Andy's biological grandmother, even though neither had known of the other's existence until last year. Andy had moved Beth Ann and Randy Keith, his biological father's twin, to a new home on the Blackwater property where they could have more room, better access to medical care, and more regular visitors. Randy Keith loved being in the midst of the renovation efforts and helping out with weddings and other special events.

As Sarah drove up Signal Mountain, she thought about how uncomfortable Artie's suggestion of a gift had made her. Part of her discomfort was uncertainty. Why was he buying her random gifts? Was she supposed to reciprocate? When she'd told Liam and Elizabeth about her reaction, Elizabeth had said gift giving was probably Artie's love language. *Love language! Too early for that.* Sarah bristled at the memory. *Artie should just accept that I don't like gifts and not buy them for me. He can give other people gifts.*

Liam had said Artie's willingness to talk about what happened was a good sign though. *Unlike me. I avoid confrontation like the plague, especially the small stuff, which is stupid. I should be more open. What was it Liam said? Name and claim? I need to name and claim my feelings.*

Sarah merged onto US-127 toward Signal Mountain, wondering when her aversion to gifts had begun. Family gifts had never been an issue. *Boyfriends, though.* She remembered giving Blake a jacket she'd found for him at an outlet store. He'd barely glanced at it. He'd thanked her but had never worn it. She'd never questioned why but remembered her own dismay at the chunky jewelry he'd given her one Saturday before a football game. *On trend at the time, but definitely not my taste. But I wore it to make him happy.*

Sarah's thoughts wandered as her car chugged up the mountain. *Ethan. Ethan gave me gifts all the time.* She'd liked the gifts at first. The bangle bracelets he'd bought, though impractical for her career, were still a favorite accessory. He'd showered her with gifts of flowers, jewelry, and gourmet foods, but then football season started. The gifts stopped, his mood darkened, and he started working a lot more hours. They'd broken up before the season ended. *Stupid sports gambling.*

Sarah slowed as she drove through the small town of Signal Mountain. *Maybe that explains it. I just don't trust gifts. I should tell Artie.* As the road narrowed heading into the valley, a view opened up on the left. Sarah turned into the overlook and stepped out of her car. A few puffy clouds in the brilliant blue sky cast shadows on the patchwork of farmland below. *I'd forgotten how beautiful this valley is.* Heading back to her car, Sarah noticed a trail sign. *Bridal Veil Falls. Maybe Artie and I can hike that someday.*

She stopped at The Green Grocer in downtown Belford. The family owned grocery had a well-worn green and yellow tile floor, but the shelves were stocked with fresh produce and familiar brands. Sarah found the yogurt she liked for breakfast and some sandwich supplies for her lunches, then went looking for a box of candy for Beth Ann and Randy Keith. Choosing a box of Belgium chocolate seashells, Sarah had a sudden flashback to Brandon handing her a similar box, calling it an obligatory three-month anniversary gift. *He didn't even have the date right, but gifts shouldn't be obligatory.*

Well aware she was buying a gift while figuring out why she didn't like gifts, Sarah added the chocolates to her basket and went to the register. She saw a truck pull up outside and laughed at the sign on its door: Vin's Pots of Zen. *What are the odds?*

Sarah exited the store and stood on the sidewalk, wondering if she should speak to ol' Vin. She glanced his way again and realized that he'd seen her looking at him.

"Hey. What's up? Did I park wonky?" He spoke without a trace of an Italian accent as he closed his car door and moved onto the sidewalk.

Sarah sucked in her breath. *Dang, he's GQ model handsome.* Dressed in a blue slim-fit suit with a floral shirt and brown Ferragamo shoes, the man radiated confidence and confusion.

"What are you doing in Belford?" Sarah asked.

"Do I know you?" he asked at the same time.

Sarah laughed. "Not exactly, no, but I wasn't expecting to see you here." She shook her head. "Sorry, I'm not making sense. Bee Branch Trail? That truck," she said, pointing, "trapped us in a parking lot a couple weeks ago. Does that sound familiar or are you in the habit of blocking people in?"

"Ah, bellisima. Of course, of course," he said, grinning, his accent temporarily restored. "I wanted a quick run after a long drive but hadn't expected the lot to be so crowded. What's a man to do?" He cocked his head. "Your hair's different, and you're smiling, which you definitely weren't doing last time. You should always smile." He held out his hand. "Vin Fabbri."

Generally, Sarah did not like being told to smile. No one ever told a man to smile after all. But somehow, even though he hadn't apologized for his behavior at the trail, Sarah couldn't help but smile at the shameless beguiling man with the incongruous accent. She shook his hand as she admired the cut of his suit. Last time, he'd been wearing basketball shorts and an over-sized jersey that had done nothing to hide his muscular shoulders and arms.

"I'm Sarah. So, you live here in Belford? That's an amazing coincidence."

"I don't believe in coincidence. I believe in destiny," Vin said as he stepped closer, reaching for Sarah's hand again. "We meet twice in two weeks. It must mean something. How is it that I've never seen you around town before? I've only been back a few weeks, but Belford is not big."

Sarah pulled her hand free and briefly explained about working in town and visiting friends out near Blackwater Pond.

"Blackwater Pond, now that is an interesting twist. My three or four times great-grandfather worked on the manor house out there."

"You're kidding. He helped build it?" Sarah asked.

"He was a craftsman. I don't know if it's still there after all the renovations, but he carved the rinceau molding in the dining room."

"Ran-zoo? Is that what you call it?"

Vin placed his hand over his heart and stepped back. "Stop, please. Rinceau."

"Rin-sew?" Sarah laughed at Vin's horrified expression. "Sorry, I don't know anything about architecture or design. My sister got all those genes. The molding's still there. I mean, some of the fruit or flowers or vines need restoring, but it is lovely. So, did he like stand on scaffolding and carve the plaster for hours at a time?"

"No, that's not how the rinceau is done. Perhaps I will show you sometime," Vin said, reaching into his breast pocket. "Here's my card. Come by the studio anytime. It's behind the white house just over there," he said, pointing up and across the street.

"I might take you up on that," Sarah said, tucking the card into her purse. "I should get going. See you around."

On her drive to the house at Blackwater Pond, Sarah thought

about Vin and the coincidence of running into him. Would she see him around? Was seeing him today a coincidence? She wanted to see Artie more often this month, but maybe the universe had other plans. How curious that after a dearth of men for seven months, trips to Belford had led her to two interesting men. Maybe there was such a thing as destiny.

Vin was awfully cute. It had been rude to block them in at the trail, but using a fake accent was kind of funny. A little mean, a little sneaky, granted, but maybe the accent wasn't fake, just exaggerated and convenient. She smiled again. It was cheeky, that was the word. She didn't know if there was an American equivalent, but the Brits would say cheeky. She wondered what Artie would say about Vin being in Belford. She'd find out tonight when he called. If he called. He seemed really stressed lately.

Sarah turned left onto Blockhouse Road. *Almost there.* She felt excited and a little anxious. A month was a long time to stay with anyone, especially someone you barely knew.

There's the pond and the manor. She drove past the imposing house she'd last visited when James and Meg married. *When I met Artie. Gah, I so misjudged him.* Arriving at the simple house Andy had built for his grandmother and uncle, Sarah gave herself one last pep talk. *It's going to be fine. I've got this.*

Intentionally designed to enable Beth Ann and Randy Keith to age in place for as long as possible, the one-level house was situated in a wooded area near the base of the ridge that formed the back border of the property. A screened room at the back of the house overlooked a creek that fed into the nearby Igohida River. The home's doorways were wide, and safety bars had been installed in all the bathrooms. Sarah parked her car and waved to Randy Keith, who was waiting, sitting in one of the rocking chairs that lined the front porch.

"Hey there, young'un. Come on in," he said, hurrying to help her with her bags. "Ma's probably in the kitchen. She's been making cookies."

Sure enough, Sarah was greeted with the aroma of chocolate chip cookies as she walked inside. "You didn't have to make cookies! I don't want to cause you any trouble," Sarah said.

"Oh, law, it's no trouble. Young people should have cookies." Beth Ann gave Sarah a hug. "We know you're going to be busy, but we are so excited to have some company. You get settled, then we can visit a spell."

Sarah put away her groceries, then went to one of the guest rooms and unpacked. It felt odd to think about being here for a month. She appreciated their hospitality but didn't want to impose or feel obligated to spend all her free time with Beth Ann and Randy Keith. She would have to make that clear right up front.

Returning to the living room, Sarah said, "Beth Ann, I've got two surprises for you. First, these chocolates. And my second surprise is right here." Sarah held up her laptop. "Every other Sunday, I Zoom with my mom and siblings."

Sarah was surprised to learn that Beth Ann and Randy Keith were familiar with Zoom. "My great-grandsons have Zoomed with me," Beth Ann said proudly as she opened the box of chocolates. "Course, Andy generally has to be here to work it. It is a marvel."

"You all can say hello to Mom and Andy, then I'll move into my room so I won't disturb you," Sarah said.

"Why, that's just fine," Beth Ann said. "Don't feel you have to entertain us. We're glad you're here, but you just make yourself at home and don't worry about us old folks."

At two o'clock, Sarah logged into the Zoom session with her family. It was always good to catch up in these bi-weekly chats. Often it was just Sarah, Elizabeth, and their mother, Jillian. Since the wedding, Meg had been joining more frequently and James sometimes popped in for a few minutes. It wasn't unusual for Andy or Liam to at least say hello.

After Beth Ann and Randy Keith had an opportunity to speak to everyone, Sarah moved to her bedroom to continue a more private conversation with just Elizabeth and their mother.

"You won't believe who I ran into at the grocery store in town a while ago," Sarah said. "Remember the guy who blocked Artie's truck when we were hiking? He lives here in Belford. Can you believe that? His name's Vin Fabbri. He had a relative who did that fancy molding in the dining room, and let me just say, the man is hot."

Even on the computer screen, Sarah could see the looks Elizabeth and their mother exchanged.

"That's wild, sis. Uh, have you heard from Artie?"

"Not today. Not yet, anyway. He's working in Kentucky again this week. By the way, I think I've figured out why the whole flower syrup thing set me off." Sarah explained the syrup story to her mother, who agreed with Elizabeth that she should gently tell Artie that she appreciated him thinking of her but would prefer he not buy her presents.

"Giving or receiving gifts may be the way he expresses love," Jillian said. "If you prefer quality time or—"

"You know what," Sarah interrupted, "it's way too early to be expressing love in any way, shape, or form. We're just getting to know one another. It's too much, too soon, and it's making me uncomfortable. I like him, but I want to enjoy this fun, flirty stage of getting to know each other without the weight of worrying about the future. I mean, it's great that we've finally kissed, and I'm excited about seeing him while I'm in Belford, but I'm trying to break my old pattern. It's too soon to jump in with both feet!"

Sarah felt both frustrated and defensive seeing the looks on her mom and sister's faces. *They don't think I know what I'm doing, but I've learned a lot being single for almost nine months.*

"Are you saying you plan to pursue Vin?" Elizabeth asked.

"Whoa! I never said anything about dating Vin. I just said he was cute and that I'm doing things differently this time," Sarah insisted. "I'm not pursuing anyone. I'm letting things happen as they will without trying to control them. Mom knows what I mean."

"There is wisdom in relinquishing control, Sarah," Jillian started, "but there's a difference between trying to manipulate people and circumstances and drifting aimlessly."

"I'm not drifting aimlessly," Sarah protested. "I'm working toward a goal of home ownership. That's why I've worked so many hours the last few months and why I'm working through my vacation."

"I think Mom meant drifting in relationships. Meg and James speak so highly of Art, and you really seem to like him. It seems risky—"

"I've told you both and I've told Artie that I really like him, and I do, but I, well, I don't want to rush things, and if the universe keeps putting good looking guys in my path, then maybe I'm not supposed to be with Artie. It makes sense to me to go with the flow awhile and see where I wind up."

"Then I'm going to say one thing more, Sarah," Jillian said. "Months ago, Amy encouraged me to remain open to opportunities. She told me to go with the flow and not to get out of the river. If your focus has changed to simply enjoying the dating scene again, then there's certainly no harm in going with the flow. If your focus is a healthy long-term relationship, I still think Amy's advice was wise, but I'd add that you should beware of side channels. They may look inviting, but you don't want to get mired down in something that fizzles out."

Sarah considered Amy's advice for a minute. Despite her sort of hippie-ish vibe, her mom's older friend was very sensible and down to earth. "I'll keep that in mind, Mom," Sarah said, wondering how she would know a side channel from the main river, "but we've had enough river analogies for one day. Can we please talk about something else?"

Elizabeth talked a bit about her work, and Jillian shared plans for a master bathroom addition she and Andy were undertaking. Sarah was glad her mom and Andy had decided to renovate Jillian's house rather than move. Right before they said good-bye, Jillian asked

Sarah if she had Vin's contact information. "I'd love to find out if he knows anyone who can restore the rinceau molding, and I'd like to verify what little information we have about his relative who worked at Blackwater."

"Oh. Vin may actually know how to do that. He said he'd show me sometime. Why don't you Google *Vin's Pots of Zen*. Probably quicker than waiting on me to find his card."

They'd barely disconnected when Artie called.

"Artie? I'm surprised to hear from you so early. I just finished talking with Elizabeth and Mom. I'm still unpacking." Sarah hung some clothes in her closet. "Are you driving?"

"Nah. Giving my leg a break in Chattanooga on my way to Lexington. Naturally, I thought of you and decided to call."

Sarah knew that on long drives, Artie would remove the prosthesis and elevate his residual leg to prevent swelling. "Oh, so you need a reminder, huh?" Sarah teased as she stowed her suitcases in the closet. "Do I need to add my name to your calendar?"

"It might help, busy as I am," Artie said. "Nah, I'm kidding. Neither of us would get any work done if I called every time I thought of you."

Sarah smiled, sitting down on the bed. "That's really sweet, Artie. Thank you."

"So, how's Belford?"

"Oh, Artie, you won't believe it. You'll never guess who I ran into earlier. Do you remember that guy, the one who blocked us in at Bee Branch Trail? He lives in Belford!"

"You're kidding. I really hope you're kidding," Artie said with a groan. "The zen guy?"

"Yes! His name's Vin Fabbri, and get this, he doesn't even have an Italian accent. He sounds like every other person in Belford." Sarah went on to tell Artie the whole story of meeting Vin and finding out about his connections to the house at Blackwater Pond. When Sarah mentioned that her mother wanted Vin's contact information, Artie grew quiet.

"Are you still there?" Sarah asked.

"I'm here, Sarah, but I wish I wasn't."

Sarah frowned. "What do you mean?"

"Just that I wish I was with you," Artie said. "Look, I better get back on the road. I'll call you tomorrow if I get half a chance, or you call me."

Well, that was weird, Sarah thought. Artie didn't usually end calls so quickly. Shaking her head, Sarah decided she'd see if she could help with supper. Her new temporary vacation job started tomorrow.

Chapter Seventeen

Sarah wasn't expected at the clinic until nine o'clock on Monday morning, so she delighted in sleeping late, then wandered into the kitchen for coffee. Even though it was after eight, the house was quiet, and she briefly wondered if Beth Ann and Randy Keith were still sleeping. The pot of coffee indicated otherwise, so Sarah poured a cup and added some granola to her yogurt and carried both to the front porch, where she spotted Randy Keith digging in the front flowerbed under Beth Ann's direction.

"Good morning, sunshine!" Beth Ann greeted her. "I guess you slept okay. We're planting these impatiens before the day heats up. They should be real pretty out here and bloom until first frost." Approaching ninety, Beth Ann sometimes used a walker but stayed busy. At seventy-one, Randy Keith seemed to have more energy than many younger men. Both had worked hard all their lives, but as Beth had once said, that was just part and parcel of living.

Sarah sat in a rocking chair, listening to the early morning bird calls, looking out across the valley toward the big house, and relishing the cool breeze while watching the older pair.

They'd always lived in rural areas of Tennessee and Kentucky, never traveling very far from home. Although new to Belford, both seemed very happy in the valley. Sarah would tell Andy that the next time they talked. She finished her breakfast, packed her lunch, and cleaned up the kitchen. "I'll be back about five-thirty, I guess," Sarah said as she waved goodbye.

"That's fine. We'll see you when you get home. You have a good day now," Beth Ann said before pointing out some weeds for Randy Keith to pull.

Home. This place couldn't be more different from my home in Chatta-nooga, but it sure is pretty. Sarah drove slowly on her brief commute to the clinic, admiring the beauty of the fields lush with growing crops. The long narrow valley was bordered by steep slopes on both sides. Wire fences lined the narrow road and separated farms and small country homes. To her right, the ridge stood in stark relief against the bright blue sky, fog rising from the river in front of it. Nearing the downtown area, the road narrowed even more and dipped, crossing a narrow bridge over a creek. *Next right*, Sarah remembered. *Then left past the farmer's market.*

She drove past the small brick pergola where farmers sold their wares on Saturdays and pulled into the parking lot of the rural clinic. Sarah parked on the far side of the lot and walked toward the small white-framed building, wondering if it had once been a family home. When she opened the door, she was sure it had.

Although a wall had been removed to form a waiting room and office area, the original fireplace remained. The room smelled a little musty and could use a coat of fresh paint. Sarah rang a bell that sat on the counter surrounding the reception desk.

"Just a sec," came a voice from the back. Moments later, a tall black woman wearing pink scrubs patterned with llamas and rainbows came through a swinging door, balancing a cup of coffee and a stack of files. Placing both on the counter, she held out her hand. "I'm Janelle Williams. You must be Sarah."

Sarah glanced at her own blue scrubs patterned with brightly colored turtles of pink and yellow. "I am. I guess the scrubs gave it away," she said, smiling. "Is there any more of that coffee?"

"Yeah, come on back," Janelle said, leading Sarah through the swinging door. "This is our kitchen and break room. You can put your lunch in the fridge there. We collect change for the coffee in this can and take turns making it. Whoever is first on the schedule makes it, last name cleans up. Only staff is allowed back here, so you can stow your things in any of the empty lockers. We've never had an issue with theft, but if you're worried, you can lock your purse in the supply closet or bring in a padlock.

"This being your first rural clinic experience, let me just remind you that things are a little different. We're lucky to have a tiny little hospital here in Belford, unlike about a quarter of rural counties, but we still perform a lot of functional diagnoses and create treatment plans here. I'm guessing most of your clients were physician referrals."

Sarah nodded. "They were. I'm comfortable designing treatment plans, but I haven't made many diagnoses."

"No worries," Janelle said. "I'll handle that. Let me show you around."

Janelle pointed out a hall bathroom, then entered the therapy room. Two smaller rooms had been combined to form a rectangular space with four therapy tables separated by retractable curtains perpendicular to the longest wall. A filing cabinet and desk stood in a corner.

"Supplies here." Janelle opened a storage cabinet filled with first aid supplies, reflex hammers, stethoscopes, belts, and bands. Squeezed in beside a standing desk, a wheeled wire basket held exercise balls and mats under a finger ladder mounted on the wall.

"We're a little cramped. Well, a lot cramped, but we do the best we can. Supposedly, we'll be getting a new building within the next year or so. Sometimes all the tables are in use but mostly just one or two." Janelle laughed. "We don't like to be outnumbered. Usually there's just a couple of us, plus someone at reception. You're filling in for Lacey, who's on maternity leave. I can't tell you how grateful we are to have someone to fill in for a whole month. We've been hard-pressed to find reliable interim workers."

A bell rang as the front door opened. "Just me, Janelle."

"Come meet Missy. She's been working the reception desk for a couple years now." Janelle and Sarah walked back to the office. At first, all Sarah saw was a wide expanse of flowered fabric as the woman put her purse under the desk. Missy straightened and blew out a breath, causing her bangs to float up. She was short and round, with curly brown chin-length hair and cheeks almost as red as her lipstick. Wide blue glasses framed her dark eyes.

Introductions were interrupted by the arrival of the day's first patient.

"Clive, what brings you in?" Janelle asked. "Your name's not in the appointment book."

Dressed in overalls and a T-shirt, Clive was led by a teenager with bright pink hair, who struggled to keep him upright.

"He can't walk good," the girl said. "Says he's real dizzy."

Janelle nodded and told them to come on back to the exam room. "Do you have any experience with vertigo or vestibular problems?" she asked Sarah.

"No," Sarah admitted.

Janelle nodded. "I'll check for stroke, but Clive's had trouble with vertigo before. You can listen and learn while we see what's going on with him." Janelle asked Clive to smile, then raise both arms. She examined his eyes and ears, palpitated his neck, and asked if he had a headache, fever, or any vomiting. She verbalized the reasons behind her questions, explaining to both Sarah and the patient her diagnosis and the treatment plan.

"We're going to do a few exercises here, ones that you can also do at home. At first, you're going to feel very dizzy, like you're about to fall over or pass out. But we won't let either one happen, okay?" Janelle had Clive sit in a chair, leaning forward on his elbows. She directed him to look at the floor for a minute. "Now look up at the ceiling."

Clive did as directed, grabbing the chair arms as dizziness hit.

"Okay now, Clive. You're all right." Janelle led him through the same exercise four more times. "Good, now sit up straight. Look here, Clive." Janelle put a yellow sticky note on the wall. "I want to you look at that paper. Keep your eyes on it but turn your head to the right. That's it. Come back to the left."

Janelle continued working with Clive for ten or fifteen minutes, adding a couple more simple exercises. "Jasmine, you'll need to lead him through these exercises." She handed the girl a printout. "Look over this and let me know if there's anything you don't understand. You're in charge of seeing that he does them twice a day, you hear? Make sure he's drinking plenty of water." Turning to the old man, Janelle said, "Clive, Jasmine's in charge. I don't want to hear about any sass coming from that old mouth of yours. I will see you back here next Monday morning. Tell Missy to write it down."

Sarah watched as Clive and Jasmine left. "Granddaughter?"

"Great-granddaughter. Clive's eighty-nine years old. In pretty good shape, but still. Jasmine lives with him," Janelle said, shaking her head. "Okay, we've got about five minutes before the diabetic exercise class gets here. I'd like you to lead them through the exercises." Janelle stood in front of the computer and printed off a sheet for Sarah. "We have to use the front room to fit everybody in. I'll introduce you and then go make our healthy snacks for after class."

"Snacks? You give them snacks?"

"Yes, it's a good way to introduce healthier foods. Things that are easy and appetizing. They're more likely to try them here, since they don't have to buy a bunch of ingredients they're not sure they'll like. Plus, they're more likely to show up if there's food."

"That's a great idea, but isn't it expensive?" Sarah asked.

"We've got a grant. We partnered with the schools in a community food grant program. Healthy habits start young, and diabetes and obesity often go hand in hand. Working with the adults can change family habits." Janelle stood and dusted her hands together. "Sometimes, it seems half of our work here is writing grants to keep the clinic open and functioning."

Sarah studied Janelle as she spoke, guessing that she was in her early forties. "I had no idea. How long have you been here, Janelle?"

"Seventeen years. I'm from Memphis originally, but my husband is a local boy." Janelle smiled. "We met at UT Martin, standing in line for a parking pass, if you can believe it. Can't nobody that knew me in high school believe I married a farmer. I was 'destined for greater things'." Janelle laughed, stretching, then lifting her heavy braids from her neck. "It took him a while to convince me to leave the city. I wasn't sure how it was gonna work out here in Belford, but it grew on me; it's home now."

The rest of the morning passed quickly with Sarah meeting lots of new people in the exercise class, several of whom invited her to visit their churches or meet their sons. After the group, she joined Janelle and Missy for a quick lunch in the break room. Janelle reviewed the afternoon appointments, explaining that Sarah would be on her own for a couple of hours while Janelle led some balance training at the nursing home. "Missy will be here to introduce you. Call me if you run into problems."

Fortunately for Sarah, the afternoon patients had pretty typical complaints, and Sarah felt comfortable leading them through stretching and strength building exercises. Her last patient was a walk-in, a twelve-year old boy who'd been skateboarding on the courthouse steps nearby. He'd misjudged his ability and fallen, scraping his elbow and hurting his wrist. Sarah cleaned the scrape and applied a bandage after speaking with his mother on the phone. "Well, Sam, the wrist isn't broken this time, but wearing wrist guards would be a good idea. That and finding a different place to skate."

"So, did we scare you off?" Janelle asked as they tidied up the office.

"No. It was different though. At home, I deal more with sport-related injuries than disease. And someone else handles the billing and grant writing and clean up," Sarah said as she washed the coffee pot. "I don't mind. It's different, but I kind of like it."

"We definitely wear a lot of hats around here," Janelle said, as she replaced a trash can liner. "I daresay not too many receptionists sweep or vacuum, but Missy does that and more. We all help out. Our caseload is probably a little different from what you find in the city too. Don't get me wrong, we do get sports injuries, like young Sam. Mostly teenage athletes though. Adult injuries tend to be work related. Farming is a hazardous occupation."

Sarah nodded. "I hate to admit this, but the only time I've ever been on a farm was for a field trip. We rode a tractor-pulled wagon into a field and chose a pumpkin to take home. They had goats and pigs and chickens too."

"Real working farms are a bit different," Janelle said. "If you'd like see one up close, let me know. My husband Petey could take you for a ride on a tractor or a combine. You get an urge to milk a cow, you holler." Janelle laughed, then muttered, "Got me a city girl."

"More suburbia or small town, actually, but I've definitely never milked a cow."

"I'm kidding, girl. I grew up in the city, as do most folks. Cities and towns. Supposedly, ninety-seven percent of our nation is rural, but eighty percent of the population lives in cities! Ain't that something? Personally, I've come to appreciate having space."

"It is beautiful here. And so quiet." Sarah grinned. "Not a single mooing cow out at Blackwater Pond."

They collected their belongings, then Janelle set the alarm. "Growing up, I didn't know one end of a cow from another, but I have learned a bit being married to a farm boy. I'm not a farmer by any stretch of the imagination, but I garden and raise a few hens." Janelle ushered Sarah out the door. "You'll likely see some farm injuries before you leave, but pain management is a lot of what we do."

Sarah was tired. Getting used a new routine, new people, a new place, all those things took mental energy. Although she'd been walking to and from work for years, it felt good to sit as she drove back to Blackwater Pond. The day was warm, but Sarah kept the windows down, enjoying the different sounds and smells of the countryside. When she arrived back at Blackwater Pond, she noticed a small green sedan in the drive.

Sarah was surprised to see Randy Keith in the open concept kitchen with Sue Ellen Ramsey, whom she recognized from her brother's wedding. "Oh my gosh, something smells wonderful!" Sarah said.

"We'll be ready to eat in about twenty minutes," Sue Ellen said, before directing Randy Keith to set the table.

Sarah took a quick shower and changed before joining everyone for the tomato, zucchini, and yellow squash casserole Sue Ellen had prepared. She sat beside Beth Ann and joined hands as they asked the blessing.

"Did you have a nice day?" Beth Ann asked.

"I did. We were busy but not overwhelmed. I think I'm going to enjoy working there." Sarah passed the salad and bread to Randy Keith. "Those impatiens you planted sure look pretty."

"Ma likes them," he said. "She always had them out front. Course, back then she called them touch-me-nots."

"Well, they will spray seed if you touch them. Folks round here call them jewelweed," Sue Ellen said. "Speaking of jewels, how's Janelle, Sarah?

"She's great. Very easy to work with. How do you know Janelle?"

"Oh, everybody knows Janelle. She married Petey Marsh from out my way."

"Wait," Sarah interrupted. "Marsh? I'm working with Janelle Williams."

"She kept her maiden name," Sue Ellen said. "Roger Marsh wasn't exactly welcoming at first, but Janelle won him over. She won a lot of folks over. She's kind of indirectly responsible for me being here tonight."

Sue Ellen stood and started removing things from the table. "About ten years ago, I started having some spells. My sugar wasn't good, and my doctor said I needed to get more exercise and eat better. Diabetes runs in my family, so I listened. Janelle invited me to one of her classes."

As Sarah carried plates to the sink, Sue Ellen pulled a bowl of mixed berries from the refrigerator.

"So, I try to eat better. I've been doing meatless Mondays for a long time now." Sue Ellen put her hand on Randy Keith's shoulder. "A while back, Randy Keith and I got to talking about healthy eating, and I offered to cook for him one night." Sue Ellen blushed. "Then we decided to have regular dinners out here so we can take a walk or sit on the porch awhile afterward. It's real nice."

"It sure is, sugar," Randy Keith said, gazing at her.

After the kitchen was cleaned, Sarah walked to the back porch with Beth Ann. Randy Keith and Sue Ellen were already sitting side by side in the porch swing. Sarah sat in a wicker chair near Beth Ann. "I love that I can hear the creek from here. Do you ever see deer or anything out there?"

"Oh, ever now and again. The deer come by in the morning, mostly. Randy Keith has seen their tracks. Those and raccoon." Beth Ann smiled, remembering. "I do believe the boys ran them off for a bit, but they're back now."

Randy Keith chimed in. "Andy and those boys played in the creek ever day they was here. They dammed the creek and made a little pool. I've been known to take a dip out there now and again on a hot day."

"I'm sure they had a great time. Andy's boys are neat kids." Sarah peered out the screen. "It's only seven o'clock. How is it already getting dark?"

"This here's the gloaming. It's not really dark, won't be 'til about nine," Randy Keith said. "The sun's hiding behind the ridge there." He gestured across the creek at the steep incline and opened the screen door. "I believe we'll take a little walk, then let Sue Ellen get on home."

Beth Ann sighed contentedly. "She's a good woman. Just what my boy needed."

Sarah watched the fireflies flickering and listened to the frogs and jar flies making their night noises. "It's so peaceful here," she said quietly to Beth Ann before realizing she had nodded off. "I may never leave."

From across the yard, she heard Randy Keith and Sue Ellen quietly singing "Down in the Valley." Sarah smiled. *Something else to tell Andy. Randy Keith has found love.*

Sarah continued to sit, basking in the peace of the quiet evening until Randy Keith returned. She went to her room, intending to call Artie but fell asleep instead.

Chapter Eighteen

"Tuesdays must be knee days," Sarah said, dutifully completing her notes after her fourth patient recovering from knee surgery.

"It seems that way sometimes." Janelle agreed. "We get a lot. Unfortunately, gout and osteoarthritis of the knee are very common here."

"Is it farming or obesity or what?" Sarah leaned back, stretching.

"Obesity and a bad diet certainly contribute. Both problems here, as in much of our nation, unfortunately. As you know, every pound of body weight puts about five pounds of pressure on the knees. Exercise, weight loss, and a plant-based diet can help, but some folks are resistant to all three." Janelle closed the file she'd been working on. "Then there's our farmers, who are bending and lifting heavy things all the time. Repetitive motion and even riding tractors contribute to knee problems."

Janelle broke off, hearing some commotion in the reception area. She grinned and shook her head slowly but continued. "Around here, bad knees are seen as a fact of life, so getting someone to seek help before they deteriorate further is kind of a victory in itself."

Looking behind Sarah, Janelle said, "Speaking of victory, will you look at what the cat dragged in? Lord have mercy, boy. You are a sight for sore eyes. Get your sorry behind over here and give me a hug."

Sarah turned. "Vin? What are you doing here?"

Janelle looked at Vin, then at Sarah in surprise. "Girl, you don't waste time. You know this rascal?"

"You're looking good, Janelle," Vin said, giving Janelle a hug.

"Don't you start with me, boy. Back in town six weeks and this is the first time you're darkening my door? Here I am, thinking you finally come to find me, but it just takes you two days to call on this girl! Hmph. I know when I'm not wanted." She patted Sarah's shoulder on her way out of the room. "You watch yourself with this one, Sarah."

Sarah felt both confused and a bit embarrassed by Vin's presence but noticed how his tight black T-shirt emphasized his muscles. "Are you looking for me? How did you even know I was here?"

"There are no secrets in a small town, Sarah. I asked Lisa."

"Lisa? Who's Lisa?"

"Lisa Green, from The Green Grocer? Apparently, you mentioned the clinic or how long you'd be in town or something. When I chatted with her after running into you Sunday, she was disappointed that I didn't know much beyond your first name and where you'd be staying." Vin laughed at Sarah's face. "She called me Monday morning to fill in the details. News travels fast."

Sarah wasn't sure how she felt about that. It felt a little stalker-ish. "Weird. I didn't realize I'd be a topic of gossip. I'm not used to people talking about me."

"Don't think of it as gossip, Sarah. It's just being friendly. We like to know what our neighbors are up to." Vin grinned. "I came by to thank you for the referral. Andy Harrison from Blackwater Manor called me this morning to discuss the rinceau molding. It caught me off guard. I had no idea you were so well connected. I'm supposed to meet the caretaker next week to assess the molding. So, I'd like to take you to lunch to say thanks. Are you free?"

"She's free!" Janelle and Missy called from the break room before bursting into laughter.

"I guess I'm free," Sarah said with an embarrassed laugh.

She'd expected to walk to a place in town, but Vin opened the door of a gray Mazda Miata for her. For about half a second, Sarah wondered about the wisdom of getting into a car with Vin. *I'd never do this in Chatty, but Janelle knows I'm with him. Probably half the town knows.* "Where's your truck?"

"My sister Angelina has it, so I borrowed her car. She's clearing out some things from the attic today. I thought we'd go to The Sand Witch Shoppe, if that's okay. It's a five-minute drive, and I need to drop off some things." Vin drove in a direction Sarah had not been before, pointing out a new manufacturing facility and the road to the jail. "This side of town isn't as picturesque as out your way, but the town was glad for the new jobs."

"I've never heard of that company."

"Hmm. They manufacture, sell, and lease various agricultural implements. I wouldn't know what you call them individually." Vin laughed. "I'm an oddity in Belford, not living and breathing farm knowledge."

"That does seem to be the norm." As Vin pulled into the restaurant's parking area, Sarah saw a little witch on the restaurant's sign. She laughed. "I thought you said 'sandwich'. What's the story behind the name?"

"Well, Deanna, the owner, is a transplant from Florida. She's not a witch, but she carries a lot of crystals and tarot cards in the shop, along with sand art, fairy art, and essential oils and things. My Nonna wouldn't even eat a sandwich from her shop without crossing herself."

When Vin walked in, Deanna ran from the kitchen to give Vin a big hug, and several other customers stood and shook his hand. Sarah was amused by the fuss. After they were seated, she asked, "So, are you a town celebrity or what?"

Vin looked a little sheepish. "I was the high school quarterback. We had a winning season my senior year, which, believe me, was unusual. People haven't forgotten."

"Oh, that explains Janelle's comment about victory. That's cute," Sarah said, opening her menu, which featured a cartoon of a little girl on a beach wearing a pointy pink witch's hat. Sarah perused the sandwich choices, noting they were named for witches from books and movies. "Oh, this whole menu is cute. The Circe is ham and cheese. Wasn't Circe the witch who turned Odysseus's men into pigs?" Sarah took a quick picture, thinking she'd send it to Elizabeth.

"Uh, I'm not sure. The Ursula is good too if you like fish," Vin said.

"I guess the turkey in the Maleficent makes people sleepy." Sarah looked up from the menu. "What's actually in chutney?"

Vin laughed. "Depends on who makes it. Deanna uses apples mixed with sugar and vinegar or something to make it kind of sweet and sour. It's pretty good on that sandwich, but I like the Morgan le Fay better. Avocado grilled with goat cheese on Irish Soda Bread."

Sarah made a face. "Is that what you're getting?" Sarah asked. "I can't make up my mind."

Vin said he was letting the fates decide as he ordered Cassandra's Choice, Deanna's method of trying out new sandwich creations. Sarah chose the Good Witch, a platter of quartered cream cheese sandwiches with different breads and toppings.

After they placed their orders, Vin asked about Sarah's connection to Blackwater Manor. Sarah was deliberately vague, saying only that her mother and Andy had inherited the property and decided to create a museum and wedding venue. After a sip of water, she said, "So, tell me your story, Vin. How did you get interested in pottery? What's happened since your high school glory days? What are you doing back in Belford, and where have you been?" When she stopped herself from adding 'inquiring minds want to know', Sarah remembered a little guiltily that she had neglected to call Artie last night.

"Well, there's not much to tell. I grew up in town, middle child. My dad taught history at the community college over in Dunlap. Mom taught art at the elementary school." Vin waved as someone he knew came in the restaurant. "Dad got me started throwing pots. I played football, raised Cain with my friends, then left for college."

After their sandwiches arrived, Vin explained that he had gone to UT Martin for both his undergraduate degree and a master's of fine arts in ceramics. Then he'd taught classes and led workshops in Memphis and Little Rock. "It took me a while to figure out how to make a living as an artist. Met a girl and followed her to New Orleans. It wasn't the scene for me, so I moved back a while ago."

"This sandwich is really good," Sarah said. "So, what happened to the girl?"

"She decided to stay." Vin shrugged. "It wasn't meant to be."

"So, you believe things are meant to be or not to be?"

"Well, 'that is the question'." Vin laughed. "Not exactly. I believe in free will, but I also think there's a greater plan. If things don't work out the way I want, well, I think it wasn't meant to be." He drummed his fingers on the table. "I believe in destiny but a destiny we bring upon ourselves, not some plan etched in stone that we can't avoid. Our choices either lead us toward or away from that greater plan." Vin made a face and scraped a few onions from his sandwich. "My mom used to quote what St. Augustine said all the time: 'Love God and do what you will.'"

"I don't understand," Sarah said. "What does doing whatever you want have to do with loving God?"

"No, it's not whatever you want; it's what you will. If you truly love God, you will act with love and your actions will be in line with God's will," Vin explained.

"Oh. That's really deep." Sarah paused for a minute. "So, parents both teachers. Did you ever consider teaching full time?"

"I lead workshops, which is as close to teaching as I want to get. So, no, I'm a potter, not a teacher. It's not the easiest way to make a living, but I get by. Festivals and family commitments will keep me busy between now and Thanksgiving."

They stood, getting ready to leave. "I'd love to see some of your work," Sarah said, before noting that Vin hadn't finished his sandwich. "Did you not care for Cassandra's Choice?"

"You win some, you lose some. Too many onions this time. I'll let Deanna know and take care of the bill while you look around. She has some of my work here," Vin said. "Which reminds me, I need to get that box out of the car."

Sarah reached for her purse. "Vin, let me give you money. You don't have to buy my lunch."

He waved her off, so Sarah thanked him before wandering through the small shop set off in a corner of the restaurant. She saw the crystals and tarot cards Vin had mentioned, as well as a display of tin signs featuring everything from cycles of the moon to uses of herbs. She was admiring a display of fragrant soaps when Vin joined her. "Look, these are shaped like the meditating Buddha on your sign."

"Yeah, my sister actually makes these."

"Angelina?"

"No, her twin, Adelina. She's local. Married a guy that works out at the prison. My work is over here," Vin said, guiding her to a nearby display.

Sarah stiffened a little at the feel of Vin's hand on her back but forgot her discomfort as she looked at his work. A swirl pattern stood in relief on the front of small rounded wall vases with bright green, turquoise, and orange crackle glazes. A larger footed version of the same design was tagged as a cauldron. Small incense burners shaped like snakes lay in between mugs with moon and star designs, owls or cats. "That line is specifically for The Sand Witch Shoppe," Vin said almost apologetically as they left the shop.

"I wouldn't want you to judge my ability by those pieces, Sarah," he continued. "They're very commercial, which makes me feel a little defensive sometimes, especially in conversation with my parents, but I have to make a living. Or maybe I just feel guilty. I'd like to show you my better pieces, actual pots."

"I don't get why you'd feel guilty. Those vases were beautiful, and surely your parents understand you need to earn a living. I mean, we all do that, right? I doubt you'll be making things for Deanna's shop forever, but surely it takes a while to establish yourself as an artist."

"Yeah, the guilt is mine, not theirs. It's complicated. I'm an artist. I want to make a living with my art. With the art I want to make. Not useful products people will buy or junk they collect. I want to push the boundaries, create things that reflect inner beauty. I don't exactly get in the zone when I'm replicating designs for Deanna."

"I'm not an artist, Vin, but that sounds, well, it sounds admirable but also really difficult to accomplish. I mean, a pot is always going to be useful, right?"

"Yes, but I want to create beauty in the useful items. I'd much rather fire one beautiful vase than a dozen coffee mugs with silly sayings. Perhaps if you see some of my Pots of Zen, it will make more sense."

"I'd like to see them sometime." *He's an interesting guy, talented and charming, but I don't think he's asked me a single thing beyond my connection to Blackwater Manor. Then again, I did pretty much ask for his life story.* "Do you show your work at other places in town?"

"Oh, a couple places but not the more serious pieces. I just don't want my whole market line to be chintzy or witchy, you know. I already feel a little guilty about that because I grew up in the Church, yet here I am, selling items in a store seeming to promote a belief in witches. Perhaps the guilt is grounded in religion, perhaps in fear of disappointing my family. It's a fine line I walk." Vin pulled into the lot. "Perhaps I'll see you next week?"

"At Blackwater Pond? Maybe," Sarah said. "Thanks for lunch."

Sarah had enjoyed Vin's company and definitely thought he was cute, but she wondered what had brought him back to Belford. Was he running away from something or back toward something?

In between patients that afternoon, Janelle talked about Vin. "That boy's a charmer. Always has been. I guess it'd be hard not to be looking that way. It's a wonder he's not spoiled rotten. Do you know the family?"

"No, but he mentioned that his parents were teachers."

"Yes, they've retired and are traveling a bit but bought a place up in New Jersey, where Vinzetta's from. That's his mom."

"And he's got twin sisters, right?

"Yeah, two of the six are twins," Janelle said.

"Six kids or six sisters?" Sarah asked.

"Six sisters. Can you imagine? He's the only boy, right smack in the middle. Alessia, Adrianna, Antonia, Vin, the twins Adelina and

Angelina, and finally Aleonora."

"Wow. I can't even. You seem to know his family well," Sarah commented.

"Oh, sure. We all went to the same church over in Dunlap. Plus, his grandmother was a patient here, and through the years, every one of them brought her in for one ailment or another. She was a little bitty thing, spoke only Italian, but ruled the roost. She died about six months ago. I hear Vin's here to clean out the house, maybe renovate it."

"Do you think he'll stay after that's done?" Sarah asked.

Janelle gave Sarah an appraising look. "I have no idea. No one seems to know. That big old house has been in the Fabbri family forever. Vin's the only son. It might even be his now. With Vinzetta and Tony moving, they may have called him home. Have you been in it?"

"No, I really don't know Vin at all. We met in a parking lot a few weeks back, then I ran into him at the grocery story, then lunch today."

"Explain the parking lot, please, ma'am," Janelle said.

So Sarah explained how she'd been hiking with Artie and how they'd been blocked in by Vin's truck. While she'd never expected to see him again, she'd spoken to him at the store and been surprised at how charming he was.

"Well, he is that," Janelle said. "He's a sweet boy, really. His mother and grandmother had their hands full when he was growing up, but he is a genuinely nice guy who loves his family." Janelle started the end-of-day chores but turned to Sarah. "If you've already got a boyfriend, why are you going out with Vin?"

"Oh, today's lunch was to say thanks for a referral, and Artie's not my boyfriend. Not really," Sarah explained, a bit flustered. "It's complicated. I mean, I really like Artie, but we just met four months ago, and I've barely seen him because we live in different states and seem to always be working."

Sarah walked to the kitchen and started washing the coffee pot. Sighing deeply, she turned to Janelle. "I have a history of rushing into relationships with the wrong men. I'm working on figuring things out so I don't make the same mistake this time. I'm not chasing after anyone, but I'm also not running away. Does that make sense?"

Janelle nodded. "It does. I barely know you, much less the other guy, but I do know Vin. You be careful with my boy, there. Don't put him in the middle and then break his heart."

"Oh, Janelle. I don't even know if I'm interested in dating Vin. He's nice, but he's awfully young, and I don't know that he's interested in me."

"Hmm. I guess you'll figure that out soon enough. He's twenty-five. Around here, that's plenty old enough to settle down. All of his sisters are married and starting families."

Sarah thought about Janelle's comments as she drove to Black-water Pond. Twenty-five wasn't that far removed from twenty-nine. *I think Artie's thirty-one. Does it matter?* It shouldn't, Sarah decided. She couldn't imagine 'settling down' at twenty-five. Was she ready at twenty-nine? She did want children. One day. At almost thirty, she worried that her time was running out. Most of her friends were married. *Maybe it's time. But if it is, why does Artie's talk of the future scare me so?*

Chapter Nineteen

arah had hoped to spend her first weekend in Belford exploring the countryside with Artie. When they'd FaceTimed Thursday, he expected to arrive on Saturday, but called on Friday to say he wouldn't make it to Blackwater Pond after all.

"I wouldn't be good company anyway, Sarah," Artie griped.

"Why, what's wrong?"

"Work stuff."

"What kind of work stuff? Maybe I can help."

Artie sighed. "I appreciate the offer, but I'll deal with it. This project is an effing nightmare. I'm sorry to ruin your weekend. I'll be there next weekend, come hell or high water."

"Oh, Artie, I'm sorry too. I'll miss you. Hey, why don't we FaceTime tomorrow?" *I wish he'd tell me what's going on. I probably can't help, but I can listen.*

"I'd love that. It'll have to be after eight though. I've got a full day, then a dinner meeting with the client."

Sarah slept late on Saturday but felt restless and a bit uncertain what to do with herself. When she called her mother to talk about the house hunt, Jillian suggested they walk through a few homes that would be listed in the coming week. "I've been researching homes in the area, and my friend Patti sent me information on these. Do you want to meet at your apartment in a couple of hours? You never know, one of these houses could suit you."

"ALL THE HOUSES are in Rossville, Georgia," Jillian said as they got in her car. "It's just across the state line, less than twenty minutes to the center of Chattanooga. It's more rural than you're used to, but after a week in Belford—"

"I'm really not ready for farm life, Mom," Sarah laughed.

Sarah found things she liked and disliked about all three homes. One was too large, another too isolated, but she liked the layout of the third.

"So, you like the new one best?" Jillian asked.

"Well, no," Sarah said. "It was cute, and a garage is nice, but the neighbors were so close! I liked the second one but don't need three acres."

"Well, all three are within your budget. The one with acreage would be the least expensive as it's only two bedrooms."

"To be honest, Mom, none of the houses feels like a good fit for me." Sarah sighed. "Am I being too picky? I keep looking online but find flaws with everything."

"Oh, honey, house hunting is a process. You don't have to settle for something you hate, but don't look for a 'perfect' house." Jillian rubbed Sarah's back. "It's normal to feel overwhelmed. Some agents limit the number of houses they show buyers for that very reason. We'll keep looking, but things are shifting, quickly moving to a seller's market. You may have to adjust your expectations or widen your search area."

"I know, I know. I'm just not sure a long commute is something I'm willing to accept."

WHEN LIAM AND ELIZABETH joined Sarah for dinner that evening, they laughed at the notion of her living in Rossville. "I can't imagine you living outside the city," Elizabeth said. "You love living downtown."

"Definitely a different kind of night life," Liam added. "No honkytonks or rooftop bars in the country."

"Too true," Sarah agreed. Yet as she walked back to her apartment, she realized that she missed the quiet of Belford. Did she already prefer fireflies to streetlights, the hoots of owls to car horns, and the cool breeze off the creek to the hot exhaust from passing cars?

"HEY, YOU. Did your day get any better?"

"Sarah! It just did. Find something fun to do today? You look pretty well moved in."

Sarah looked around in confusion. "What? Oh, I'm actually back in Chattanooga. Mom and I looked at houses, so I decided to stay over."

"Tell me about them."

As Sarah shared her thoughts about the houses, she realized how talking with Artie calmed her. Even on FaceTime, which could be distracting for her, all the noise in her head went away as she drank in his quiet attention. She didn't second-guess her comments or attempt to gauge his mood. She just talked, until a car horn sounded outside. "That's something I don't hear in Belford. It's a lot quieter there. I kind of miss sitting on the screen porch, listening to the quiet."

"That sounds great," Artie said. "I'd like to sit there with you sometime."

"I'll see if I can fit you in. My schedule's so full these days," Sarah joked.

ARRIVING HOME after her second Tuesday in Belford, Sarah was surprised to see Vin and Randy Keith in the living room. Beth Ann was in the kitchen, putting together a salad. Vin greeted her with a big smile and an admiring glance.

"Want to ride over to the big house?" Randy Keith asked. "Vin here wants to look at that fancy molding in the dining room."

"It would be nice to see the manor again without all the wedding guests. I didn't really look at the molding then. Beth Ann, do you need any help with dinner?

"Oh, no, hon, it's almost ready. You go on if you want to."

Sarah put her things away, then joined Randy Keith and Vin for the short ride to the manor. The golf cart rolled along a well-worn path, with Randy Keith pointing out the barn, the pecan orchard, and the pond. Vin didn't say much but appeared to be taking it all in.

Randy Keith led the way through the big front entry doors and down the black and white marble hallway into the dining room, turning on lights as he went. "I'll grab the ladder and be right back," he said, declining Vin's offer of assistance.

Sarah heard the elevator descend to the basement as she walked through the rooms on the first floor, remembering James and Meg's wedding, remembering meeting Artie.

Vin came up behind her quietly. "So, there's something I need to ask."

Sarah turned. "Okay. Ask away."

"It's about that guy you were hiking with the first time we met. Is he your boyfriend?"

"We're dating, but we're not a couple."

Their conversation was interrupted by Randy Keith's return. Vin took the ladder from the older man and carried it into the dining room. He carefully leaned it against the wall, then climbed the ladder as Randy Keith held it. At the top, Vin took a small tape measure from his pocket and dictated dimensions of the molding to his phone before carefully examining the molding with a high-beam flashlight and taking several pictures. "I'll talk to my uncle about the repairs. It really is remarkable craftsmanship."

Vin insisted on helping return the ladder to the basement closet, so Sarah had a few moments to think about Vin's question. Was Artie her boyfriend? They'd never said they were exclusive. Artie's feelings were clear, but Sarah's were not. She'd really enjoyed FaceTiming with him on Saturday but didn't think she was in love with him. Not yet, anyway. She'd maintained all along that she wanted to see other men. So, she could date Vin if she wanted to.

Did she want to? Was she not in love with Artie only because she hadn't allowed herself to be? Sarah sighed heavily. *This is making me crazy. I just need to live in the moment and let things play out as they will.*

Sarah was quiet as they rode back to the house. She laughed when Vin imitated her mispronunciation of rinceau, even though it hurt her feelings a little. She was surprised when Vin joined them for the summer soup and green salad Beth Ann served for dinner.

"This is one of Sue Ellen's recipes," Beth Ann said. "She's been teaching me some about eating healthy. The hardest thing about it was peeling the butternut squash. I had to get Randy Keith to do that."

"You'll have to give me the recipe," Sarah said. "It's delicious."

"Great dinner, Miss Beth," Vin said. "Thanks for inviting me. Would you mind if I wander down to the river before I leave? Some of my high school buddies and I used to fish out there."

Sarah thought a walk was a great idea. "Can I join you, Vin? I'd like to see the river, and I could use some exercise. Somehow, I haven't made time to run since I've been here."

When Sarah stood to help clear the table, Beth Ann shooed her away. "You-uns go on, we'll get this.

"You know, you talk about this place like you've been here a month." Vin laughed.

"Time just moves differently here at Blackwater Pond," Sarah said. "It hasn't even been two weeks, but it feels much longer."

Vin and Sarah followed the creek behind the house the half-mile or so to the river. A small trail led to a spot where the creek merged with the Igohida River. "Do you think it's safe for swimming?" Sarah asked.

Vin shrugged his shoulders. "I wouldn't recommend swimming alone, but yeah, I think so. Are you worried about pollution?"

"Oh, no. I hadn't really thought about pollution. I was thinking about hidden depths and fast moving currents."

"Either way, I think the river's safe enough. You're pretty near the headwaters, so it's probably unaffected by any runoff from farms. This river's not very deep, maybe five, six feet in some stretches, but here, probably about four feet."

"Any white water? It might be fun to go rafting."

"You'd need to go over to Dayton for white water rafting. This river's really slow moving. Back in high school, we'd put in at John's Creek and float down river about three miles every summer. That took about three hours."

"Maybe I'll stick to running," Sarah said.

"I'd love to join you," Vin offered. "Tomorrow evening?"

Sarah shook her head. "I have plans. I said I'd join Beth Ann and

Randy Keith at church tomorrow. Wednesday night dinner, you know."

When Vin didn't respond, Sarah looked at him, holding his gaze, wondering what the universe intended. "Maybe Thursday?"

"Thursday then. I'll be here."

SARAH MET VIN at the little house after work on Thursday. She'd explained to Beth Ann that she wouldn't eat with them because she was going running with Vin.

"Well, that's fine, Sarah. We'll be eating a little late tonight, but if you're not back, I'll save you a plate."

Vin was wearing basketball shorts and a loose jersey, much as he had been the first time they'd met. His curly hair was pulled into a man-bun. Sarah had always thought the hairstyle looked silly, but on Vin, it worked.

They stretched a bit, then jogged down the long driveway past the pond, neither saying much. As they neared the manor house, Vin picked up speed before doubling back along the river and circling back to the creek behind the little house.

Sarah stopped running as she caught up with Vin. "Whew!" she said, leaning on her knees. "Either I've gotten out of shape after two weeks of no running or you set a faster pace than I'm used to. I think it's the latter."

Vin wasn't breathing as hard as she was, but he was dripping with sweat. "I had to push to stay ahead of you." Vin peeled off his shirt and mopped his face. He held up his hand for a high five. "Good run, Peters."

Sarah tried not to look at Vin's bare chest, but she couldn't help noticing his sculpted torso. She checked her Fitbit. Three miles, almost exactly. "What are you doing?" she asked as Vin suddenly sat down and starting removing his shoes.

"That creek is calling my name." Vin stood and hobbled on bare feet across rocks toward the creek, where he shamelessly removed his basketball shorts and waded into the water, wearing nothing but a pair of tie-dyed boxer briefs.

Sarah felt a little attracted and a lot conflicted. Obviously, joining Vin in the creek would signal her interest in being more than a running buddy. *Is that what I want?* After a moment, she sat down and removed her shoes.

Vin stood in the small pool Andy and his boys had created. He watched Sarah wading carefully into the creek. "You're overdressed," he said, splashing her.

"Um, I think you're under-dressed," she retorted, noticing the water encircling Vin's muscular legs, lapping at the fabric of his boxers.

"Hey, eyes up here." He pointed to his face. "I'd be skinny-dipping if we weren't within sight of the old folks. Don't want to give them a heart attack."

"But you don't care about giving me one." Was she flirting? She felt out of practice. Fully dressed but holding her shirt above the level of the water, Sarah joined him in the pool. Vin crouched suddenly, then rolled on his back to a floating position.

"Thank goodness you're still somewhat clothed," Sarah said. But floating in the cool water seemed enticing. She pulled her T-shirt over her head and tossed it to the bank.

Vin sat up abruptly and looked at Sarah in her nylon shorts and sports bra.

"It's been years since I've done this," Sarah said as she sat in the creek.

Vin snaked an arm around her waist and pulled her into his lap. "It's been a while for me too."

"Vin!" she protested, pushing his arm away.

He released her, and they both sat facing each other as the water swirled around them. Vin grinned. "I'd like to kiss you."

Sarah held his gaze, breathed out slowly, and said, "I think I'd like that."

Vin stood and reached a hand to Sarah, pulling her up out of the water and holding her close. He put his hand behind her head and kissed her long and hard, pushing his tongue into her mouth. Sarah's long-dormant passion ignited, and she returned his kiss with urgency. Vin pulled her closer.

"Stop," Sarah said, stepping back. "I shouldn't be doing this."

"Why not?" Vin reached for her hand. "We're obviously attracted to each other. Why shouldn't we explore that attraction?"

"Oh, God, I've got to go, Vin. I'm sorry. I'm sorry for everything." Sarah climbed out of the creek, grabbed her shirt and shoes, and ran for the back porch, not noticing the forest green truck in the driveway, nor the horrified expression on the driver's face.

Chapter Twenty

Sarah wouldn't have been surprised to find Beth Ann and Randy Keith on the porch having witnessed everything, but it was empty. A neatly folded towel lay on the arm of a chair near the door. Someone had seen her in the creek. Someone had, perhaps, seen her kissing Vin.

Sarah stood, hands folded in front of her mouth, eyes open wide. *What have I done?* When she realized she was biting her fingers, Sarah grabbed the towel, dried off as best she could, and hurried to her room, vaguely aware of raised voices and slamming car doors from the front of the house. She showered and dressed quickly, then returned to the kitchen, hoping to make a cup of tea without having to talk to anyone.

"Oh, there you are, Sarah. Right on time," Beth Ann said. "I wasn't sure you'd make it. Randy Keith said you were splashing in the creek. Our company's getting settled."

Sarah noticed the table was set for four. "Company?"

"Why, yes. Your friend Art. Andy said he was coming to town to study on the landscaping, so I said there weren't no need for a family friend to go to a hotel. Not when we've got room."

Sarah's thoughts were spinning. *Artie? Here? Now?* She was still processing her thoughts about kissing Vin. *It wasn't cheating. Not really.* Then why did it feel like a betrayal? Hearing footsteps behind her, Sarah bit her lip and turned. "Hey! I'm, um, I'm surprised to see you, Artie. I didn't expect you tonight."

Artie nodded without smiling. "Yeah. I think we both got a surprise."

Sarah's insides grew cold. *Oh, God. He saw me kissing Vin.* She fought the instinct to cover her face in shame. *I can kiss who I want. He's not my boyfriend. I don't have to feel guilty.* But she did.

Beth Ann looked from Sarah to Art as if wondering why the room was suddenly filled with tension. "Sarah, why don't you fix our drinks?"

"I thought you were staying in town. I thought you were coming Saturday," Sarah said as she pulled glasses from the cabinet.

"Change of plans and no room at the inn," Artie said. "Sorry for intruding."

"Well, we're always glad for company," Beth Ann said. "Won't this be nice? Art, would you care to put the casserole on the table?"

An awkward dinner with somewhat stilted conversation followed. Artie was pleasant enough, but his remarks were brief, and Sarah's face burned the few times he looked at her. When dinner was finally over, Beth Ann encouraged them to go for a little stroll before settling in for the night.

Sarah slipped on her shoes and followed Artie out into the gloaming. Her emotions were jumbled. She was glad to see Artie, anxious about his behavior, and unsure of her feelings for Vin.

Artie rapidly strode some fifteen or twenty yards from the house before turning toward her. "What the hell, Sarah?"

"What? Why are you acting like this? You won't even look at me. I don't understand."

"Don't you?" Artie closed the distance between them. "Well, let me be blunt. I'm pissed." He turned and walked away again. Still not facing her, Artie swore and then said, "I mean, I've been counting the minutes until I could see you, Sarah, see your beautiful face. Been imagining it all week. I grab my bag and—I stand there like a fool, trying to make sense of what I'm seeing."

He shook his head. "I didn't believe it at first. Didn't want to believe it. Wouldn't, until you got out of the creek." Turning to face her, he continued. "You said you ran into him. You never said you were seeing him."

As was her instinct, Sarah disguised her discomfort with scornful disdain. "So what? You and I have been on two dates, Artie. Two. We're not exclusive. I can kiss whoever I want."

Artie turned to look at Sarah. "Are you sleeping with him?"

"I don't believe that's any of your business, Arthur Gladstone," Sarah said, covering her hurt with anger.

Artie stared back, trying to find an answer in her eyes. He swore again softly and turned away from her. "You're right. It's not." Artie glanced back at her, shook his head, and started to walk away.

Sarah stepped forward and put her hand on Artie's arm. "Artie, wait."

Artie looked at her hand but didn't say anything.

"Artie, I'm not—we're not. We were just having a bit of fun. I didn't mean to start anything with him, it just happened." Sarah gestured at the creek. "We'd been for a run and then cooled off in the creek. I hadn't planned on kissing him. It just happened," she said again, moving closer to him.

"These things don't just happen, Sarah. You choose to act or not act."

Sarah's hand dropped. She bowed her head and protested. "He kissed me first."

"Did you kiss him back?" Artie asked quietly.

Sarah backed away. Her voice, conflicted with anguish and defiance, shook. "Yes, yes, I did. What do you want me to say, Artie? What do you want from me?"

Artie stepped close to Sarah, put his hands on her waist, and pulled her close. "Haven't I made that clear?" Moving one hand to her face, Artie tilted her chin so he could stare into her eyes. "Sarah Peters, I want you to be my girlfriend. I want to date you and only you and kiss you and make love with you and see where the future takes us."

Sarah froze. Her heart soared. *He wants us to be together.* If she stepped closer, maybe everything would be okay. She watched him watching her and started to smile. *Maybe Artie can be my boyfriend. Maybe he'll forget I was kissing Vin and we can build a future together.*

Artie moved his hands to her hips and pulled her even closer, looking into her eyes. "Sarah," Artie said quietly, bending his face toward hers.

A future. No, he can't possibly mean that after what I did.

He stopped, backing away, shaking his head.

Perhaps he saw her uncertainty, her fear, her guilt because she wasn't really sure she wanted to forget about Vin. Sarah stood a foot away from Artie, wanting to reach for him but filled with uncertainty. *Isn't it too soon to be exclusive? Haven't I always moved too quickly? Hasn't it always ended badly when I did?*

"You know what I want from you, with you." He jerked his head over his shoulder. "But in case I haven't been clear about him, I for damn sure want you to send that inconsiderate bozo packing."

"He's not a bozo," Sarah protested. "He's actually really smart and sweet and talented."

"Yeah? He wasn't so sweet when it was my truck blocking him in."

"Oh, Artie." Sarah stepped closer. "If you'd give him a chance, I think you'd like him."

"Jesus, Sarah!" Artie threw his arms up in disbelief. "I'm not going to be best buds with a guy who's been kissing the woman I—" Artie paused, gesturing to himself and to the creek. His voice grew quiet. "The woman I can't stop thinking about." An owl hooted, silencing the jar flies.

Sarah had startled at Artie's outburst. Now she stood watching him, biting her lip in uncertainty, hands upturned, shaking her head slightly. She didn't know what to do, how to feel.

Artie stilled, watching her. "Despite everything I said about wanting to be with you, you defend him. You've chosen him. After twelve freaking days, you've chosen him. I can't believe this." Artie stepped away, then turned and looked at her, waiting for what she would say.

Sarah raised her eyes to look at him, silhouetted in the growing darkness. "No, no, I haven't, Artie."

"But you haven't chosen me either, have you?" Artie stood, arms stiffly at his sides, the pain in his voice evident.

Sarah turned in a circle, throwing up her arms. "Four months ago, I didn't even know you. Three months ago, I decided I liked you. However many weeks ago, I realized I really, really liked you, but that scares me, Artie. What if I'm fooling myself again? I need more time."

"Time to choose between me and Fabbri? Is that it, Sarah?"

Sarah's eyes didn't leave Artie's face. She was hurting because he was hurting, because her own heart ached. Shaking her head in confusion, she said, "No. Well, maybe? I mean, I need more time to figure out what I want. I didn't mean to hurt you. I like you, Artie. So, so much, but you scare me sometimes. How can you be so certain so soon? How can I trust your feelings when I don't trust my own?" Sarah brushed at the silent tears rolling down her face. "Please don't hate me, Artie, but I don't know if I can give you what you want."

Artie moved toward Sarah, stopping before he touched her. "I could never hate you, Sarah." He reached toward her but again stopped and shoved his hands in his pockets. "Please don't cry. I know I've been mad as hell, but I won't ever, ever hate you."

Sarah stood shivering with emotion. She sucked in a breath, trying not to cry and wrapped her arms tightly around herself. "I'm so scared."

Artie came to her then, wrapping his arms around her, shushing her, kissing her hair. "Shh, it'll be okay. You're okay." After a few minutes, he asked, "What are you so afraid of?"

"Losing myself. Making a wrong choice. Messing things up with you. Wondering 'what if' about Vin."

Artie stiffened. Sarah held him tightly. "Can we pick up where we left off?" she asked softly.

"No."

Sarah's arms fell, and she stifled a sob of hopelessness.

Artie shook his head. "You're asking too much of me, Sarah. I need time to think. I know we hadn't talked about being exclusive, but I felt like we were. And now, I can't forget what I saw."

Oh, God, please don't go.

Lifting her chin, he said, "I don't know what to do, to say. My mind is still reeling, but I'll say this much. I'm mad and I'm hurt, but I'm not ready to give up on you. On us."

Sarah's eyes widened in disbelief, in hope. She wasn't sure she would be so forgiving. In her mind, he was obviously the better person. *I don't deserve him.*

Artie stepped back and looked off into the distance. "I'll be around until Saturday, maybe Sunday. Maybe by then we'll have figured something out. It's getting dark. We should go inside. I need to unpack and get some work done."

Chapter Twenty-One

arah's alarm woke her from a restless sleep. She showered and dressed quickly, hoping to repair some of the damage she'd done to her relationship with Artie before leaving for work.

The house was quiet. Sarah knocked on Artie's door, but he didn't answer. *I hope he's at work and not on his way back to Acworth.* Sighing deeply, she pulled out her phone and texted him. "Sorry I missed you this morning. Sorry for everything. I'm really hoping we can figure something out. Talk soon?"

Sarah tried calling Elizabeth but had to leave a voice mail. "I screwed up, sis. Artie saw me kissing Vin. Why do I always do stupid things? I like Vin. I liked kissing him, but I like Artie too. I don't want to lose him. I'm attracted to them both. Is that so wrong? Please call me."

At the clinic, Sarah struggled to keep her feelings contained as she went through the motions of her job, unable to interact effectively with her patients. Janelle asked if she was sick. Sarah truthfully said she hadn't slept well. When her phone buzzed mid-morning, she left her patient exercising and went into the restroom to see who it was from.

Vin. "Are you okay?"

"I've been better," Sarah responded, realizing the truth in that statement. She was crying again. How could a person feel so many contradictory emotions all at once? She was disappointed in not hearing from Artie, and at the same time, happy to know Vin cared enough to check on her. Attracted to both, uncertain how to proceed with either.

"Talk tonight?" Vin texted.

Sarah grimaced as she texted Vin. "I can't. Maybe Sunday?"

She hated that she'd hurt Artie so badly. She should've been upfront with him and said she wanted to see other people, that she wasn't ready to commit to a relationship. She shouldn't have kissed Vin without talking to Artie first. Why had she done that? *Maybe because Vin reminds me of every other guy I've dated, and I've always jumped straight into relationships.*

Sarah winced. Artie had been so mad, so hurt. *Will Artie ever forgive me?* He'd said maybe they could figure something out, so maybe there was a chance to salvage the relationship. *I'm not ready to give up on him. Do I even want to go out with Vin? Yeah, maybe. Kind of.*

Aware that she had a patient on the table and that she had been in the bathroom awhile, Sarah washed her hands and face and went back to work.

At noon, Janelle confronted Sarah again. "Girl, I don't know what's going on with you today, but you need to get on out of here and figure it out."

"I know I've been out of it, Janelle. I'm really sorry. It's just, it's just a bad headache. I didn't sleep well last night, but I can finish out my shift."

"Hmm. I suspect I know what kind of headache. Sign out, and I will see you Monday morning, when I expect things to be back to normal."

Sarah nodded. "I'm sorry for being so unprofessional. It won't happen again."

"Lucky for you it's a light schedule this afternoon. Go on now. Do what you need to do and get your head back on straight."

Sarah could sense Janelle watching as she gathered her things and walked to her car. She didn't want to go back to the house and face questions, so she drove slowly through the town and pulled into a church parking area. *I need to talk to Elizabeth.*

Sarah wasn't surprised when her phone rang. She and her sister often shared almost telepathic moments. Sarah wandered among the tombstones as they talked, explaining everything that had happened.

"Oh, Sarah, I don't even know what to say. What are you going to do?"

Sarah sank onto a bench at the side of the graveyard. "I don't know what to do. That's why I called you."

"What do you *want* to do?"

Elizabeth's simple question unleashed a storm of pent-up emotions. "I want to be you! I want to stop acting impulsively and just, you know, be normal! I want to stop forgetting what I'm doing in the middle of doing it because of all the backtalk in my head and be able to make a decision without getting lost as I try to analyze every freaking possible outcome, but I just can't. I want to be with the man who is right for me and *know* that we're right for each other, but right now, I'm too afraid of being wrong to know who's right."

"Are you done now?" Elizabeth asked calmly.

Somewhat pacified by Elizabeth's calm voice, Sarah took a deep breath. "Yeah, I'm just so over screwed-up relationships."

"Hmm, I get that, and I'm trying to avoid stating the obvious here, but you do realize you kissed Vin about five minutes after you said you weren't going to pursue him. What changed?"

"I told you. It just kind of happened."

Elizabeth waited.

"Okay, I wanted to kiss him. I like Vin. He's funny and flirty and, well, I like how I feel when I'm around him. But I like Artie too. I really do. I know I need to make a choice, but I'm afraid of making any kind of decision. What if I'm wrong again?"

"I don't know what to tell you, Sarah. We agreed that I haven't been in your situation, and you only listen to about half of what I say anyway, and—"

"I always listen!" Sarah protested. "But—"

"Let me finish, please. Sometimes you act without thinking. Maybe it's your ADHD or whatever, but that impulsivity gets you into some crazy situations. I tried to warn you. If you hadn't kissed Vin, then—" Elizabeth stopped. "Never mind, there's no point in going there. It happened.

"This morning I asked Liam if, in general, he felt it was wrong to pursue a relationship with two people at the same time." Elizabeth's voice grew quiet. "Sorry, people walking by. Liam said 'wrong' was a judgment, which he wouldn't make because it would depend on the people and circumstances, but," Elizabeth sighed, "he said that it can actually be beneficial. It's difficult though."

"No joke," Sarah said, twirling a small twig with leaves. "How can it be beneficial?"

"Well, do you remember saying that you knew past boyfriends were jerks, but they were your jerks? If you'd been dating someone else, you would've been more likely to send the jerk packing because it's easier to see a person's flaws and assets when there's someone to look at in comparison."

"That . . . actually makes sense," Sarah said.

"So, although my instinct is to say choose one, maybe you should try dating both." Elizabeth blew out a breath. "Don't blame me if it doesn't work out though. Honesty and transparency are super important. You've got to talk to Artie and Vin to make sure they're both okay with it."

Elizabeth paused, waiting on Sarah to say something. "You can't go behind their backs on this, Sarah. You've seen how angry and hurt Artie felt. Meg will flip if you hurt him again, and honestly, I wouldn't blame her. I don't understand why you didn't tell Artie you wanted to see other people to begin with."

"I think I just assumed he knew. We've talked a lot, but it's been hard to see each other in real life. Plus, Vin and I went for a run. That's not exactly a date date."

"Really, Sarah? Who are you trying to fool?"

Sarah blushed. "Okay, maybe it was a date. Maybe I realized what could happen, but Artie and I never said we'd be exclusive, Elizabeth, even though I kind of knew how he felt."

"Sarah, you told us what he'd said about seeing a future with you.

And you told us you thought you should see other people. I'm just trying to understand why you didn't tell him that."

"Jeez. Okay, well, I, uh, maybe I was afraid he wouldn't agree, and I really like him, Elizabeth."

"So, you were afraid Art would end things if you said you didn't want to be exclusive. But you weren't sure enough about your feelings to be his girlfriend. Is that it?"

"Gah, that sounds so horrible. Am I really that bad? Oh, Elizabeth, I should've talked to him. I feel so guilty about hurting him."

"You're not horrible, but yes, you should've talked to him," Elizabeth said. "But listen. Maybe you're feeling guilty because you're worried about other people's expectations of your actions and behaviors. You have to live in your own expectations. Where do you draw the line?"

"I need to sit with that a minute." Sarah paused. "I've told Artie I like him, and I know he likes me. He's ready to be exclusive, but I'm not." She sighed. "I haven't been as open with him as I should've been. I should've said I was feeling rushed, but I didn't because I didn't want him to leave. The thing is, there are times where I, well, I feel nervous, uncertain around him."

"Nervous, how? Are you afraid of him? Afraid of displeasing him?"

"No. No, nothing like that. It's more that I don't know what to expect. With Vin, things are more familiar and predictable, yet unexpected at the same time. With Artie, things, even little things, seem more momentous, more important. Like saving a first kiss for a special place or hearing all these meanings in little things he says. Even "I'm here" seems to mean more—like I see you, I've got you, you're not alone. It's exciting but a little nerve-wracking."

Sarah leaned back on the bench and looked up, beseeching the sky. "Oh, I'm not explaining any of this very well. I've never felt this way before."

"Captain Obvious again, Sarah, but maybe you're feeling loved for the first time."

"What? I've felt love before. What do you mean?"

"You've been in love, but maybe those other guys weren't so much in love with you. Or maybe you were just in love with the idea of being in love or having a boyfriend. Maybe that's why you've always moved on so quickly."

Sarah blew out a breath. "OMG. I don't even know what to say to that, but it's not helping my current situation. Can we get back to that? I've never tried to date two men before. I'm afraid of losing Artie."

"Well, you may. One or both of the guys could decide to walk away. Are you willing to take that risk?"

Sarah stood and walked a few feet away from the bench. "I think I have to be. If I tried to choose now, I'd always wonder if I'd chosen the right man. I don't want to lose either one, but I'm not ready to choose. Any words of wisdom?"

"Oh, sis. I don't know. Maybe just see what Artie has to say. Vin too, for that matter. And keep working to figure out what you want and are willing to accept. In the end, what matters is what's in your heart. Do you feel secure? Seen and appreciated? Can you be yourself? Can you envision a future with this person? Do you respect each other?"

"Well, that's the thing, isn't it?" Sarah said. "I don't know. This may be the most important decision I'll ever make, but I haven't known either one that long. It's too soon for me to make up my mind, but they're both here now. I'm feeling a lot of pressure." Sarah began walking back toward her car. "I think I need to try dating both and get to know them better."

"Um, about that getting to know them business, Sarah." Elizabeth paused.

"Stop, please. I know where you're headed, but no, that won't be happening with anyone until I've made a decision. I'm hoping to talk with Artie tonight. During our fight, he said maybe we could figure something out. So, I have hope."

"Well, hang onto that, but don't push a conversation before he's ready. Let him know you want to talk it out. Listen to what the man has to say. Really listen, Sarah. Hear the emotion behind the words and remember that emotions aren't right or wrong."

"Okay. Anything else?" Sarah asked, starting up her car.

"I hate to say it but be prepared to let him go. Even if he agrees to back down on the exclusivity thing, you can't do this forever, you know. A couple months at the very most. It's not a game."

"I know that," Sarah said.

"I KNOW THAT," Sarah thought again, as she drove to a grocery store she and Vin had passed on their way to The Sand Witch earlier in the week. No point in giving people at The Green Grocer more to talk about. Sarah planned to cook for everyone on Sunday, so she bought ingredients for a summertime cheese lasagna, salad, and French bread, then added some lime sherbet for dessert, thinking it might be a little healthier than ice cream.

As Sarah shopped, she thought about dating two men at once. She'd never done that but knew other people did. *Just casually, probably. Is that what I want? Just a casual thing?* Sarah bit her lip. *Vin definitely feels more casual, but could he be more? Am I even ready for more?*

Sarah paid for her groceries and loaded them into the car. *I do want more. I'm not looking for a casual fling. If I just ended things with Vin now, maybe Artie . . . But doesn't kissing Vin prove I'm not sure about Artie? Ugh. If I can't decide, I need to date both. That's what I want.*

When Sarah arrived at Blackwater Pond, she could see Artie behind the manor house with Randy Keith, apparently measuring sections of the yard. Sarah unloaded her groceries and visited a little with Beth Ann before going to her room, thinking she would make another attempt at understanding her attraction to Artie and Vin. Sarah sat on the bed and opened her journal, but the words wouldn't come. After ten minutes of staring out the window, getting nowhere, she yawned fiercely, then turned the journal sideways and began doodling without thought.

SOMETIME LATER, Sarah woke to the sounds of doors closing and a shower running. She hadn't meant to fall asleep but honestly hadn't slept well Thursday night. She looked at her phone. *After seven. Nothing from Artie. I guess he's not ready to talk.*

Sarah opened her door and peeped out. The bathroom door was closed and the shower still running. No lights were on in the kitchen, so she assumed everyone else was on the porch. Sarah crept into the kitchen and quietly grabbed some fruit and yogurt. She didn't feel like talking to anyone either. She'd eat in her room and start fresh in the morning.

Settling on the bed with her snack, Sarah looked over her doodles. She'd sketched a creek bisecting the page. Roses and other flowers partially obscured a bridge on one side, where a gate with Artie's initials stood open, revealing his truck outside of a cartoon house. *Two windows, one door, pointy roof with smoke billowing from the chimney. How many times have I drawn that house?*

On the other side of the paper, a swooping line running from Vin's name formed a meditating Buddha surrounded by pots filled with flowers and ivy. Vin wore a football jersey and stood in the middle of six figures. *Sisters or admirers?*

Sarah smiled, shaking her head at the path the doodles had taken. *Wait, does Artie have a sword? Is he fighting bees or are those question marks?* She looked more closely. *Is that poison ivy strangling the roses? But it has thorns.*

One of Sarah's teachers long ago had suggested doodling as a means to focus her attention. She had discovered it also helped her pull together fragments of memory and make sense of different situations. As she examined her drawings, something Liam said months ago about deliberately, albeit unconsciously, choosing the wrong men came to her mind. Sarah thought about past boyfriends, wondering why she might've done that, then realized that her 'type' hadn't changed but she had. *Huh. I think I grew up, but my expectations for a boyfriend didn't change. No wonder I was frustrated. I was dating guys in their mid to late twenties who still acted like teenagers, especially Brandon.*

Sarah continued thinking and experienced one epiphany after another. Her self-esteem had taken a major blow when Blake, her first serious boyfriend, had broken up with her. He'd basically said she wasn't good enough for him. She'd immediately formed a relationship with Brad to prove that she wasn't hurt. But she had been, and apparently, she'd believed Blake, internalized the message he and his mother had given her.

When things didn't work out with Brad, she'd chosen Ethan. Liam was right. She'd chosen the wrong men because she did not trust that the relationships would last and she wanted to be able to survive the breakups. *Basically, I wanted to dump them before they dumped me, and I didn't want to really care for them so it would be easier to move on. How horrible.*

Sarah paced about her room, thinking about her behavior. She hadn't treated the guys badly to punish them. She'd been punishing herself for not being good enough for Brad. *Wow.*

Sarah remembered something else Liam had said. He'd said she was worthy. That she should figure out what she wanted and not settle for less. "Easier said than done," Sarah whispered as she picked up her journal again.

This time, Sarah thought about her own personality, her worth. She wasn't going to listen to Blake's voice anymore. She did deserve better. Turning to a fresh page, Sarah wrote, 'My life is too precious to waste.' Then she added her name in the center of the page and started linking bubbles in which she wrote things she liked about herself, unconsciously mimicking the mirror activity her counselor had suggested so long ago.

"I am worthy of love," she said as she reviewed her work. She had some good attributes. She worked hard, she stood up for her beliefs, she loved her family, she was smart and liked learning new things, she was fairly even-tempered—well, sometimes—she had friends, she liked to laugh. Sarah tore out the page and laid it aside, thinking she'd tape it to the bathroom mirror later. *I need to remember this*, Sarah thought before turning to her next task.

Liam had also said to think about why Artie's intensity scared her. At the time, she had no idea. But now it seemed simple. *I'm afraid of commitment because it hurt so much when Blake dumped me. I don't want to feel that way again. I don't trust myself or my ability to choose someone who's right for me. I haven't trusted Artie's feelings for me because I haven't trusted myself.*

Sarah heaved a huge sigh. She thought about Artie and how she'd violated his trust and wondered if he could forgive her. She thought about Vin and how everyone in town seemed to like and admire him. Two good men. Two good men who were cute and smart and kind and hard working and who liked her.

Sarah glanced at her phone again. Almost ten. She'd been

working through everything for three hours. *At least now I know the answer to Elizabeth's question. I am willing to risk losing them since that's being true to myself.*"

She stood and looked in the bathroom mirror. *I will figure this out. I will get to know them both better before trying to decide. I'm worth the effort.* Sarah got ready for bed, hoping she would remember that and that both men would believe she was worth the effort too.

Chapter Twenty-Two

When Sarah awoke the next morning, everything felt different. She lay still a moment, remembering dreaming of looking in a mirror, seeing first her reflection alone, then with Artie, then Vin, and behind them, one after another, reflections of past boyfriends quickly falling away. Was this dream reflective of the progress she'd made in deciding what she wanted, if not who?

As Sarah remembered other dreams, of kissing Artie, who turned into Vin, of seeing Artie and Vin leaving in a car together, laughing as she ran after them, she decided it was time to get up.

She pulled on a robe and checked her phone. There was a text from Artie. "We should talk. Tonight, here, 6 PM? LMK."

She blew out a breath. *Okay, good. At least he's willing to talk.* Sarah started to respond but didn't know what to say. Thanks? Looking forward to it? Eager to hear what you have to say? Hope it's good news. *Argh. Stop overthinking!*

"I'm not ready to give up. See you at 6." Sarah hit send. As bad as she felt about hurting Artie, she found strength in her resolve to risk losing him by being true to herself. *I'm not ready to be exclusive. Wanting to date both men does not make me a terrible person. Just an uncertain one.*

Even though she'd been in Belford for almost two weeks, this was the first day she'd had free of work or other obligations. Feeling restless, Sarah decided to ride into town, maybe visit the farmers market or an antique store, maybe just ride around and explore the countryside. *I'm not going to waste my Saturday hiding and worrying about tonight.*

She dressed quickly in shorts and a T-shirt, waved to Beth Ann and Randy Keith, who were already working in the garden, and got in her car.

Driving by Blackwater Manor, Sarah saw Artie near the manor house, notebook in hand. She waved, but he either didn't see or didn't respond.

The area near the farmer's market was more congested than she'd expected. Apparently, a lot of people came to town on Saturday mornings to buy and sell and visit with one another. Suddenly having no desire to interact with people, known or unknown, she drove past the market, continued beyond the outskirts of town, and turned up the road across Signal Mountain. She'd hike that trail back to the falls she'd seen on her way into town. It was only a few miles up from the valley. She'd hike it, even though it was a little overcast, then figure out what to do with the rest of her day.

At the overlook, Sarah leaned against the hood of her car and looked out over the valley at the patchwork of farms, ponds, and pockets of forest intersected by a few roads. She could see the ridge that ran behind the house at Blackwater Pond and the river that marked the border of the property but not the creek that had gotten her in so much trouble. A lone hawk whistled and spiraled overhead.

She watched, wondering how many other people in other times and places had done the same. Farming and foraging. Survival, that's what it came down to. The means were different in the city, but people were still scrambling to survive. Somehow, she would figure out this mess and not just survive but thrive.

Sarah took a picture of the trailhead, which she sent to Elizabeth, along with a quick note about her location, then retrieved a water bottle and hat from her car and started up the path. Fortunately, the trail wasn't muddy, but when it turned sharply downhill after a few yards, Sarah slid a bit and wished she'd actually bought the hiking poles she'd planned to purchase after her hike with Artie.

Things would be so different if Vin hadn't been there that day. Would I have run from Artie if Vin hadn't been waiting in the wings? Sarah wasn't sure, but as she walked, thinking about getting to know Vin, she remembered the pivotal moment at the creek—not the kiss but the moment she'd joined Vin there. That had been the moment she'd known, truly known, that she wasn't ready to be exclusive with Artie.

She thought about all her epiphanies about boyfriends and relationships during the last twenty-four hours. *Taking time away from men, free of relationships, was good for me. I feel more capable, more confident, more comfortable doing things on my own. If they both walk away, it'll hurt like hell, but I'll survive. Alone if I have to. But I hope I won't have to.*

Nearing the falls though, doubts crept back in. Delaying a

decision could cause a lot of heartache. Should she try to decide now? She rounded the corner and found the falls. Sarah sat for a few minutes, communing with nature, trying to come to peace with her situation. Maybe the universe had different plans in store for her. Things she hadn't even imagined. If only it would send her a sign. The water cascading down the rock face of the mountain seemed to offer a litany of advice. "Trust the process. You know what you want. Believe in yourself. You are worthy." Over and over, the words repeated in her head and echoed in her heart. Sarah stood, suddenly eager to return to Belford.

Rushing from the falls, she startled a young couple on the trail. "Are you okay?" the woman asked.

"Not yet, but I will be," Sarah called over her shoulder. She heard the hawk's call again. This time it was answered by two others. Were they hunting together? In competition with each other? Siblings? Sarah didn't know anything about hawks, but when one flew off alone, she wondered if it felt lonely or free.

Sarah drove back down the mountain toward an antiques store she'd seen off Main Street. It might be fun to browse, get some ideas for decorating her future house. She wandered among the furniture and odds and ends for a few minutes, but her heart wasn't in it.

Returning to her car, she realized she was just around the corner from The Green Grocer, which meant that Vin's studio was basically across the street. He'd told her to come by any time. Should she talk to Vin now? No, she'd talk to Artie first. She owed him that.

Chapter Twenty-Three

After deciding to talk to Artie about dating other people, Sarah drove toward Blackwater Pond but impulsively turned down the next road she saw. The terrain grew a bit hillier and the road a little narrower. At a crossroad, she spotted a small restaurant and turned into a crowded lot. She squeezed in beside a red pickup and went inside.

Sarah froze at the sudden onslaught of noise. Almost every table was occupied by diners laughing and conversing with their neighbors. A little boy's crying competed with Dolly's voice coming from the jukebox. Each differently colored wall—red, yellow, blue, green—was covered with framed paintings.

A waitress exited the kitchen. "You need a menu, hon?"

Sarah stepped closer to the display case that served as a counter. "No, thanks. Can I just get a sweet tea to go?"

While waiting on her drink, she perused the paintings hanging behind the counter, each tagged with title and artist. "What's up with the fish and chickens?" Sarah pointed to the paintings.

The waitress glanced back over her shoulder. "I don't even notice them anymore. The owner's wife teaches art at the community center. Her students painted them. These aren't for sale, but the others are.”

“Oh, thanks,” Sarah said as she paid. “Do they all have fish and chickens too?

The waitress laughed. “You’re funny, but no. People bring us all kinds of work. If we’ve got room, we display it.” She held out Sarah’s change.

“Keep it,” Sarah said.

“Thanks for stopping by!” The waitress dropped the coins in a tip jar that looked suspiciously like one of Vin’s pots.

Outside the restaurant, Sarah sat in her car a moment, not quite ready to go home but not sure where she was headed. Should she turn around, go back to the familiar or should she continue exploring? Sarah shrugged and continued driving away from town.

Seeing an arrow-shaped sign pointing to Robbins Chapel, Sarah turned at the next left. She remembered meeting Nola Robbins, Belford’s elderly town historian, who’d been instrumental in getting the townspeople behind the renovation efforts of the house at Blackwater Pond. Both Miss Nola’s family and her husband’s family had been early settlers of the area. *Gotta be related.*

Her car struggled a little up some of the steep hills that punctuated the winding road to the chapel. Another sign pointed her down a one-lane dirt road and one more uphill climb before she reached a small white clapboard church situated on the grassy green plateau. Sarah parked, hers the only car in the lot, and walked to the front door, where a bronze plaque provided a brief history of the chapel.

Originally built of logs in the 1820s, the chapel had been

destroyed by fire and rebuilt as a frame building. Then Union troops had stolen the lumber to build barracks a few miles away. The small church had been rebuilt again after the war.

Sarah was reminded of the history at Barnsley Gardens, but reading about this chapel brought the idea of Union occupation a little closer to home. Some families in Tennessee had been divided by their differing loyalties and continued feuding even after the war ended. She wondered how many had lived to regret their inability to make peace with each other.

Choices have long-lasting consequences. Thoughts of choosing between Artie and Vin intruded, but Sarah pushed them back. This place seemed timeless somehow, but it wasn't. It was beautiful, restful, and serene, but it hadn't always been. It had seen happiness and heartbreak, weddings and funerals, prosperity and poverty. Somehow, amid the struggles of daily life, sickness, death, and even war, people found the courage and strength to survive and to continue building and rebuilding.

Sarah found those thoughts strangely encouraging. Troubles are temporary, after all. What had once been the scene of havoc and destruction was now a place of unbelievable peace. She walked around to the back of the church to a small graveyard and strolled among the markers, noting fairly recent dates, then much older ones. At the back boundary of the church property stood a large tree.

Sarah found a bench under the tree and looked out over the pasture, beyond hillocks and creeks to the ridge that blocked her view of what lay beyond. The hustle and bustle of her adopted city lay in that direction. The city was small as cities go, fewer than

200,000 inhabitants, yet moments such as this one would be impossible there. Had Sarah ever been this alone? No one in sight, not even a car creeping along the road, barely visible in the distance. A leaf-rustling breeze and a hawk's shrill cry broke the silence before the hawk was joined by another and flew off toward the ridge.

WHEN SARAH GOT BACK to the house mid-afternoon, Beth Ann stopped peeling potatoes long enough to ask about her day.

"It was really nice. I stopped at an overlook up on Signal Mountain with a beautiful view of the valley. We'll ride up there sometime. Then I took a short hike and saw some hawks flying around."

"Oh, I do love to see a hawk. My Granny used to say that hawks were lucky."

"Lucky?" Sarah bit a celery stick. "Well, maybe I'm due some luck because I sure saw hawks today. Three on Signal Mountain and two out at Robbins Chapel."

"Three means courage, strength, and wisdom," Randy Keith said. "Ain't that right, Ma?"

"That's what my Granny said. I don't believe I've ever seen but one at a time." Beth Ann placed the chopped potatoes in a pot and covered them water. "Put this on the stove for me, son. That pot's awful heavy."

Randy Keith moved the pot, then asked, "Where's that Robbins

Chapel at?"

Sarah laughed. "That I couldn't tell you. I was out driving around. I stopped in town this morning and then headed west, I think. I bought some tea at a little restaurant at a crossroad. It was loud with crazy colors."

"Oh, sounds like the Fin and Feather," Randy Keith said. "It's quieter through the week. Pretty good food."

"Fin and Feather," Sarah said. "Oh, well, duh. That explains the paintings. Anyway, I just drove on from there and followed the signs. The road curves around a bit and climbs up to the plateau. The land up there is different from here somehow, but it sure is pretty."

Sarah yawned, then offered to help Beth Ann in the kitchen, but when the older woman said she was about finished, she retreated to her room, intending to read for a while. It wasn't long before she was asleep again.

SARAH WOKE AT ABOUT FIVE-FIFTEEN. She was supposed to meet Artie at six. She didn't know where they were going or how she should dress. Did 'meet me here' mean they were eating here? Surely not.

Sarah hadn't been anywhere in Belford that was fancy, but she decided to put forth a little effort and chose a knee-length dress with cap sleeves. The yellow and white daisy print nearly obscured the navy background. Sarah brushed her dark hair but left it loose, found some navy flats, and added lip gloss as a final touch.

She was waiting in the living room when Artie emerged fresh from the shower. He looked at her, then at his own shorts and T-shirt. "You're overdressed."

Sarah cringed, remembering Vin saying those words to her before they kissed in the creek. "Should I change? I didn't know what we were doing."

"You're beautiful," Artie said. "You don't need to change."

"Why, you're pretty as a picture, Sarah," Beth Ann said coming in from the back porch. "Art, I put some of that lemon tea in a thermos for you."

Sarah watched as Artie gave Beth Ann a hug before adding the thermos to a cooler. She felt oddly out of place. Beth Ann was her 'almost' relative, yet she and Artie seemed to have bonded in less than forty-eight hours.

When Artie picked up the cooler and a blanket, Sarah rushed to open the door for him. "We're taking the golf cart," he said. "I felt like a teenager asking Dad for the keys to the car, but it makes a lot more sense to take this thing than my truck. I thought we'd sit in the pecan grove near the river."

"That sounds nice. Very romantic," Sarah said uncertainly.

"Private, anyway." Artie sighed. "And quiet, so we can talk while we eat."

Sarah didn't know how to respond to that. "Oh, okay. Um, I saw you out working on the property today. Did you get a lot done?"

Artie glanced at her. "I did. I took some soil samples, made some notes, and sketched a few ideas. I'll have to get some help for the actual tilling though."

"Will Bruce help you?"

"Pfft. Bruce wouldn't help me cross the street. He's been reassigned, but this isn't a company job anyway. I'm working on my own now. That's why I've been so busy."

"Oh, I'm glad?"

"Yeah, it's a good thing." Artie turned from the gravel drive onto the grass of the pecan grove and parked the golf cart between two rows of trees. Sarah waited while Artie spread the blanket, then sat, pulling her dress down over her knees, expecting him to join her. When he started unpacking the cooler, she said, "Can we talk first? I'm too nervous to eat."

"Yeah, okay, sure," Artie said, setting the food aside. He sat on top of the cooler facing her, leaned forward, and rested his elbows on his knees. "You don't have to be nervous though. I'm not mad anymore." Artie looked away briefly, shaking his head. "I won't say that I wasn't hurt and angry after seeing you kissing the Zen guy, but I've calmed down, and I think we've both got a lot of listening to do. Over the last forty-eight hours, I've recognized that my feelings for you are stronger, deeper than your feelings for me."

"And that scares me, Artie. I've made so many mistakes in the past, choosing men wrong for me, rushing into relationships that went nowhere. I can't go down that road again."

Artie took a deep breath and exhaled slowly. "If you want to be with him, I'll step aside."

Sarah turned quickly to look at him. "I don't want that."

Artie reached out, touching her arms still encircling her knees.

"What do you want, Sarah?"

"That's the big question." Sarah looked out over the river before looking back at him. "I like you, Artie. I really do. Like-like you, you know?"

He gave a small grin. "Like-like, like in sixth grade?" He looked off toward the road, then turned back to her, more serious. "But you don't want to be exclusive. Am I reading the situation right?"

Sarah bit her lip. "I need to be sure. I have to know I'm choosing the right man this time."

"I'm not surprised, but I gotta say I'm not too happy about that, Sarah. I also need to say that I'm partly to blame."

"What? How? Why would you say that?" Sarah protested.

Artie stood and walked away a few steps, looking off toward the river again. "I think I scared you off. If I'd kept my mouth shut and not crowded you, maybe none of this would've happened. You'd been on that long break from men. I should've realized that maybe you weren't quite as ready for a relationship as I am." Artie moved back to the cooler. "I think my confession drove you right into the other guy's arms. If I could go back in time, I'd—"

Sarah moved suddenly to her knees, reaching for him, touching his arm. "Artie, I should've said something then, but I just couldn't process what you were saying. I enjoyed that day so much, please believe that. I thought I was ready, but I got scared."

After considering each other's words in silence for a minute, Artie said, "I called Meg last night."

Sarah bit her lip. "Is she mad at me?"

"Surprisingly, no," Artie said. "She said all this was just a hiccup and not to worry. She also suggested I call my brother Rob."

"Rob?" Sarah looked at Artie in confusion. "Why? I mean, I didn't think you were all that close."

"We haven't been, but Meg reminded me of some things, so I called Rob and told him about you, and he shared some thoughts. It was the best conversation I've had with my brother in two decades." Artie looked up at the sky. "Wind's picking up. I think it's going to rain."

"What did he say?" Sarah asked, ignoring the weather report.

"Doesn't matter," Artie said, shaking his head. "I can't take his advice. Our situation's a bit different anyway."

Artie stood, then offered Sarah his hand and helped her to her feet. "Look, my offer stands. You want Fabbri, I'll pack my bags and go back to Acworth." He brushed her hair back from her face. "I like-like you enough to want you to be happy."

"What was Rob's advice, Artie? What did he say?" Sarah insisted.

"He said to bring out my A-game and fight for you. The thing is, Sarah, it's not a game. It's not a situation of letting the best man win. You're not a, a conquest, a prize the victor carries off." He stepped back. "That doesn't sit well with me. I'm not fighting this guy or anyone else over you, Sarah. You get to choose who you date."

"I've never expected anyone to fight for me," Sarah said quickly.

"Please hear this, Sarah," Artie said slowly, moving to face her, rubbing her arms lightly. "I will fight with you and for you, every day if necessary, but I won't fight over you. There's a difference in those little words. I already know how I feel about you."

Sarah's shoulders raised, and she shook her head slightly as if in disbelief. "I wish I had your certainty, Artie, but I don't. It's too soon. How can you possibly know?"

Artie tilted her face upward. "Sarah, I'm not suggesting we run off and get married. I'm saying that I want you to be my girlfriend."

Sarah's eyes filled with tears as she shook her head. "We've only had two real dates."

Artie stepped away and picked up the cooler. "You say two dates, I say four months. That's long enough for me. I know. I've known a long time. Come on before we get drenched. We can eat back at the house."

"Artie, wait." Sarah stood beside him at the back of the cart, arms wrapped around her middle as the wind blew her hair across her face again and whipped her skirt. "Can we date other people? Still see each other but just not be exclusive?"

Artie shoved the cooler onto the back shelf and tied it down. "I don't know that I can be just one the guys you're dating, Sarah. I've got this image of you kissing him in the creek. If I hadn't seen that—" Artie broke off, swearing under his breath as thunder rumbled around them. "I'm struggling with this, Sarah. My head, my pride, says walk away. But my heart." Artie patted his chest, looking in her eyes. "My heart says we're worth fighting for."

The short ride back to the house was quiet, each lost in thought. As Artie parked the golf cart, Sarah turned to him. "Do you believe in soulmates?"

Artie rubbed his chin and spoke slowly, thoughtfully. "I don't know. I'm not sure that I believe certain people are destined to be together, but I think when there's a spark, an attraction, that maybe the universe has something to do with it. If those two people meet and meet again, maybe destiny plays a role in providing the opportunity. Are they soulmates? Maybe they choose to be. I don't know, but if people are meant to be together, want to be together, they'll find a way." Artie took her hand. "I believe that. We'll find a way."

Did the universe have something to do with me meeting Artie? Meeting Vin? I'm attracted to both. I kept running into both. Sarah sighed. She'd hoped for a sign, not a competition.

They walked into the house as the first raindrops fell. Randy Keith and Beth Ann, who were settled in front of the television watching a movie, invited them to come watch, but Artie declined, saying they'd finish up their picnic on the porch, sheltered from the rising storm.

Sarah went to get a sweater. By the time she made it to the porch, Artie had pulled out the sandwiches and potato salad and poured glasses of the lemon tea, placing everything on the small table between their two chairs.

Sarah closed the sliding door and asked, "Why did Meg tell you to call Rob?"

Artie turned from the table and looked at Sarah. "Because of her sister, Trish. Rob and Trish dated off and on for years. One or the other would break it off, and they'd hate each other for six or eight months. Then they'd be back together." Artie shook his head. "About a year ago, Rob was dating both Trish and Pamela."

"Oh. When you say dated—" Sarah broke off. "Do you mean they didn't . . . ?"

"Right. Neither one knew about the other. Rob fell head over heels for Pamela but had this history with Trish, so he kept it going for a while. It didn't end well."

Sarah looked at Artie, fearing the answer to her unspoken question. Had Rob lost both? "In what way?"

Artie sighed. "Rob would probably say it ended fine. I have no idea how, but he managed to convince Pamela to give him a second shot about six months after she found out about Trish and dumped his ass. They're engaged now. Trish, though, she's still furious with Rob. Primary reason he didn't come to Meg's wedding."

They ate in silence, watching the empty porch swing swaying in the wind. The rain fell heavily, drowning out the sound of the creek, and thunder rumbled in the distance. "It's very peaceful here," Artie said after he had eaten. "Even with the storm. I don't remember the last time I sat on a porch or listened to the rain."

"On my first night in Belford, I almost fell asleep sitting right here with Beth Ann, listening to the crickets." Sarah paused and frowned. "You know all those sayings about crickets in the country? I thought they were implying crickets were silent, but that wasn't it at all. They're meant to say that we only hear the crickets when the other noises fade away. Crickets are not quiet."

"No, they're not. I can hear them clearly through the windows of my room here." Artie laughed, then was quiet for a while longer. "Sarah, it's very convenient, me staying here while working at the manor, but if that makes you uncomfortable, I can stay in town somewhere. Andy said he knows some people who have extra rooms if the inn is booked."

Sarah looked up quickly and reached for him. "No, please stay here, Artie. I mean, this situation is hard on both of us, and I'm starting to recognize that I don't always consider what other people think or feel. But if you're comfortable here, I hope you'll stay. I enjoy your company, and I want us to get to know each other better."

"Okay."

After a few minutes, Sarah said, "Artie, I feel like I'm betraying you by wanting to go out with Vin. I feel guilty, which makes me snarky. And then I get defensive. I'm trying to be more open and honest with you and myself about my feelings."

Artie rubbed his jaw. "Okay, well, I don't want you to feel guilty, Sarah. Unpleasant as it was for me to witness, and despite the anger I felt, I was the only one in a relationship." Artie leaned forward and looked at her. "You aren't there yet emotionally; you may never be, so it's unfair to say you betrayed something that existed only in my imagination."

He sat back and blew out a breath. "I honestly don't like the idea of us seeing other people, but if that's the only way we can move forward, then okay, we don't have to be exclusive. Just don't expect me to sit at the dinner table with the guy or make pleasant conversation with him."

"No, I won't," Sarah said. "If I go out with Vin—" Sarah cocked her head. "Wait, did you say 'us seeing other people'?"

Artie nodded slowly. "Well, yeah. If we're not exclusive, then we're both free to see other people."

"Like Rachel?"

Artie shrugged. "I don't know, I haven't thought that far ahead. I guess it could happen if—"

"Are you doing this to hurt me? You said you weren't interested in Rachel."

"And I'm not. I would never intentionally hurt you," Artie said, slowly. "I hope one day you'll believe that." He paused. "I said *if*. It could happen if she stopped seeing Craig. The point is, Sarah, that I'm not going to be the sad clown in the corner watching you come and go. I don't have anyone in mind, but that's how this works. If we're seeing other people, then you don't get a say in who I see."

Somehow, Sarah had never considered that Artie would see other people. But of course he would. Oh, she didn't like this. She didn't like this one bit.

"No, of course I don't. I'm sorry, Artie. It just caught me off guard for some reason. This is all new to me, but I'm grateful you're still willing to see me. I want to spend time with you while you're here."

"About that. Things have changed a bit. I'm not going to be in Belford all the time, but I do expect to be around most weekends. My schedule here depends on my workload at my real job, so I won't know for a while."

Sarah's brows drew together. "I thought you were going to be here for three weeks."

"With Bruce gone, everything's changed. I can squeeze in some vacation time, but it won't be a long stretch. Maybe that's for the best now." Artie reached over and took Sarah's hand. "I want to see you while I'm here though. Spend some time on the porch, go hiking, explore the countryside, stop for lunch.

"Oh. Well, I'm a little sad about that," Sarah admitted. "I had hoped for more time."

"Look, this situation, this agreement, isn't ideal in my mind, but we'll see how it goes," Artie said, letting go of her hand and shaking his head. "I don't want you to feel bad about needing time or space or whatever." He stood. "I'm rooting for us, but no matter what, I will never hate you. That's a promise."

Chapter Twenty-Four

Sarah woke several times during the night. Each time, she lay in the dark room, listening to the rain before drifting back to sleep. Around ten, she finally got out of bed, remembering she'd promised to prepare Sunday dinner. They'd eat when Beth Ann and Randy Keith got home from church.

Sarah hurried to the kitchen. Artie was sitting at the counter working, coffee cup in hand.

"Good morning, sleepyhead. Need some coffee?"

Sarah, hair mussed, still in her pajamas, nodded. "It was so quiet, I thought you'd already left."

"I wouldn't leave without saying good-bye, Sarah. We're still friends. Even better, we're friends who like-like each other." Artie grinned, getting up to pour her a cup of coffee. "Here you go." He handed her the coffee he'd prepared with brown sugar, cinnamon, and a pinch of ginger. "Strong, sweet, and spicy, just like you."

"Mmm, thank you, Artie. It's just the way I like it." Sarah was surprised that Artie was so cheerful, even flirtatious, after their talk last night. She moved to the window. "It's still raining."

Art joined her there. "Not stormy though. That's a good sign."

Sarah turned and looked up at him, wondering if they were just talking about the weather. "I need to get dressed. I'm making dinner today."

"Beth Ann mentioned that," Artie said, taking her empty cup.

"Will you still be here?"

"I'm not going anywhere, Sarah. Not yet, anyway."

Sarah smiled a little uncertainly. *Am I reading more into his words than he means?* "I'm glad you're here."

She showered and dressed quickly before returning to the kitchen, where she started opening cabinets and drawers, pulling out pans and utensils and ingredients she needed. Sarah opened a can of crushed tomatoes, some tomato paste and sauce, and poured them in a large pan on the cooktop. She peeled an onion and began chopping it.

Artie wandered in from the back porch, where he'd been watching the rain. "I think it's going to clear off. Can I help? I'm pretty good at chopping things."

"Could you dice some carrots really small? About a cup? I need to get the sauce put together quickly. It's supposed to simmer almost an hour." Sarah peeled and chopped several cloves of garlic. "I can't believe I slept so late." She added some olive oil to an iron skillet and began to sauté the freshly chopped ingredients.

"You're probably still catching up on sleep from all your overtime." Artie pulled out his phone, fiddled with it a minute and said, "Maybe some music will pep you up."

"Who is that?" Sarah asked. "What is that?" she added, laughing as she realized the song was about vegetables.

"It's an old sixties group, the Beach Boys. Just a goofy little love song to their favorite vegetables. I've heard tales about Paul McCartney sitting in on the recording session, but I don't know if they're true. Speaking of Sir Paul, he's up next," Artie said.

Sarah listened as the Beatles song started slowly speaking of a working girl hitting the big time. When the song transitioned to a faster tempo, Artie took her hand and spun her around, singing "Honey Pie," but when the lyrics took a turn toward love, Sarah pulled away and turned back to the garlic.

"Are the carrots chopped fine enough?" Artie asked.

"They're perfect. Add them to the sauce," Sarah directed. "They cut the acid without adding white sugar. Would you mind sautéing the onion and garlic while I add the spices?" Sarah touched Artie's back as she moved around him to rinse some basil, which she quickly chopped and added to the tomato mixture along with fennel seeds and oregano.

Artie's playlist continued with songs about food from a few artists Sarah recognized and many she did not. Artie named each one: Patty Griffin, Jack Johnson, Marvin Gaye.

"Did you create that playlist? I had no idea so many food songs existed."

"Nope, it was already put together. I just saved it to listen to when I'm cooking. It's mostly oldies, but the music is solid." Artie stirred the pan and turned off the heat. "I think the onions and garlic are ready. Should I add them to the pot?"

"Yep. It's time." Sarah took the lid from the pot. "Hey, finally someone I recognize." She laughed as John Legend's "Slow Cooker" played.

Artie added the ingredients and stirred them into the sauce, which was starting to bubble. "It smells good already."

Sarah smiled at Artie. "Thanks. It's one of my favorites. It just needs to simmer a while."

"A lot of things do." Artie nodded. "I miss cooking. Being on the road so much lately, I'm eating out more than I like." He found ingredients for a salad and started washing the lettuce and other vegetables.

Sarah pulled a large pan from under the counter and moved to the sink. "I need to fill this for the noodles."

Artie took the pan from her, filled it with water, and carried it to the stovetop. "Have you ever had lasagna with zucchini instead of noodles?" Artie asked as he moved back to the sink.

"No, I didn't know there was such a thing. Have you tried it?"

"Not yet. Maybe we'll do that next time," Artie said.

Sarah glanced quickly at him but didn't respond at first, wondering if there would be a next time. Artie seemed his usual self this morning, but she worried that he might grow tired of her indecisiveness and decide to move on. "Maybe we will," she said at last. "Maybe we will."

"No meat in this lasagna of yours?" Artie asked, interrupting her thoughts.

"No, it's supposed to be lighter for summer, so it's just cheese. Still pretty high in carbs and calories, but I'm using part-skim mozzarella and cottage cheese instead of ricotta to be a tiny bit healthier. I'll use the immersion blender after it's been simmering a while so the sauce seems lighter too."

As Sarah told Artie about Meatless Mondays and Sue Ellen and Randy Keith, Artie abandoned the salad preparation and leaned on the counter near her, listening. "They're really sweet with each other. I don't know if Sue Ellen's been married before, but Randy Keith lost his wife really young."

They both were quiet for a minute, watching the pot of water, waiting for it to boil, thinking of love and loss. When a Neil Diamond song about red wine started playing, Artie took Sarah's right hand in his left and drew her close, placing his hand on her hip and whispering, "Dance with me, Sarah."

The lyrics were not particularly romantic, but somehow, as Artie's eyes never left hers, it felt very sensual. They danced in a simple box step as the music played. After a couple of minutes, Sarah smiled slowly and moved her arms around Artie's neck. Artie froze for a moment and backed away, shaking his head.

"I forgot to add the wine," Sarah said suddenly, babbling to cover her embarrassment. "The recipe calls for a cup of white wine in the sauce. I had to buy cooking sherry for the first time in my life. I actually got carded buying it. They don't sell wine in Belford. Did you know that?"

When Artie didn't respond, Sarah realized she was alone in the kitchen.

THE RAIN MOVED OUT BY TWO. Artie had stayed for lunch and been very complimentary about the lasagna. Shortly after the meal, though, he left, hugging Beth Ann but just waving to Sarah.

Sarah thought long and hard about her conversation with Artie. His response had surprised her a bit. He'd been calmer than she'd expected. Kinder, more considerate. Nicer than she'd deserved. His hurt had shown, though, when she'd tried to kiss him while they were dancing. Was it really worth risking her relationship with Artie to date another man? Sarah sighed in frustration. Now that they'd had the difficult conversation, she felt almost obligated to try. She texted Vin.

"Can I come see you?"

"Sure. Come to the studio behind the house."

Sarah drove past the large white house and turned down the narrow unpaved lane to its right. She parked in front of a large free-standing garage and got out of her car. Hearing a whirring noise from inside, Sarah approached the open door. "Vin?"

He came from around a back corner wearing a navy blue apron splattered with clay. "Come in, come in. I'm just finishing up. Let me wash some of this off." Vin walked to a sink along the wall, hung his apron on a nearby hook, and began scrubbing his hands and arms. "Are you here to see my pottery?"

Sarah shook her head. "We need to talk. Is this an okay time?"

Vin made a face. "Conversations that start that way usually don't end well, but now's as good a time as any. Follow me. We'll sit on the back porch."

He led her to a screened porch that ran the length of the large white house. "Have a seat," he said, motioning to some wicker furniture. "I'll get us something to drink."

Sarah took a seat on a wicker settee with a red floral cushion, then reconsidered and moved to a chair. She didn't want to be too close to Vin for this conversation.

He reappeared carrying a tray with lemonade and a plate of cookies dusted with powdered sugar. He set the tray on the coffee table between them and took a seat on the settee.

"Oh, that looks very nice, Vin. Thank you," Sarah said as he handed her a lemonade.

"Of course. So, do you want to start or do you want me to?"

Sarah looked at Vin in surprise. She hadn't considered that he would have anything to say until hearing about her proposal. Once again, she'd been thinking only of herself and had been oblivious to others. "Why don't you start, Vin? I'd like to hear what you have to say."

Vin nodded. "I'm glad you're here. I apologize for whatever trouble I caused by kissing you in the creek. I wasn't aware we were being watched. But Sarah, I did ask if that guy was your boyfriend. You should've been honest with me. I wouldn't have acted on my feelings if I'd known he was."

"He's not. Not exactly, anyway." Sarah bit her lip.

"He obviously thinks he is."

"I know," Sarah moaned. "We really, truly have only been on two real dates. Artie's a great guy, and I like him a lot, but we've talked and I'm not sure."

When Sarah paused, Vin asked, "Not sure of what?"

"If he's the only one I want to be in a relationship with." Sarah looked at Vin and continued. "I've made a lot of mistakes, a lot of bad choices when it comes to men." She stood and walked closer to a faded photograph on the wall depicting seven children on the front porch of the big house. She touched the image of little boy Vin in the midst of six girls. Turning back, she said, "I met Artie at my brother's wedding last February. We've run into each other a few times since then, and like I said, we've been on two dates. He's ready for a relationship, but I'm, well, I'm conflicted. I'm also attracted to you."

"So, what are you saying, Sarah?" Vin asked, head tilted and eyes narrowed.

"I'm saying that I'd like to date both of you."

"Whoa." Vin sat back. A minute passed in silence. "I don't know that that's a good idea, Sarah. I'm not saying no, but do you mean like a threesome?"

Sarah laughed out loud. "God, no. Did you really think that?"

"I wasn't sure, Sarah. You said date both of us." Vin shrugged. "I like you, but maybe you should just, you know, date the other guy. He got there first, I can step away. I don't believe in stealing another man's girl."

"Let's get one thing straight, Vin. I'm not anyone's girl, and I'm not an object that can be stolen," Sarah said fiercely.

"Gotcha. It was a poor choice of words." He grinned. "I like your spirit." Vin stood and put his hands on her waist. "So, I'm in. Can I kiss you now?"

But for some reason, Sarah wasn't feeling it. This was what she wanted. Why wasn't she happier? She shook her head. "Not now, Vin. I just want to go home."

Chapter Twenty-Five

On Monday morning, Sarah felt sticky and uncomfortable in the increased humidity left by the passing storm, so rather than listening to the morning sounds through open windows, she turned on her air conditioning. The radio in her old car hadn't worked in years, but before long, she was humming "Red, Red Wine," wondering about Artie pulling away and wishing he hadn't.

Sarah walked into the office. *Can't think about that now. After Friday's fiasco, I need to be one-hundred percent professional today, or Janelle may send me packing.* But Janelle didn't seem inclined to discuss Sarah's personal problems or her breakdown on Friday. It wasn't until Sarah received a text at lunch that she acknowledged the situation.

Sarah glanced at her phone. *Vin.* "Yo, Peters, meet me outside." Wondering why Vin was there, she said, "I need to step outside a minute. I'll be right back. Excuse me, please."

Janelle raised her eyebrows. "He could come inside, rather than tom-catting around. I won't bite his head off."

Vin was waiting in the parking lot without his truck. Sarah looked at him questioningly as he backed away when she attempted to hug him. Had he decided he didn't want to date her?

"I'm a sweaty mess. Angelina's had me moving stuff out of the attic all morning, but I wanted to see you and make some plans. I figured it was better to talk about it in person on your break than come in and get Janelle riled up again."

"Oh, thank goodness. I thought 'meet me in the parking lot' was your equivalent of 'we need to talk.'" Sarah laughed in relief. "Janelle's fine. She said you could come inside."

"Angelina's gonna find out I flew the coop any minute and track me down with a horse whip." Vin rolled his eyes. "Excuse my mixed metaphors." He reached for her hand. "I'd like to take you to dinner tomorrow night. We'll ride over to Dunlap and eat at a nice restaurant. What do you say, want to dress up and let me wine and dine you?"

"That sounds really nice, Vin. I'd love to." Sarah smiled, relieved to have plans with Vin. *Maybe this will work. Maybe I'll figure things out.* As she rejoined Missy and Janelle at the table to finish her lunch, both looked at her expectantly.

After a few minutes of silence, Missy spoke. "I think you've kept us in suspense long enough. Are you going to go out with him or not?"

Sarah looked up in surprise. Missy had rarely spoken to her beyond office business and hadn't seemed inclined to get to know her personally. She nodded. "Yes, we're going to a restaurant in Dunlap tomorrow night."

"Ooh," Missy said. "Fancy."

"I guess," Sarah said. "He mentioned wining and dining." She continued eating her sandwich, watching the two women exchange glances. "What?"

"There are a couple standard reasons people drive to Dunlap or Dayton for dinner," Janelle said. "One, to avoid the prying eyes, and thereby gossip, of the good folks of Belford, and two, to impress a date with a more special experience. You know, tablecloths, real china, wine with dinner. No point in driving all that way if you're gonna eat fast food. We have some unique eateries with good food here in Belford, but they're not what I'd call date night places. Most folks around here, if they're going to eat out, do so at lunch."

"Is that habit or availability?" Sarah asked.

"Probably both," Janelle answered. "If we had a nice restaurant downtown that was open for dinner, I think people might patronize it. An Italian place or maybe a steak house."

"I'd like a place with lots of options," Missy said. "Somewhere I could get meatloaf and potatoes one night and stir-fry another. I get tired of cooking dinner night after night. Dining out on something healthier than fast food would be nice."

Hmm. Maybe the limited dining options in town are part of the attraction of Wednesday night potluck dinners at church. Sarah had been to a few of those at Beth Ann's church. The food had been good and plentiful, and leftovers were boxed up and delivered to the homebound. One thing she'd noticed about Belford was how its residents looked out for each other. Maybe the gossip was just keeping tabs.

Sarah was grateful the afternoon was busy enough to prevent her from dwelling on her upcoming date with Vin or her worry over

Artie. *What if he finds someone else?*

She texted him that evening, saying that she'd enjoyed some leftover lasagna for lunch and thanked him for his help in making it. He'd replied with a smiley face and a note that he was in a meeting. *Is he avoiding me? No, Artie wouldn't do that. He's the most honest person I've ever known.*

THE NEXT AFTERNOON, Sarah hurried home to shower and dress before her date with Vin. Since the 'fancy' restaurant was thirty minutes away, she chose a wrinkle-free turquoise knit dress with a halter-neck that fit her curves and fell to her knees. Sarah added earrings, a touch of mascara and some lip gloss, and hoped she wasn't overdressed.

Her fears were allayed as Vin walked onto the porch wearing a cream-colored double-breasted linen suit with a floral shirt. Sarah smiled, attempting to picture Brandon or Ethan or really anyone she'd dated wearing a similar suit. None were very fashionable. "You look very nice," she said, opening the screen door.

"Ma come sei bella!" Vin said, stepping back to look at her. "You look beautiful. These are for you, bellissima."

"Oh, these are beautiful, Vin. Thank you." Sarah put the bouquet of brightly colored lilies in a vase and took his hand for the short walk to his truck, wondering how she felt about those flowers. They were pretty, but it seemed a little cliché.

"We're going to My Buddy Jack's Place," Vin said. "It's just on the other side of Dunlap, in an old Victorian house they converted."

"What's it called?"

"I just told you," Vin said, grinning. "My Buddy Jack's Place. He had a different name in mind, but everyone was calling it that as he was renovating, so he just went with it. They've done pretty well."

"Hmm. What kind of food do they have?"

"Oh, a mix of traditional American food, steak, seafood, and some limited upscale offerings. I keep trying to talk him into serving cioppino," Vin said as they drove through the countryside.

"What's that?"

"My absolute favorite food, a traditional Italian seafood stew."

"I'm not crazy about seafood, though I do like crab and some fish. Not shrimp though. Something about the texture."

Vin made a face and lifted his hands from the steering wheel as if she'd wounded him. "I thought everyone liked shrimp. I'm not sure we can be friends," he joked. "My Aunt Gina in New Jersey makes the best cioppino I've ever had. She sautés vegetables and spices and red pepper, then adds calamari and cooks that low and slow. All the juices blend together. Ecco qua! It's got clams and mussels and shrimp and fish. Makes my mouth water thinking of it."

Sarah made a face. The thought of seafood in a stew made her a little queasy. "Do you go to New Jersey a lot?"

"Yeah, a good bit. Dad's family is from Belford, but a lot of my family on Mom's side lives near the Jersey Shore. That's why my folks moved there. Have you ever been?"

"No, we always went to the beach in North Carolina." They

spent a few minutes talking about beach vacations and family before Sarah asked if Vin had been to New York City.

"Oh, sure, it's a two-hour train ride from the family, so growing up, I went there often. I'll be your tour guide if you want to go." He spent the remainder of the ride discussing some of his favorite places.

Sarah enjoyed hearing about some of the iconic sites often seen in movies or television shows but grew impatient as he described food from restaurants she'd never visited.

They approached Dunlap, and the monologue slowed as Vin drove through the historic district. Red brick buildings, many with green awnings, lined the street. A few had large white block letters painted across the top, still advertising long gone businesses.

"Dunlap's a coal town. There's a museum and big park with coke ovens. We can go sometime if you like." Vin turned into the parking lot of the restaurant, once a two-story Victorian home complete with turret and gingerbread trim along a porch lined with rocking chairs. Vin held the door, then waved to the hostess heading their way. "Julie, good to see you. This is Sarah. Sarah, Julie, Jack's wife."

Julie led them to a table in the front parlor and asked if Vin wanted a menu. "Yes, I'm afraid to order for her. She doesn't like shrimp," he mock-whispered with a horrified expression. "But maybe I can order some wine?"

Julie returned with menus. "Jack will come say hello as soon as he can. He said to tell you he's got some good-looking shrimp tonight. And, Sarah, he promised the salmon looks good too."

Sarah smiled and thanked her, then looked around the restaurant as Vin and Julie talked about common friends. Commercial dining tables and chairs mingled with antiques which were both decorative and functional. An antique podium served as Julie's reception station. A large dining room buffet housed a coffee service and rolled napkins. Fresh flower arrangements were artfully displayed on a fireplace mantel and a player piano in the main dining area. Sarah also noticed that other diners were dressed far more casually than they were.

After Julie left to seat other diners, Sarah said, "This is a really cute place, Vin." Then she leaned forward and whispered, "But you tricked me. We didn't have to get dressed up."

Vin grinned. "It's true, but I couldn't pass up the chance to see you in a sexy dress."

Vin's compliments pleased her. Dressing up for a date was a pleasant change from her daily uniform of scrubs and a ponytail. Previous boyfriends, with the exception of Blake, had rarely bothered to dress up for dates.

A young waitress came to take their order. "Have you decided, Sarah?" Vin asked.

"Yes, I'll have the salmon—no, wait, I want the Primavera Fettuccine." Secretly, Sarah was proud of herself for not ordering what Julie had recommended. She was sure the salmon was delicious, but she was tired of making decisions based on what other people thought. Small steps, Sarah reminded herself.

"You can get salmon on top of it if you like," the waitress said.

"No, thanks. Just the pasta and fresh vegetables. The lemon sauce sounds delicious."

"And for you, sir?"

Vin ordered the shrimp and grits, which was served with a mushroom gravy. "I often get the shrimp scampi, but it has a lot of garlic."

Sarah made a face at the thought of shrimp. "So, you have family in New Jersey. Do you see yourself staying in Belford or moving there?"

Vin shook his head. "Neither. Several of my sisters are there, two here, so I'll visit, but it's time to move on. I like Belford, I like it better than I did Memphis or Little Rock or New Orleans, which weren't bad places, you understand, just not what I'm looking for."

"So, what are you looking for?" Sarah asked touching his arm.

"Other than you?" Vin asked with a smile, putting his hand on top of hers.

Ahh, he's sweet.

"I think a small city would be ideal. Small enough to get around without a lot of traffic. Big enough to be able to go out to eat without driving a half hour each way. Small enough to know my neighbors but big enough to provide opportunities for my art." Vin shrugged. "I kind of want to stand out while blending in. That shouldn't be a problem, right?"

Sarah laughed. "Well, you know Chattanooga is a nice little city."

"Maybe we'll go there next time. Find somewhere to dance?"

Sarah liked that idea. She told Vin about several places where she'd done exactly that.

"I'd like to explore the city more. Most of the time, I just drive through. The congestion, construction, and traffic don't appeal to me." Vin looked at Sarah, cocking his head. "You, on the other hand—" He grinned. "I've been looking at Asheville and Berea because of their locations, size, and commitment to the arts. Perhaps you'll convince me to give Chattanooga another look."

Their conversation was interrupted by the arrival of their drinks and dinner. "Yum. This is really good, Vin. How's your shrimp?"

"Tasty. Want to try it?" Vin offered, holding out a forkful.

"No, thank you. I've never met a shrimp I liked, and I have tried them, boiled, fried, and barbecued." Sarah took a sip of her wine and looked at Vin. "So did you and Jack get in a lot of trouble in school as teenagers?"

"Me? In trouble? No, no, Jack and I were at different schools, but I was an angel in school. A little lazy, but I didn't misbehave. My parents are teachers and wouldn't have put up with misbehavior in school. Neither would my coaches." Vin grinned and shook his head. "Now, outside of school, well, a lot of practical jokes, cow tipping, fights, you know, usual stuff."

"Don't let this guy bullshit you, ma'am. Cow tipping is just a rural legend," interrupted a big burly man wearing a chef's jacket.

Vin stood up, shook his hand and introduced Sarah. "This is Jack Ramsey, a good friend from way back. Pull up a chair if you've got a minute," he said to Jack.

"It'll be about that long, but I wanted to see how you're doing, Vin. It's been a while." Jack pulled over a chair over from an empty table. "I heard you were back in the area, cleaning out the old homestead. Sorry to hear about your Nonna. Man, she was something else."

"She was that," Vin said. "Remember that time she chased us out of the kitchen with a rolling pin?"

Jack laughed. "Pshew, didn't nobody mess with Nonna's kitchen after that."

"Right? Oh, hey, man, Sarah's working with Janelle," Vin said.

"Janelle? Wow, I haven't seen her in ages. Give her a hug from me. Hate to rush, but I need to get back in the kitchen. Great meeting you, Sarah. Vin, don't be a stranger."

While they were waiting on the check, Sarah asked Vin how he knew Jack and how Jack knew Janelle.

"From church. There isn't a Catholic church in Belford. The closest ones are in Dunlap or Dayton, about the same distance from Belford. The Catholic population around here is too small to have parochial schools, so all us kids had religious training together. Jack's a little older, but we got to be good friends, and even though we eventually became rivals on the football field, we always looked out for each other.

"We lead very different lives these days. He married his high school sweetheart, has three kids, another on the way, and a mortgage, the whole bit." Vin shrugged. "Glad it's not me."

"Do you want a family?" Sarah asked.

"Eventually, sure. Five, ten years from now, maybe. Plenty of time."

Not for me. In ten years, I'll be 39, kind of old to think of starting a family. Sarah was quiet as they walked out to the truck. Was not being ready for kids a deal-breaker? *He might change his mind, and it's not like I want a baby next year.*

When Vin unlocked the truck, Sarah turned toward him and drew his face to hers. "Thank you for dinner," she said softly before kissing him without heat or passion.

Vin pulled back a little and said, "A goodnight kiss usually comes at the end of the date, you know." Then he pulled her closer and nuzzled her neck. "We should go."

Feeling a little lost and confused but not understanding why, Sarah slid closer and reached for Vin when he got in the truck. He kissed her again, laughed and backed out of the parking lot. "You're a bad influence on me. Public displays of affection, drinking on a school night. Next thing you know, we'll be rolling somebody's yard or letting crickets loose in their house."

Sarah cringed. She'd been acting like a teenager, trying to reignite the spark she'd last felt with Vin in the creek. "Those seem very specific pranks, Vin."

"I will neither confirm nor deny having participated in either."

Sarah smiled and gazed out the window. She had enjoyed dinner, enjoyed laughing and talking with Vin, but the kisses hadn't forged the connection she'd been seeking. Maybe they just needed more time together. Dancing would be fun, and they'd have lots of time to talk and get to know one another better on the way to Chattanooga and back.

"You've gone quiet on me, bellisima."

"I know, I'm sorry. I think I'm just tired."

Vin nodded and turned on the radio, singing along with some country tunes. Sarah joined in on the ones she recognized, holding his hand and feeling better about their date. They pulled into the long drive of Blackwater Manor. He helped her down from the truck, walked her up to the porch, and turned toward her. "I had a really nice time, Sarah. I hope you did as well."

Sarah smiled and nodded. "I did, Vin. Let's go dancing Friday."

"I'd like that," Vin said, then leaned in for a kiss.

When the kiss deepened, Sarah pushed him away. "Sorry, I suddenly had this vision of myself making out on the porch of my mother's husband's grandmother's house. It's so ridiculous. I can't even." Sarah started laughing. "I'm going inside now."

"Okay," Vin said slowly. "Sometime you'll have to explain the mother's husband's grandmother's bit. I got a little lost."

I'm sure I've explained that before. Even though it was still early, Sarah went to her room after speaking briefly with Beth Ann and Randy Keith, telling them a little about the restaurant and Vin's friends. Vin was nice, charming and fun, with life-long friends, friends who were pursuing adult goals, and he had goals of his own. His desire to leave Belford wasn't motivated by disdain for the country life but by ambition for his career. She understood that and his desire to postpone children, but did he feel the same way about a relationship? And if he was moving out of state, was she even interesting in seeing him again?

Chapter Twenty-Six

Sarah drove to work the next morning still thinking of Vin and their date. He was cute, well-mannered, and fun. *Gosh, it's been a while since I've been dancing.* When her phone rang, she expected it to be Vin, but it wasn't.

"Artie! Hey!"

"You're in a good mood."

Sarah paused. Hearing from Artie did make her happy. "Just looking forward to going to work on this beautiful morning."

"Right, well I wanted to let you know I'll be back at the pond tonight. I hope to see you while I'm here."

"I, I'd like that, Artie. I'm going to Chattanooga on Friday though. How long will you be in town?"

"Possibly through the weekend. Going house hunting, huh?"

And dancing. Gah, this could get awkward. Am I supposed to tell him about every date? "Hope to." Sarah slowed as she passed the farmer's market. "I'm almost at work, Artie. I'll see you tonight, okay?"

"Oh, okay, sure."

Missy bombarded Sarah with questions about her date as soon as she walked into the office. Sarah told her about the restaurant, Vin's friends and their meal, but not about his desire to leave Belford or their shared kisses. Sensing that Janelle was watching her closely, Sarah cut it short and got to work.

A few minutes before noon, the bell over the door rang and voices sounded in the reception area. *Is that Vin? What's he doing here?* Feeling confused and a little irritated, Sarah finished updating her patient's file and followed the noise to the break room, where Missy was unpacking aluminum pans, salsa, and chips.

"I brought everyone lunch," Vin said, grinning.

"So I see."

Vin handed Missy a pan. "Veggie fajitas, and for you, Janelle, spinach quesadilla. Sarah, I wasn't sure what you'd want, so you can choose: cheese enchiladas or Camarones al Mojo de Ajo."

"I don't even know what that is, so enchiladas, please."

"Are you sure? Camarones are Mexican shrimp in a buttery garlic sauce. They're really good."

"I'm sure. I don't like shrimp." Sarah frowned. "Thanks for lunch. It's uh, unexpected."

Vin began opening his food. "Yeah, I called Missy earlier and got her and Janelle's order. Figured I'd surprise you and pass along Jack's greetings to Janelle."

Janelle raised her eyebrows. "I heard you went to Jack's place last night. How's that boy doing? Better question, how's Julie doing?"

"They're both great. Julie's getting big. I think the baby's due in August." Vin stood suddenly and gave Janelle a hug. "That's from Jack. He said he hadn't seen you in a while."

"Oh, stop being crazy," Janelle said, although Sarah thought she looked pleased.

They talked about the restaurant and people from church while they ate. Missy wasn't Catholic but seemed to know the people being discussed or know their families. Sometimes Vin or Janelle would rattle off the connections before Missy asked. "Cassie is John Dawson's daughter, used to date Bobby Owens but married Ben Jackson's boy—what's his name? The second one. Bill. No, Justin."

Sarah sat with a bemused smile, thinking that maybe her mother's husband's grandmother wasn't such an odd connection after all.

After Janelle finished her meal, she leaned back and looked at Vin, eyes narrowed. "Thanks for the food. Why don't you tell us why you're here?" As Vin opened his mouth, Janelle continued, "It's not just to catch up. What are you after?"

Vin laughed. "I am innocent of any nefarious plans this time, mia cara. I simply want to talk to Sarah about a change in plans that was too complicated to text." He stood and hugged the other women. "So, I will say my goodbyes and speak with Sarah outside. Shall we?"

"Is something wrong, Vin?" Sarah asked as they walked toward his car.

"No, but I wanted to talk to you in person. I got a call from a gallery over in Chattanooga that's agreed to show some of my work. I'm headed to Asheville on Saturday, so I thought maybe we could go dancing tonight or tomorrow instead of Friday, and I'll deliver the pots while I'm in town."

"Oh, uh, yeah, I think that could work," Sarah said, wondering when she'd be able to see Artie. "Thursday might be better. I'd hoped to see some houses while I'm in Chattanooga. Maybe I'll do that while you're at the gallery?"

"Of course. We can work out the details later."

Sarah meant to give Vin a quick hug, but she froze in his arms when a familiar green truck drove by the clinic. She recognized Artie, but who was the woman beside him? Suddenly she didn't want to see Artie tonight. Her head spun. *Is he seeing someone? I mean, he can, but why call me to say he wants to see me, and then——*

Sarah's hurt and confusion made her reckless. "Vin, forget what I said. Let's go tonight, okay? I'll meet you at your house at 4:00."

Janelle was standing by Missy's desk when Sarah walked back into the clinic.

"Everything okay?"

"Oh, yeah, we just needed to change some plans. Vin has a delivery to make to a gallery in Chattanooga today, so I'm, uh, going to ride with him."

"You look a little flustered," Missy observed.

Sarah rubbed her forehead. "Yeah, I, I need to confirm some things with my realtor. That's all."

Janelle twisted her mouth. "Still a city girl, huh? I thought maybe the call of the wild would take hold of you after a few weeks. We could sure use you. Lacey's having second thoughts about coming back at all," Janelle said of the physical therapist out on maternity leave.

THE CLINIC CLOSED EARLY ON WEDNESDAY, so Sarah left at three and drove to Blackwater Pond, wondering if Artie would be there. He'd sounded eager to see her, but who was that woman?

Driving past the manor house, Sarah looked for Artie's truck. *It isn't here. Maybe he and the mystery woman are on their own date.* Sarah parked beside Artie's truck outside the little house. *Has he brought her here?*

Drawing in a fortifying breath she walked into the house, where Artie was in the kitchen pouring two glasses of tea.

"Hey, you're home. Want some tea?" he asked, reaching for a third glass.

"No, thanks. I'm in a bit of a rush. I'm leaving for Chattanooga as soon as I change."

"Tonight? I thought . . ." Artie shook his head. "Never mind, do you have a minute to meet someone?" Artie took the tea and motioned for Sarah to follow him to the back porch.

Seated at a wooden table just outside the sliding door was the woman Sarah had seen in Artie's truck earlier. As Artie handed her the glass of tea, she said, "Thanks, love. I was parched." Then she looked up at Sarah and smiled. The warmth in her eyes seemed at odds with her jet-black hair, thick layers of mascara, and harsh red lipstick. "You must be Sarah. Art's been talking about you all afternoon. I'm Ansel."

"Oh, uh, it's nice to meet you."

"Ansel's helping set up my website."

So, it's not a date. Sarah smiled. "A website?"

"Yep. Moving one step closer to the reality of Arbor Gate

Landscaping Services."

"Really? That's great, Artie. I'll have to look at the website later though. I'm in a hurry."

AFTER HER SHOWER, Sarah paired some skinny jeans with a silky pink camisole. For now, she'd wear flats and a flowered blouse over the cami; later she'd add a little makeup and heels and lose the blouse. She usually dressed up a bit more for dancing, but they'd have to leave before things got cranked up anyway.

As she left the house, Sarah glimpsed Artie and Ansel laughing, huddled together in front of Artie's laptop, and wished she could trade places with Ansel.

Chapter Twenty-Seven

Sarah drove to Vin's house feeling frustrated that she'd made impulsive plans. She'd honestly prefer sitting on the porch with Artie over dancing with Vin. Still, it couldn't hurt to look at houses. The clock was ticking. Six weeks until Liam moved in.

Vin met her at her car. "Want to take my truck?" he asked, kissing her cheek.

"No, I'll drive, Vin. I'm more familiar with the area and parking a car will be easier than parking that big truck."

"All right, give me just a minute." Vin gingerly placed a box of his pottery in the trunk and two in the back seat. "They're carefully wrapped, but don't go all NASCAR on me."

Sarah laughed. "I promise. Hey, is it okay if I drop you at the gallery while I look at houses with my mom's friend? It'll take about an hour, maybe ninety minutes."

"Absolutely. I'll take care of business and have time to browse. No worries on my end. I'm eager to see how the gallery compares to what I'll see in Asheville this weekend."

Sarah's mind wandered. She'd visited Asheville with Brad. They'd gone contra dancing, which he'd hated, and hiking, which they'd both enjoyed. *I wish I was dancing in the kitchen with Artie right now. Wonder what he's doing tonight.*

Vin was still talking. "It can't really compare to Berea in terms of numbers. I mean, over eight hundred artists exhibit at the Kentucky Artisan Center. Everything from modern and traditional art forms to music, film, and even specialty foods."

AFTER DROPPING VIN AT THE GALLERY, Sarah drove to a nearby realty office to meet her mother's friend Patti. They talked a bit about Sarah's wish list, particularly the short commute.

As they drove, Patti said, "I understand, but your budget doesn't really allow for downtown, so we'll look at houses here in Redbank today. We're about five miles from the Aquarium; with traffic, that's ten to twenty minutes, depending.

"We're also looking at older homes because of budget constraints. You're smart to buy now, since prices are steadily increasing. This one was built in 1964 but has been updated. It's three bedrooms, two baths, 1100 square feet."

"Is that a garage?" Sarah noticed a detached building.

"Yes, but it's currently full of boxes," Patti said as she opened the door.

The home was empty, so Sarah struggled a bit to envision furniture arrangements. "Those big windows are nice, but I'd almost have to put a couch there, which would block half of the view," she said before walking into the kitchen.

"White cabinets, all new stainless steel appliances. The bathrooms have also been updated. What do you think so far?"

"Ceramic tile in the kitchen worries me," Sarah said. "Every dish I drop would shatter, and the floor feels cold. Other than that, it's okay, I guess." She opened the back door and walked outside. "Not much of a yard."

"The lot actually extends several hundred feet," Patti said, pointing up the steep hillside. "If you wanted to, you could dig out the hillside to create more usable space."

"I think that would be too expensive." Sarah shook her head.

"Well, maybe not. This house is priced lower than others in the area, and the money you save could pay for extending the yard." When Sarah didn't say anything, Patti opened her iPad. "Sometimes a comparison helps. Here's a two bedroom that's closer to your work and the riverfront, but you pay for the location. Although older and smaller than this one, it's in the middle of your budget. Should we go look at it?"

Sarah looked at the pictures and shook her head. "No, I see what you're saying. I'll keep this house as a maybe, but I don't need to see the other one. It's expensive, the lot's too steep, and it has on-street parking, which I'd like to avoid."

They returned to the car and drove down the street. "The next house is at the top of your budget, but the sellers are motivated. It's larger, with three bedrooms, two baths, built in 1935. The lot is hilly, but it has a driveway and attached garage, so you wouldn't be carrying groceries uphill in the rain."

Sarah laughed. "Add three little kids and that's my mom's nightmare situation. The house I grew up in was like that."

"It's an important consideration," Patti said, turning into a steep driveway. "The backyard is small but fenced. Shall we go inside?"

Sarah walked into the living room and stopped. A huge asymmetrical section of the wall surrounding a small fireplace was covered in dark stone with a harsh white mortar. "Ugh, that's not really my taste."

"Well, the room would look completely different with darker mortar, a decorative mantel, and a different wall color."

Sarah wasn't convinced but continued looking at the house, noting the small closets, updated baths, and new laminate floors.

"What do you think, Sarah?"

"Maybe I'm being too picky, but the flooring in this room is two different colors. It feels like a bad DIY job, which makes me wonder about the other renovations. I think I'll pass."

"I'm sensing that an older home is not really what you want," Patti said.

"It's not that," Sarah protested. "Not really. I mean, I actually like older homes with personality." She paused. "Can you say personality when it's not a person? Anyway, I'd like to put my own stamp on a place, you know? These feel like they're trying to copy the finishes in new houses."

Sarah paused again, remembering Artie's rant about home-owners in Acworth all wanting the same plants and features in their yards. She sighed. "Maybe it's the area. I didn't realize it was so hilly here. I'd like to be able to see more than ten feet out of my back window. Here, the view is blocked by hills. I feel hemmed in, trapped almost."

"Buying a house is scary," Patti said. "It's hard to commit when you haven't seen everything that's available and can't truly know what life will be like in this house or that house. I understand your hesitancy. But since you're under a bit of a time constraint, you may have to make a now choice instead of a forever choice."

Sarah stared at Patti. *Has that been my pattern? Settling for a now choice because I wanted a boyfriend?*

"I have an idea," Patti said. "My office just signed a listing agreement out in Lookout Valley. I haven't seen it, but the house has been unoccupied a while. The former owner's heir is mailing the key, so we won't have access but can walk around and peer inside the windows. It's about ten minutes from your work. Do you want to take a look?"

Sarah's mood lifted. She hadn't considered Lookout Valley because of its proximity to the interstate, but she knew a couple who lived there, and it was closer to Belford, so she could see Artie when he was there, or Vin, maybe.

As they drove, Patti explained that the house was just under a thousand square feet with three bedrooms and one bath. "It's an older home on a small lot, but there's a park on one side. The seller doesn't want any of the furniture or personal belongings. He's out of state and may be willing to take a reduced price to not have to deal with all that."

As they neared the property, Sarah noticed a few churches, fast food restaurants, and a grocery store. *There's a library. Everything I need is close by*. Homes in the area were small but maintained, and the lots were flatter than some she'd seen. "I like the area. It has kind of a small-town vibe."

Patti turned into an unpaved driveway and parked beside an older one-story home with faded blue siding. "No garage, but you can always add a canopy."

Sarah nodded but didn't speak as they walked toward the house. Her mind was racing. *It's kind of plain, but replacing the concrete steps with a porch and adding shutters would really change its look. I could repaint, maybe white with black shutters. Maybe Artie would help me with landscaping.* She followed Patti to the front window and peered inside. "I doubt I'd keep the floral sofa, but the tables and lamps are okay. I never even thought about furnishing a house."

"There's always Craigslist or second-hand stores," Patti said. They looked through another window. "The kitchen cabinets look original."

"I kind of like them," Sarah said. "The yard is small but fenced. I could get a dog!"

Patti smiled. "It sounds like you're considering making an offer."

"Oh, I'd need to actually go inside first and talk to my mom, but maybe."

"Well, don't wait too long. The market really is picking up," Patti said, "which means prices could escalate quickly."

Sarah nodded. "Yeah. Thank you. I have a lot to think about, but I'll be in touch soon."

FEELING HAPPY ABOUT THE LITTLE HOUSE and excited to show Vin all her adopted city had to offer, Sarah thought a drink at O'Shea's would be fun. She pointed out the building as they drove past. "We'll start our evening with a drink at the rooftop bar once we find a parking place."

They found a spot near the Main Street Honkytonk. "This is perfect," Sarah said. "We'll probably end up there eventually, even though I prefer Bootleggers." They started walking back toward O'Shea's with Sarah sharing information about the places they passed.

"You're excited to be back," Vin observed.

"Yeah, it feels like I've been gone forever. Tell me about Gallery 1401."

"Oh, it's a great place with a lot of high-end work from numerous artists: painters, woodworkers, potters, metal workers, and textile artists. I'm really pleased to be accepted. I talked to some artists who work a few hours a week to get a better commission. The place has good vibes," Vin said. "I hadn't really considered Chattanooga before, but it's a growing scene and you'll be here. There's something to be said for getting in on the ground floor."

"Yeah, there are a lot of galleries around town," Sarah said slowly, wondering why she felt crowded by Vin's comment. "I think we're early enough to be able to get in without a wait. It gets crowded closer to sunset," she said as they rode the escalator to the rooftop bar.

"Great view." Vin suggested a selfie with the river and mountains behind them. Back at their table, Sarah ordered one of O'Shea's specialty vodka cocktails. Vin ordered whiskey for himself and a cheese tray for them to share.

"Tell me about Chattanooga. What's so appealing?"

Sarah spoke at length about the small city's charms, how she loved walking to work and to restaurants and bars and theater, and how so many of her friends had settled in the area. "It's a young city, for one thing, and by that I mean the people, not the actual city. I think the median age is around thirty-five. So it has a good mix of trendy places, tourist attractions, and old-school historic sites. And you can buy just about anything you'd ever need within five miles of the city."

They talked a while longer, debating the merits of the small cities Vin was considering. As the evening waned, the bar grew more crowded. Sarah pulled out her phone and found that Bootleggers didn't open until nine. "How do you feel about line dancing?"

"I just wish I'd worn my cowboy boots. Are they even going to let you in with heels?" Vin teased.

As they walked hand in hand several blocks to the Honkytonk, Sarah looked at everyone they passed, half expecting to see someone she knew, but it appeared the city had moved on without her.

When they walked in the bar, "Wagon Wheel" by Darius Rucker was playing. Vin pulled Sarah onto the dance floor, and they joined in the line dance. After a couple more numbers, the DJ introduced a two-step number. *Finally, I get to dance with a partner.*

Sarah enjoyed dancing with Vin, but she couldn't help noticing how much younger the crowd seemed than the last time she'd been there. When had she last been dancing? Two years? Had it really been so long? Maybe it had.

When the DJ announced a return to line dancing, Vin suggested they split a basket of chicken fingers and fries. The food was good, but conversation was impossible because of the loud music. A slow song began, and Vin led Sarah back the dance floor and held her close. When the lights flashed and another fast song began, he asked, "Do you want to get a drink and sit this one out or go to the other bar?"

"I don't think so, Vin. Let's just head back over the mountain. Do you mind?"

"Not at all. I'm with you, that is enough."

Sarah kissed Vin on the cheek. "You're really sweet."

Vin looked at her curiously. "That felt like a good-bye."

"Oh, um, no. Sorry. It wasn't meant to be." *Was it? Are we moving in different directions? Are we meant to be together or is it time to say good-bye?*

When Vin offered to drive, Sarah readily agreed. He asked her if she'd found a house, so she told him about about the houses she'd seen and her concerns with each. "I like the Lookout Valley house best, but it needs work."

"I grew up in an old house and lived in a new one in New Orleans. Both had their problems. No house is ever going to be perfect, but if you spend enough time there, they become home."

"I'm just ready to find something," Sarah said, thinking that sounded like settling. "I suck at making decisions."

"Well, let's go over them again. Think about the pros and cons."

"I'd rather not." Sarah leaned against the door and closed her eyes. *Maybe I need to give up on perfect. Maybe good enough or good enough for now is enough.* Sarah thought about the houses, but before long her thoughts turned to Artie and Vin. *Vin is sweet, but he——*

"Do you mind if I listen to the radio?" Vin asked.

"It's broken," Sarah said without opening her eyes. Before long, Vin was singing softly, thumping his hand on the steering wheel. *Did spending time with previous boyfriends make them feel like home? Is that why I put up with them, even though I knew they weren't right? I'm not perfect either. Not by a long shot.*

As Sarah thought about her faults, she suddenly recognized the Eli Young Band song Vin was singing. It was one they'd danced to. Had she broken up with him in a bar? *I wish I'd never started anything with Vin. He's fun and flirty like I thought I wanted, but there's no emotional connection like I have with Artie.* Tears slid down her face. *I'm not good enough for Artie. I betrayed him, his trust, his belief in our future, then believed he'd brought a date to Blackwater Pond. Even though he said it wasn't a betrayal, it feels like it was. Like it is. What am I doing with Vin?*

Twenty minutes later, Vin pulled in his driveway. "Do you want to come in?"

"No, I need to go home. Work tomorrow, you know." Sarah walked around to the driver's side and took the keys from Vin. "Thanks for tonight, Vin. You're a good dancer. Sorry I've been so preoccupied."

"You have a lot on your mind, bellisima. I understand." Vin wrapped her in a hug. "Will you join me and my aunt and uncle for dinner Sunday? My uncle is coming to repair the rinceau at the manor. I think you would enjoy meeting them."

"Oh, I don't know, Vin. Can we talk about it later? I want to go home."

"Well, think about it. Jack gave me his recipe for shrimp primavera. It will be wonderful," Vin said with a chef's kiss.

Sarah stared at him disbelievingly, then got in the car without another word. *Is this my future? Dating a guy who can't even remember that I don't like shrimp? What the hell am I doing?* All of her fears and frustrations and uncertainties bubbled up. Sarah pulled to the side of road and sobbed, then turned toward home, toward Artie.

Chapter Twenty-Eight

A lamp's soft light drew Sarah through the dark house to the back porch where Artie sat alone at the table, focused on his laptop. "How's the website coming?"

"Just putting on the final touches," Artie said, eyes still on the screen. "There, saved and ready to go." He looked up, his smile fading rapidly. "You've been crying. What's wrong?" He stood quickly, holding the table for balance.

Sarah's eyes watered, and her face crumpled as she struggled for control. "Nothing. Everything. I don't want to talk about it."

"Sarah." Artie breathed her name, quiet as a whisper, soft as a kiss on her eyelids, and held his arms wide.

Sarah choked back a sob, then wailed, "He, he, shri-i-i-mp," before stepping into Artie's embrace with such force that he fell heavily into the chair behind him, his crutch clattering to the floor. Sarah landed in his lap.

A moment passed in silence. Artie held her tightly. Sarah snuggled closer. Then they both started shaking with laughter.

"Oh my God, Artie. Are you okay?"

Artie loosened his hold and looked at her. "Yeah. Just lost my balance. Did, did you say shrimp? You don't even like shrimp."

Sarah buried her face in his shoulder again and wailed, "I know." Artie held her, gently rubbing her back, waiting for her sobs to subside.

After a few minutes, Sarah lifted her head and stared blankly at the wall. "I know that. You know that. How can he not know that? I've told him three times."

Artie's arms dropped to his side. Sarah covered her face and hiccupped, then shifted in his lap so she could see his face. "Wait, how do you know I don't like shrimp?"

"The wedding," Artie said, shrugging. "I offered you a bite of shrimp cocktail, and you made a face. That face," he said, stifling a laugh. "Sarah, what is going on?"

She hiccupped again.

"I'll get you some water." Artie looked around the floor. "I think my crutch got knocked—oh, there it is."

"I'll go." When she returned with two glasses of water, Sarah asked about his leg.

"It's fine, a little swollen. I've been on my feet a lot this week. Are you going to tell me what's wrong?"

She hiccupped and shook her head. "I need a minute. Show me your website.

"Now?"

Sarah hiccupped and nodded.

Artie shrugged, then patted the seat beside him, opened the laptop and called up his website. "So, this is the landing page." A dark-brown intertwined AG logo rested on a muted green backdrop on the left side. On the right, Artie leaned on a shovel, sleeves casually rolled to the elbow, with Blackwater Pond in the background.

"Sexy fore-hic-arms," Sarah said, suddenly aware of the heat from his body beside her.

Artie shook his head. "Is that even a thing?" He grinned as he clicked on the gallery page. "So, this is basically my portfolio—before and afters of yards and office buildings. This section is mostly plans for Blackwater Manor." He scrolled through pictures of plans and a bed of annuals he'd already installed at the front entrance. "This is a sketch of the bridge we'll put over the creek feeding the pond, and here's my rose garden plan.

"It's not the best time of year to plant roses, so we'll focus on the brickwork and soil prep now. I'll be back in the fall to do the planting. That's when this place will really come together."

Sarah realized she'd never thought about all the literal groundwork that went into creating a successful garden. "This is incredible, Artie. What other ideas are circulating in that brilliant mind of yours?"

"Eh, I don't know about brilliant, but I have lots of ideas. A kitchen garden, trees and azaleas to line the drive, magnolias, hydrangeas, and some seasonal bulbs by the pond. We'll be working in phases though. We're years away from completion, but I'm okay with that. I like Belford. I like it a lot."

"Artie, you keep saying we. Is that woman I met this afternoon part of your plan?"

"Ansel? No. She's a photographer who happens to know a lot about web design. What, did you—"

"Forget it, Artie, I thought maybe—"

"Oh, you thought I was dating her." Artie rubbed her back. "I know we talked about seeing other people, but Sarah, I wouldn't bring a woman here."

"No, Artie, I know. I just jump to crazy ideas sometimes. I've been feeling so lost. I thought I'd be happier dating you both, but I'm not." Sarah stood up. "I'm going to bed. I'm exhausted."

Artie held out his hand. "Can I show you one more picture? I'd like to use it on the website if you're okay with it."

Sarah shrugged. "Sure."

Artie opened a tab labeled 'inspiration' and paged down, stopping on a photo of Sarah standing in the little niche where they'd first kissed. The caption read, "A Rose of Incomparable Beauty— The lovely Lady Sarah." Below was a brief note: "A hybrid tea rose also known as Jardins de Bagatelle."

"But, but that's me." She sank in the chair beside him. "This is where we kissed for the first time. That rose you bought, the one you said was your new favorite." Sarah's voice cracked. "It's called Lady Sarah?"

Artie nodded. "Yeah, I've got closeups of the rose in here too, but I wanted to include this picture if it's okay."

"Oh, Artie." Sarah covered her face. "I don't know why you'd want my picture on your website. I've treated you so terribly. I don't deserve you."

Artie laid a hand on her back. "Don't say that. I'll take the picture down if you want me to, but it brings me nothing but good memories."

Sarah stood suddenly. "I've treated you like crap, Artie. I basically cheated on you, then insisted that we date other people. What is wrong with me? I'm an awful person."

"Sarah, stop this. You're not—"

"Oh my God, Artie. Do you know where I've been?" Her voice rose as she stood and pointed toward the door. "I've been out dancing with Vin while you sat here putting a picture of me on your website. How can that be okay?"

"Give me a little credit, Sarah," Artie said patiently. "I assumed you were with him. I mean, you aren't exactly dressed for house hunting." He stood and reached for her. "I don't like it, but I agreed to it. You can see who you want."

"You can too." Sarah drank some more water and stepped closer to him. "I saw you in town. I didn't know who she was then, but I was jealous of Ansel. That's why I told Vin we should go dancing tonight. I didn't want to go. Not really. But I went anyway. I shouldn't be treating you this way, Artie. You deserve so much better."

Artie reached for his crutch and stood. "Why did you go, Sarah?"

"Because I have trust issues." Sarah's lip trembled again. "I don't trust people not to leave me, so I leave them first." She breathed heavily. "I don't trust myself to make good decisions. For years I dated men who were wrong for me. And despite my best efforts at breaking that pattern, I jumped right back into it with Vin, who reminds me of every boyfriend I've ever had." Tears trickled down her cheeks. "Apparently, I'm doomed to repeat my mistakes. Seven months without a date was supposed to help me learn how to break the pattern, yet here we are."

Sarah wiped her face and motioned to the swing. "Will you sit with me?"

They moved to the swing, and in the darkness of the moonless summer night, Artie listened patiently as Sarah proceeded through tears and self-recrimination to tell the full story of her dating history. "That's what I learned on my big hiatus from men. That I'm an idiot, self-sabotaging every relationship, apparently intentionally. You should run for the door."

"Sarah, I'm not going to sit here and let you beat yourself up for past mistakes. But I need to know." Artie stopped the swing and looked at Sarah. "Why Vin? Why now, when I'm here wanting a relationship with you? You said you weren't happy. Is it me? Are you just not that into me?"

Sarah put her hands on either side of his face. "No, Artie, no. It's not that. I want you. I think I've always wanted you." She sat back. "But I don't deserve you."

"You want me?"

"Yes. But you're too good for me. You can do better," she sobbed. "You should find someone else. Someone who's not so messed up."

"Sarah." Artie shook his head. "You don't get to make that choice for me." The swing creaked a little as Artie scooted closer and put his arm around her, moving her head to his shoulder. They swung slowly, the quiet punctuated only by occasional sniffs.

When Sarah's crying stilled, Artie said, "After our ill-fated hike, you told me that the stories we tell ourselves are just stories. Can't you see you've been believing a lie for years? That Blake guy messed with your head. You didn't need to change for him, Sarah. You don't need to change for me."

Sarah sat up and looked at him. "I don't?"

"No, it's like with plants. If I left a plant confined to a pot for years, it would become rootbound and die. Maybe he outgrew you, or you outgrew him, I don't know. It doesn't even matter. The point is that plants bloom in ideal conditions. Sometimes pruning is necessary. Sometimes a change in location is all it takes to thrive— more sun, less sun, different soil. People are like that too."

Sarah snuggled against him, putting her head back on his shoulder.

"No one's perfect, Sarah. You shouldn't expect yourself to be, nor should you try to fit who you are into someone else's mold. The most beautiful rose won't bloom in the wrong soil. That's you in this analogy, in case you missed it." He laughed quietly. "You know what else I remember about that drive home?"

Sarah held onto his hand. "What do you remember?"

He smiled. "That crazy story about the woman with bugs in her hair. That mirror thing where people wrote about you? I wish you could see yourself the way I see you, Sarah."

Sarah sat up and looked at him.

Artie smoothed her hair and wiped away her tears. "You are kind and gentle and loving. Funny and smart and interested in life. You've got this magnetic energy that I find very enticing." Artie hugged her close. "I love your laughter, your big heart, and your genuineness. Your random stories and mad connections that somehow make perfect sense. I love it all."

Sarah leaned back from the embrace and cupped his face. "Oh, Artie. You are the one who's kind and gentle and loving and just innately good. You're so calm, confident, focused on your journey and deliberate with your words. With you, I can hear the crickets."

Artie laughed a little. "What?"

"When I'm with you, Artie, my anxiety fades, my mind slows down, and I feel like I can focus on the important stuff. Everything makes more sense, and somehow, I believe that I can be the person I want to be. Like maybe I am enough."

"You are, Sarah. You are enough, and you are worthy of love, and in case you missed it, I like-like you."

"You do? Even after all this?"

"Yes." Artie picked up his crutch and stood. "My balance may be off, but I'd really like to kiss you right now."

"I'll hold you," Sarah said. "I like-like you too."

Chapter Twenty-Nine

When Sarah awoke Thursday morning, she stretched and smiled, remembering talking with Artie long past midnight. They'd shared childhood memories and hopes for the future in between kisses and cuddles and declarations of love. She picked up her phone and smiled to see his morning greeting. Artie, she was sure, was already at work, finalizing plans for tomorrow's groundbreaking.

Later that day, after a very slow morning at the clinic, Janelle asked her to step into the break room. "We only have a few people on the afternoon schedule. Things will pick up after the Fourth, but that's not why I asked you in here. Lacey called me last night. She's not coming back. The job's yours if you want it."

Sarah shook her head. "Janelle, I—"

"Don't say no. Not yet. I know Belford's a big change from Chattanooga and that maybe you've found a house you want, and maybe there's more room for advancement there. All that's true, but you're good at your job here. I like working with you, and I'd like you to stay. So, take the afternoon off. Think about your options. Maybe spend a little time with that gardener I hear is back in town."

Sarah laughed. "Does everybody know everything that happens around here?"

"Just me. No, I'm kidding. I saw a friend at the library this morning who said her niece is helping that boy with web design. You should know folks keep up with all the goings on out at that manor these days."

"Yeah, I've noticed." Sarah yawned. "Janelle, I appreciate the offer and want you to know I've really enjoyed working with you, but I'm ninety percent sure I'm putting an offer in on the Lookout Valley house this afternoon."

"Well, ten percent is better than nothing. Take the afternoon. Maybe look at living arrangements around here. Enjoy the countryside."

"Okay, I'll take the afternoon and think things over." Sarah yawned again. "Maybe dream about them. I was up too late last night."

Sarah gathered her things and texted Artie: "On my way home. Do you have time for lunch?"

AT BLACKWATER POND, Beth Ann and Randy Keith were just sitting down to lunch. "Why, you're home early, Sarah. Can I make you a sandwich?" Beth Ann asked.

Before Sarah could answer, Artie came around the corner, backpack in hand. "Okay, that's all—Sarah!" His whole face lit up.

"I just got your text. I've been on the phone finalizing tomorrow's schedule. It's going to be a long day, but I've got coolers of water and that cafe in town is delivering lunch about 11:30. The tractors and tillers will be here at seven to start cultivating the garden beds and smoothing the pathways for brick-work next week."

"'Spect I won't recognize the place after that," Randy Keith said.

"It'll definitely look different," Artie said. "Sarah, want to grab some lunch, then go exploring?"

"Give me five minutes." She ran to change out of her scrubs.

Artie helped her in the truck, kissed her softly, and asked, "How'd you manage to get the afternoon off?"

After Sarah told him about Janelle's offer, he asked how she felt about it.

"Honestly, it seems like a distraction from my goal. I started all this to find a house, and while it isn't perfect, nothing is, so I'm pretty sure I'm making an offer tonight. I like it here, but I'm used to Chattanooga and I like my job there too. Belford would be a big change, and I can't live at Blackwater forever. I mean, can you imagine moving here from Acworth?"

Artie looked at her in amazement. "Yeah, I'm hoping to do exactly that, Sarah. That's what the website's for. All those dreams about a landscaping service I told you about last night? This is the place. And after all those issues at work, I decided this is the time, so yeah, today I'm looking for land."

Sarah's eyes widened. "Here? In Belford? But—"

"If I can find property, yes. I like the people, the quieter environs, the slower pace of life." They'd reached the end of the drive. "Right or left?"

"When in doubt, go left," Sarah said.

"That sounds almost like a political statement," Artie said. "Where's the logic?"

"I don't know. We may get lost, but if we keep turning, we'll eventually find our way home."

"All right," Artie said. "I'll trust your instincts."

Sarah wondered about the wisdom of that. "When you say landscaping services, do you mean designing gardens like you're doing at Blackwater?"

"Well, I'll certainly offer design, on a smaller scale, of course, but I'll also be a source for seeds, plants, landscaping ties, mulch, whatever people need. The scope of my work will change, but work at the pond's going to keep me busy for a long, long time. Establishing my landscaping business while I'm earning an income with the gardens there seems wise. Andy's also hinted about a long-term contract to maintain the gardens, so that could provide some steady income for years to come."

"But wouldn't you miss Acworth and all the restaurants and stores and theaters? Not to mention the lake and visiting with James and Meg and all."

Artie looked at Sarah quizzically as he slowed at a stop sign. "Are you trying to talk me into staying in Acworth or staying away from Belford?"

"Neither one. I'm just surprised. It's a big change."

"It is, but I'm ready. Speaking of changes, my brother called me last night before you got home."

"Rob called you? Isn't that unusual?"

"Yeah. Surprised me too. I think that's like twice this decade. He wants me to join him and some work friends for a baseball game next week when he's in town for business."

Sarah knew Rob and Artie had a tense relationship. "So, what did you say?"

"I asked if he'd be embarrassed to be seen with a cripple."

"Artie! What?"

"Yeah, that was pretty much his response. He was like, 'What the f-, uh, heck are you talking about?' I told him I knew he was embarrassed by my amputation." Artie paused, then continued in a brighter voice. "But here's the thing. Rob insists he wasn't, isn't, and never has been. He distanced himself because he felt guilty as hell. And then he was ashamed for staying away. Can you believe that? He thought I blamed him for the accident." Artie shook his head. "We talked for over an hour. It's nice to have a brother again, even if he is a big jerk."

"That's amazing, Artie. I'm happy for you."

Artie rubbed his forehead. "Yeah, I can't really wrap my head around it. I truly believed he was embarrassed by my amputation."

"Good to know I'm not the only one who believed a lie for decades," Sarah said. "Just thought I'd point that out in case you missed it."

Artie glanced her way and grinned. "Smart ass." He was quiet a minute, then took her hand. "The thing is, Sarah, when Dad said he didn't want a 'cripple' for a son, I heard that he didn't want *me* for a son. 'Cripple' implies a limitation I wasn't ready to accept. Doc told me I could be an athlete, and I believed him. And when I was considering careers, I believed I could do the field work. When I looked in the mirror, I still saw me, Art Gladstone. Even though part of me was missing, I was still me, and that acceptance made me whole.

"Do you see what I'm saying? We've got to believe in ourselves. We've got to believe in us. Even if it's not easy. Especially when it's not easy. I don't know what the future holds for us, but we'll figure it out, okay? Things with our jobs and houses are changing, but we'll make it work, find a way to be together. We may not be in the same city, or even the same state—"

"Artie, honey." Sarah squeezed his hand. "I believe you. We'll find a way."

"Okay." Artie stopped at the crossroads, leaned across the seat and kissed her. "Good."

"Wow. Um, that was getting kind of intense. How about a lunch break? The Fin and Feather's right there. Randy Keith says their food is good."

Artie pulled into the parking lot and let out a slow breath. "Yeah, probably a good idea. I'm more stressed than I realized."

"Perfectly understandable. You've got a lot going on."

"We both do." Artie opened the truck door. "Looks like we missed the lunch rush. You know, it seems an odd location for it, but I'd swear Ansel mentioned exhibiting some photos here."

The restaurant wasn't as crowded or as loud as it had been on Saturday morning, so after they ordered their chicken sandwiches and fries, they walked around looking at the artwork. Ansel's black and white photographs depicted decorative doors and fences, graveyard angels, and abandoned buildings with shadows in stark relief.

"Wow, when I asked about shots for the website, I had no idea she was so talented."

Another wall featured landscapes of mostly rural scenes, though Sarah noted a beach painting or two. She paused in front of one with a brilliant sunset reflecting on the wet shore. "How do artists get that glow? It's just paint. What makes it shine?"

"Well, the paint could have additives to make it sparkle, but it's probably just complementary under-painting or paint thinned to add a gloss."

"What's complementary under-painting?"

"Pshew. Well, if I remember correctly from my high school art class, you use complementary colors, you know, opposites on the color wheel, to block out sections of the canvas, then paint on top of it."

"What's the point of that? Doesn't the top layer cover up what's underneath?"

The kitchen door opened, and Artie said, "Our food's ready." He put his hand at Sarah's waist as they made their way back to the table.

"It's true the new paint covers the old, but it's still there, even if we're not aware of it. What's underneath always informs what's on top, and opposite colors never rest easy. I do that in gardens all the time—putting purple flowers with yellow ones is much more exciting than purple next to red."

"And that makes the paint glow?" When Artie shrugged, Sarah sat for a minute. "What's underneath informs what's on top. What's in the past informs the present? Hmm. All those layers of experiences with past boyfriends making me who I am today. I'm not sure I like that."

Artie pushed his plate to one side, took her hand and leaned close to her, smiling. "Sarah, don't worry about the past. It led us here. And yeah, parts were painful, but don't you see? Accepting our past is how we become whole. The shadows don't tell the whole story. They add to the beauty and complete the picture. The light still shines through. And sitting here, right now, knowing you love me? I gotta say, that's pretty damn special. And the best is yet to come."

Sarah leaned forward and caressed his face. "I believe you, you beautiful man."

Chapter Thirty

After lunch, Sarah directed Artie toward the area she'd explored previously. "Oh, turn left at the sign. The roads are steeper, so don't be surprised if your truck has a hard time getting up some of these hills. My car did."

"Really? Sounds like a bad fuel pump. Maybe Randy Keith can look at it." Artie's truck had no problem climbing the hills on the short drive to the chapel. "We've reached the top of the plateau," he said as they walked toward the small church. "I bet there's almost always a breeze here." He read the plaque about the chapel's history. "Reminds me of the story at Barnsley Gardens."

"That's exactly what I thought."

They walked around back to the churchyard. "Man! Look at that view!" Beyond the small cemetery, the land dropped about fifty feet. Green fields were divided by rows of darker green growth running along creek beds. Cattle and sheep roamed on some of the fields; corn and beans grew on others.

Sarah gazed out across the land. "It's like a different world here. So peaceful."

Artie put his arm around Sarah. "It is, and I think it would be a good place for me. Very few local farms grow fruits or vegetables here. I could expand my heirloom tomato operation, and there wouldn't be any competition in the landscaping or tree nursery business. Well, there's one guy who grows Christmas trees, but otherwise it's mostly cattle farms."

"Janelle's husband is a cattle farmer," Sarah said. "She invited me to milk a cow."

Artie grinned. "I'd pay money to see that."

Sarah poked him. "You don't think I could milk a cow?"

"I think you can do anything you set your mind to," Artie said. He turned back to the view. "That's Signal Mountain, right? Chattanooga's on the other side, so we can see each other more often than with me in Acworth. I can travel to work there if necessary, or who knows, Arbor Gate Landscaping Service might draw customers to Belford. Man, I'd love to find land around here. Let's drive around a bit. Maybe I'll get lucky." As they walked back to the truck, Artie whistled a song Sarah recognized from *Mr. Rogers' Neighborhood*.

Sarah was amused but a little saddened by Artie's excitement. She liked Belford, but staying in Chattanooga with its easy access to her job and restaurants and shopping made more sense, didn't it? Intrusive thoughts prevented Sarah from hearing all Artie said about planting zones and arable soil as he drove down the road. *We can see each other on the weekends, but aren't weekends the busiest times for garden centers? How will he find time for us and a new business?*

Artie braked suddenly, turning into a gravel drive. "Is that a For Sale sign?" A faded orange sign was nearly hidden by some Queen Anne's Lace growing in front of it. "Let's check it out." He reached behind him and retrieved his hiking poles, which he tucked under his arm, and stepped out of the truck. Sarah noticed that he didn't let go of the steering wheel until his right foot was securely on the ground. She followed him, watching as he used one of the hiking poles to move the weeds aside.

"Well?"

"Ten acres. There's a phone number." Artie snapped a quick picture. "Feel like walking a bit? The sign's obviously been here a while, but the land may still be available."

A large rusty gate stood at the end of the gravel drive where they'd parked and opened into a field surrounded by a barbed-wire fence.

Sarah jumped as the gate screeched. "Do you think it's safe?"

"I think so. What are you worried about?" Artie asked.

"Um, snakes, a bull, or maybe a guy with a shotgun. Take your pick," Sarah said, following him into the field.

"Fair point, but I think we'll be fine." He handed her one of the poles. "Here, you can move any briars with this. Maybe scare away the snakes, ward off bulls. Just kidding. If you see a bull, run. I will follow."

"I was kidding about the bull." Sarah looked around nervously. "You don't think—"

"No." Artie grinned as he bent down and looked at the soil. "Animals weren't kept here. The ground's uneven, furrowed. It's been a few years since the field's been plowed. See how high those weeds are?"

Sarah giggled.

"What?"

"You've gone all, I don't know, back to nature. Are you going to track wild game next?"

Artie grinned and took her hand. "I doubt I'd recognize any tracks beyond a rabbit or maybe a coyote. I want to get a feel for the property." He leaned close and kissed her. "Yell if you see a guy with a shotgun. I won't go far, and I'll stick close to the fence."

"I'm coming with you," Sarah said. The field wasn't as flat as she'd expected. From a distance, she could see a bend, a variation in the pattern of light and dark made by the overgrown furrowed rows, as if the very fabric of the earth had folded. Sarah pointed at a line of trees that ran at a diagonal in the distance. "Is that a creek?"

"Looks bigger than a creek, could be the Igohida. Either way, I'd say it's the property line." Artie took Sarah's hand as they walked back toward the truck. "I like this."

They walked in silence for a while. Sarah wondered if he meant the land or holding her hand. She heard a hawk whistle and pointed, telling Artie about her previous visit to the chapel and all the hawks she'd seen that day.

"That's cool," Artie said. "I guess somebody's looking out for us."

"Beth Ann says hawks are lucky."

"Maybe we're lucky somebody's watching out for us." Artie grinned. "Hawks are supposed to point the way too, like a spirit guide." He squeezed her hand. "I like the property. I'm going to call that number."

"Seriously, Artie? I've taken longer to decide on a new pair of shoes. I'm not even kidding," she said, when he laughed. "My mom tells this story about taking us to Walmart, specifically to spend some birthday money. Elizabeth took about two minutes to choose that game where you fit all the pieces in before the time runs out. What was it called?"

"Perfection?"

"Oh, of course. Naturally. Meanwhile, I agonized for forty-five minutes before choosing one of those fancy keepsake Barbies like my friend Jessie had. I thought I was supposed to like them, but I couldn't even play with it." Sarah looked perturbed. "I guess I've always over-analyzed things."

"Maybe you've put too much stock in what other people think," Artie said gently. "Maybe it's time to listen to your instincts and choose what you want rather than what you think other people expect."

"I don't think I have those instincts."

"I think you do. Let's circle back toward Blackwater Pond. I want to call about the land this afternoon."

As they drove on down the road, Sarah spotted an old white farmhouse to the left. "There's my dream house," she joked. "It even has a turret."

"It looks empty," Artie said as he pulled in the drive and parked in the shadow of an old oak tree cast by the midday sun. "Let's take a look."

"I really like the porch." Sarah joined him in front of the truck. "I can just imagine it lined with rocking chairs."

"Or a porch swing."

"Even better," Sarah agreed, taking his hand.

"Hang on," Artie said as his phone rang. "I need to take this."

Sarah wandered toward the house, noticing the wide stone steps, large windows, and that turret. *Turret, that's an odd word. How do I even know that word? Was Rapunzel in a turret? Or a tower? Oh, maybe turret means tower.*

"Sarah, I've got to get back to the pond. There's an issue with some of the equipment I've ordered for tomorrow, and I don't have all the figures with me."

Probably for the best. The Lookout Valley house makes more sense. Even so, Sarah didn't feel quite ready to make an offer. She'd think about it one more day.

Chapter Thirty-One

Sarah's alarm rang early on Friday morning. It was her last day at the Belford Clinic and Artie's first day of preparing the grounds at Blackwater Manor. She dressed quickly and hurried into the kitchen. Beth Ann and Randy Keith were finishing their breakfast, and Artie was going over his plan of action.

"Big day today," Sarah said.

"Yep! I'm on my way out the door. Wish me luck."

Sarah walked outside with him and kissed his cheek. "You've got this, Artie. I'll see you this evening."

A while later, she stopped in the drive to watch Artie make the first pass through the hard ground. He looked right at home on the tractor, but Sarah knew he'd pass the baton to the other workers before long. He'd told her that since the tractors weren't fitted with hand controls, braking required a whole leg movement that would stress his residual leg.

Sarah blew him a kiss she was fairly certain he couldn't see and thanked her lucky stars they'd found their way back to each other. Her phone rang as she reached the end of the drive. She was surprised to see the caller was her boss in Chattanooga.

"Hannah? What's up?"

"I'm so glad I caught you before work, Sarah. I've got some news I really need to discuss."

"You sound serious. Is it bad?"

"No, it's actually good news, but I'm a little flustered. My husband accepted a position in Wilmington."

"Oh, wow! That's great news, Hannah!"

"Yes, but that means moving. So, new job for me too."

"Ahh, I'll miss you, Hannah, but I'm sure—"

"Sarah," Hannah interrupted. "You're next in line for clinic manager. I hope you'll consider applying for the position."

"Oh, yeah, of course. Thanks for the info. Is there a scope of duties kind of document you can send me, or can we talk about it at lunch on Tuesday after the holiday?"

"I can't, Sarah. I'm actually on the road to Wilmington right now. We've got to figure out housing and schools and so forth. Things are moving fast. I've turned in my notice, so if you want the job, you're going to need to let HR know before they list the vacancy. I'll email you a job description and salary range. Look it over and text me your questions, okay?"

"Okay, sure. Thank you, Hannah."

Whoa, I guess that's the sign I've been waiting on. Sure makes the decision easier. Okay, then. I'm buying a house in Lookout Valley.

When Sarah arrived at the clinic, her phone pinged with an incoming email from Hannah. She sat in her car and skimmed the job description, frowning at the bulleted list which detailed various duties: analyze clinic metrics and key performance indicators; collaborate with internal stakeholders; budget management; billing;

collaborate with insurance. Sarah shook her head. *No. No, no, no. I don't want to do any of that.*

Inside the clinic, Sarah noticed that only a few appointments were on the schedule.

"A lot of people take time off around July Fourth," Missy said. "Farm chores still have to be done, of course, but folks cancel appointments to do a little fishing or enjoy cookouts and fireworks."

"I guess that makes sense." Sarah went to the break room to put her things away for the last time.

Janelle looked at her hopefully. "How was your afternoon off?"

Sarah told Janelle about Artie finding land, the job offer from Hannah, and her realization that she wasn't cut out to be a clinic manager. *If the job is wrong for me, maybe the house is too.* "Janelle, do you know anything about a Victorian farmhouse out past Robbins Chapel?"

"The Hawk's Nest? With the turret?"

"Well, I didn't know it had a name, but yeah."

Janelle nodded. "Yeah, a little bit. Petey, that's my husband, he knows the family. I think the oldest boy, Alex, inherited that house from his grandma. He started renovations but ran out of money. He thought he'd be able to finish it kind of piecemeal, but between work and a new baby, it didn't work out. I think they moved in with his wife's folks awhile. Do you want me to ask Petey about it? Have Alex call you?"

Sarah smiled at Janelle's hopeful grin. "Yeah? I really like the outside. But Janelle, it may be outside my budget or too big a job for me to take on, or I might just change my mind, so no promises."

"I hear you, but I've got a feeling we've moved from ten percent to at least fifty. Now let's get started on that inventory."

JANELLE HAD A PATIENT ON THE TABLE when Sarah's phone rang about eleven.

"I know you're at work and it's your last day, but I need help," Artie said. "The restaurant can't deliver lunch, and this crew is ready to eat. If they go off-site, we'll lose another hour."

Sarah started returning items to the cabinets she'd been cleaning in the break room. "What do you need me to do, Artie?"

"Can you pick up the food and bring it out here? I ordered from the little takeout cafe next to the Green Grocer. The food's ready, but the delivery guy didn't show."

"Of course," Sarah said. "I'll take an early lunch." She scribbled a note explaining everything, saying she'd be back as soon as possible. Missy was on the phone, so Sarah handed her the note and waved on her way out the door.

When she got to the manor, Artie came hobbling over, obviously in pain.

Sarah raised her eyebrows. "Looks like you overdid things this morning, Artie."

"A little, yeah. I'll be okay. I'll rest once I get the lunches delivered."

Somehow, Sarah convinced Artie to take a break from his

prosthesis and rest in the backseat of her car. She set up a table for the trays of barbecue sandwiches, chips, cookies, and drinks. It didn't take long for the workers to find the food. Sarah brought Artie a plate and gave his leg a light massage.

"You've saved my bacon today, Sarah, in more than one way," Artie said gratefully as he refitted his prosthesis. "Thanks for everything. Is Janelle going to be mad you've been gone so long?"

Sarah suddenly realized she'd been gone for two hours. "Well, it's my last day. I mean, what's she going to say?" Sarah kissed his cheek, said a quick good-bye, and drove back to the clinic, where the lot was full of cars.

As Sarah ran for the door, it opened and the afternoon exercise class spilled out, laughing as they saw her. "Here she is."

"The guest of honor!"

"Honey, you missed your own party."

"You come back anytime. You still haven't met my nephew."

Sarah looked up to see Janelle just shaking her head and laughing.

"I am so sorry," Sarah said. "I didn't know there was going to be a party."

"I guess the surprise was on us this time. You can help us clean up. Everything okay out there?"

Sarah explained the whole situation, eating a few raw veggies and the last cupcake while they straightened up the office after Missy left. "Well, I guess this is good-bye. I haven't heard anything from that guy Alex about the house. I guess it's not for sale."

Janelle gave her an appraising glance as she emptied the dust pan. "We'll see. I have a feeling we're moving toward eighty percent

Belford."

Sarah shook her head as they said their good-byes and left with no party and little fanfare.

SATURDAY DAWNED BRIGHT AND EARLY for most of the household, but Sarah slept late. She'd tossed and turned much of the night. Which house, which city, which life scenario was right for her? Strolling through the empty house, Sarah paused in the kitchen to grab a coffee and some yogurt, which she took out to the porch swing. She could hear the quiet roar of the tractors over at the manor.

Sarah was happy for Artie. She truly was. She envied his ability to go with his gut. He'd gotten a call last night. His offer on the land had been accepted. Beth Ann had insisted that he could stay with them, but Artie had said that while he'd gladly accept their offer to shower at their house, he'd just camp out at the land for a while. He planned to rent a camper by the fall and figure things out from there.

A sudden splash in the creek drew her attention. A deer, and then two more, crossed the creek and headed up the hillside. *I don't want to leave. I'm going to go look at that house.*

Sarah ran to her car feeling almost giddy, hoping to hear some-thing about the house. *Please let it be for sale. Please let it be affordable and repairable.* She drove out of Belford and turned at the familiar arrow-shaped sign. There seemed to be more cars on the road than usual. When most turned at Robbins Chapel, Sarah remembered Beth Ann talking about special Independence Day services in the area.

Sarah drove down past Artie's land, turning left at the farmhouse. *And I didn't even get lost. Could this be my house?*

She walked up the wide rock steps to the porch, where a stack of warped lumber sat with some disintegrating cardboard boxes of tiles. Sarah peeped through the window into the living room. *I love that carved fireplace mantle thing with the mirror above it. And the banister. Wonder what's upstairs.*

Sarah crossed the porch to the turret. Sunlight streamed onto recessed book shelves. She noticed a small chandelier hanging from the ceiling. "I love it," she whispered.

Sarah smiled to herself. *I'm going to tell Artie I'm reconsidering Chattanooga.*

Racing to the car without a backward look, she fit the key and turned the ignition. The car started, sputtered, and died.

Oh, no, no. This isn't good. Come on, car. Start for me. She tried again with the same result. Thinking that she'd possibly flooded the engine, she waited a minute before trying again. The car did not start. Sarah got out and lifted the hood because that's what you do, but she had no idea what she was supposed to look for. *I know I have gas. The battery looks fine.*

She closed the hood and looked around. No one in sight. *I'll call Randy Keith. No, they're at that Independence Day program.* She quickly ran through her options. Artie was working, Vin was in Asheville, Janelle was visiting family in Memphis for the long weekend. *Missy?*

I don't have her number. Hmm. The chapel? The chapel was a mile away. Sarah tried the car again, then picked up her phone.

"Artie, I drove back out to that house we saw, and now my car won't start. I know you're too busy to come get me, but can you let Randy——"

"I'm on my way."

"What? No, Artie, just tell Randy Keith and——"

"Sarah, I'm walking to my truck now. I'll be there in half an hour, tops. Just sit tight."

Sarah returned to the steps and tried to wait patiently. She texted her mom. She peered through the windows again, then checked her phone. Nothing. *I'll walk around the house.* She couldn't see in the side window but thought it might be a kitchen. She'd just reached the back door when she heard a car horn and Artie's voice calling.

"Sarah! Where are you?"

She raced around the house calling, "Back here, Artie!"

He hugged her tightly. "You scared the life out of me. When I didn't see you——"

"I'm okay, Artie. You found me. I'm just looking around. What were you afraid of?"

"Um, snakes, a bull, or maybe a guy with a shotgun. Take your pick."

Laughing, Sarah hugged Artie tightly. "Thanks for coming to my rescue. I guess there really is something wrong with my car."

"We rescue each other, honey. That's how this works. What are you doing back out here, anyway?"

Sarah smiled. "I'm having second thoughts about Lookout

Valley, Artie. I think this really could be my dream house. I have no idea if it's actually for sale, but if it is, and if I can afford the repairs on it," Sarah took both his hands, "could I be your neighbor?"

"Yes! Do you mean it? Yes!" Right as Artie cupped her face in his hands and moved to kiss her, Sarah's phone rang.

"It's a local number. I should answer it."

"Yeah, uh, I'm Alex. Um, Petey Marsh said to call you."

Sarah's smile grew as she spoke with Alex. She held her thumb up and walked back to the front porch. "Okay, I've found it," she said. "We'll look and I'll be in touch." She ended the call and knelt beside a flower bed filled with small plastic toys.

"What are you doing?"

"Getting the key." Sarah reached for an orange dinosaur, twisting and pulling it. The toy was glued to a small jar, in which rattled a front door key. "Alex said we could look around."

Sarah opened the door and quickly walked through the living room to the turret. She looked up at the small chandelier and spun in a circle. "Wouldn't this make a great reading nook?" The rounded room was open to the front hall and the kitchen.

"No appliances, upper cabinets, or countertops," Artie said. "But the lower cabinets look new."

A doorway led into a hall behind the staircase. "This must be the main bedroom," Sarah said.

"Yeah, and that corner's been framed and plumbed for a bath."

Back in the front hall, Sarah ran her hand along the banister. It was smooth and cool to the touch.

"Beautiful carving," Artie said, looking at the newel post at the base of the stairs. The top of the stairs opened onto a hall with a bedroom on either side and a bath in the middle. At the front of the house was the turret. Sarah walked into the room and ran her hands along the wall. *This would make a lovely nursery.* She turned to see Artie leaning on the doorway.

Smiling at her with love in his eyes, he asked, "Are you thinking what I'm thinking?"

"Maybe." She walked toward him and took both his hands in hers. "Artie, I don't know what the future holds or where I'll be six months from now, but I want to be with you. Whether it's living here in this house, in some other house, with Beth Ann, or camping out with you across the way, I'm staying in Belford, right where I belong."

Artie leaned his forehead against hers, and their eyes met. He grinned slowly.

"Okay."

"Okay?" she asked against his mouth.

"More than okay. I love you, Sarah." Artie cupped her chin. "I love you."

"I love you too."

Artie grinned. "Now shut up and kiss me."

Epilogue

(Sarah's journal, three years later.)

It's been three years since Artie and I first saw this house.

Three years since we planted tickseed, lobelia, coneflowers, and asters in a sunny bed alongside the driveway. It seemed silly to me to plant them before renovations on the house even began, but Artie wanted a perennial garden to be our first project as a couple. Each year, as the flowers bloom the way they are now, I'm reminded of our love for one another and how relationships, like gardens, need nurturing.

I'm not the easiest person to live with, and Artie can clam up when he's stressed, but we're making it work, learning to communicate and to accept our imperfections. He's helping me set routines and be more organized. I help him slow down and stay balanced. He doesn't have to do everything himself. We don't always agree on what should take first priority, but we're remembering to treat ourselves and each other with compassion.

That first year was tricky, as Artie worked at Blackwater Manor to establish the gardens, I worked at the clinic, and we both worked on this house. Mom and Andy helped me find local plumbers and carpenters and electricians to slowly bring this house back to life. It's taken three years, but the upstairs is finally finished, though not yet furnished.

When Artie and I moved in by the first frost almost three years ago, we basically camped out in the living room for a while. We celebrated that first night by heating soup and roasting marshmallows over the fire in our very own fireplace. We used pages from my journal about my past relationships to get the fire started.

Then I asked Artie to marry me.

He scared me a little, saying my name in that way I love but shaking his head. "Sarah, we've got a lot going on. Are you sure you want to plan a wedding now?"

I never wanted a big wedding, so we had an elopement instead, inviting our closest friends and family to Robbins Chapel for a picnic on the grounds one Saturday in early spring. Mom and Andy; Liam and Elizabeth; Meg, James, and their daughter Lily; Rob and Pamela; Artie's parents; Janelle and her husband; and Beth Ann, Randy Keith, and Sue Ellen all came. They must have suspected something was up, especially when Beth Ann's minister arrived. So we said our vows in what is still the most peaceful place I've ever known.

Over the last couple of years, we've made friends, learned to understand each other's differences, and worked together to find more projects that bring us together. We are a part of the story of the house at Blackwater Pond, just as it is part of our story. A reminder that life is constantly changing, constantly evolving, and that troubles and hard times are temporary.

Though the gardens at the pond are vastly different from our own, flowers are always a reminder of brighter days to come.

Beth Ann gave me some red bee balm. It's a nice addition to the garden, which is ablaze with color and shimmering with life every summer. Hummingbirds and butterflies and bees love the red-eyed yellow tickseed, the white asters, the purple coneflowers, and the cardinal lobelia.

Watering the flowers before each day heats up in the summer helps keep me centered, focusing on the importance of that work—life balance Hannah warned me about three years back. I've never regretted passing on the clinic manager position or moving to Belford. It's a different way of life and not one I'd ever imagined for myself, but it's home now.

One day we'll have our own children. I'll sit on the porch steps where I can smell the Lady Sarah roses and watch them play under the dogwoods Artie planted in the front yard. I can hear their laughter and feel their sticky kisses. But there's no rush.

Life is good and I can still hear the crickets.

Acknowledgements

Writing a novel is a work of love, but it is work, so I am forever grateful for those who've lightened my load: Kendra Herber, who read an early version of this novel and provided a greater understanding of prostheses and the amputee experience (any errors are mine); Linda McCune and other early readers; Christine Driver for insight and editing; Kate Winter for formatting and design; Taylor Martin, for continued assistance with my website and newsletter; Wanda Olsen, for providing a quiet space, and other family and friends for your support.

To my readers, I cannot thank you enough for joining me on this journey. It is immensely gratifying and humbling to hear that characters who've lived in my head for many months now resonate with you.

To my surprise, I have begun a third novel of Blackwater Pond. It will be a different sort of novel, told by different narrators, from different time periods, all at least tangentially associated with Blackwater Manor and the people I imagine having lived there throughout its 150-year history.

Let's keep in touch. Follow my progress, read the blog, sign up for my newsletter, or drop me a line at terrigilbertauthor.com.

9 798999 143 8223